UNRULY APPETITES

UNRULY APPETITES

UNRULY APPETITES
Erotic Stories

Hanne Blank

SEAL PRESS

UNRULY APPETITES
Erotic Stories

Seal Press
a member of the Perseus Books Group
1700 Fourth Street
Berkeley, CA 94109

Copyright © 2003 By Hanne Blank

First Seal Press edition 2003

The following stories in this volume appeared previously in other publications:

"And Early to Rise," *Clean Sheets; Best American Erotica 2001* (ed. Susie Bright)
"Severine," *Best Women's Erotica 2000* (ed. Marcy Sheiner)
"Downtown," *Scarlet Letters; Anything That Moves Folsom Street Fair Supplement; The Mammoth Book of Best New Erotica 2001* (ed. Maxim Jacubowski)
"Grenadine," *Sweet Life* (ed. Violet Blue)
"Turnabout," *Scarlet Letters*
"Lust, Debt, and a Practical Education," *Shameless: Women's Intimate Erotica* (ed. Hanne Blank)
"Debutante," *Necromantic* (necromantic.com)
"The Princess and the Tiger," *Scarlet Letters*
"Sauce for Gander," *Best Bisexual Erotica* (ed. Bill Brent and Carol Queen)
"The Graduate," *Scarlet Letters*
"Hair," *Zaftig no. 3; Best Women's Erotica 2001* (ed. Marcy Sheiner)

Library of Congress Cataloging-in-Publication Data
Unruly appetites: erotic stories/ [edited] by Hanne Blank.—1st ed.
     p. cm.
ISBN-10: 1-58005-081-6 (pbk.)
ISBN-13: 978-1-58005-081-4 (pbk.)
1. Blank, Hanne. II. Title.

PS3602.L383 U57 2003
813'.6--dc22

Book design by Paul Paddock

Distributed by Publishers Group West

Acknowledgments

To see one's book published is to owe an enormous debt to many people whose effort and presence have been instrumental to bringing it to life. I doubt I shall ever feel comfortable sending a book to press without at least an attempt at acknowledging the depth of my gratitude. So: For their reading and thoughtful comments at various points in the evolution of this collection, thanks go to my friends and colleagues Heather Corinna, Roxane Gay, Susan Glenn, Dr. Gil Rodman, Alex Pournelle, and Elizabeth Merrill Tamny. What flaws remain are entirely my fault, probably for being too stubborn to listen to the sage advice of the aforementioned. I also thank Leslie Miller of Seal Press, who is that rarest of gems, an editor who combines thoughtful editing and passionate opinion with levelheadedness and friendship. Similarly, I thank Christopher Schelling for taking a chance on an unknown quantity and for three years of faith that this collection would eventually see the light of day. For their assistance in manuscript preparation, and for helping make it possible for me to keep all the eggs in the air during the production period for this book, I thank the 2002 Intern Posse: Jennifer Bennett, Caroline Saffer, Jeannette Duffy, Julie Sabatier, Sarah Radice, and Molly Bennett. Last, but certainly not least, I thank the people who inspired many of these stories. Some of them have been my lovers, some of them have not, some of them I have never met face-to-face, but all of them have helped shape what I think about and what I do when I write erotic fiction.

For Oscar Wilde, Tess Gallagher, Colette, Vikram Seth,

Lisa Alther, Tom Robbins, Yehuda Amichai, Lawrence Millman, Nuala

Ní Dhomhnaill, Ursula Le Guin, Anna Akhmatova,

Guillaume Apollinaire, and Pablo Neruda, among many others, who

unwittingly taught me how to write; and for my beloved partner,

Malcolm Gin, to whom I owe damned near everything else.

Contents

ix Going Blind: An Introduction

 1 Turnabout

 9 And Early to Rise

19 Severine

33 What I Wanted (Cooperstown, New York)

37 Hair

47 The Cinematographer's Party

57 Waves

61 Grenadine

69 The Graduate

93 Downtown

99 Sauce for the Gander

119 Lust, Debt, and a Practical Education

131 The Princess and the Tiger

147 Debutante

157 Reasonable and Prudent

165 Virgin

173 Darling Nicky

185 Different with Your Kind

Going Blind:
An Introduction

When I was fourteen, I knew beyond a shadow of a doubt that reading dirty stories and masturbating would kill me. In the attic bedroom where I slept during my semi-willing weekend visits to my father and stepmother's house, I lay on my belly, propped halfway up on a pile of pillows, one hand smashed between my crotch and the sheet as I read the dirty parts of Lisa Alther's novel *Kinflicks*. I'd "borrowed" the book from the shelves of a family for whom I regularly babysat after discovering that I not only enjoyed the book, but that there were a variety of sex scenes in it that tossed kerosene on the fires of my pubescent libido.

There I was, diddling away, reading and rereading, giving the pertinent bits of prose the benefit of intensive literary (or is that cliterary?) scrutiny, when suddenly my brain exploded.

But not in the way you might think.

Climax did hit, yes, but with it came the sharpest, most terrifying pain I had ever felt in my young life. I was paralyzed by a sensation that seemed to stab from the base of my skull to the crown of my head, as if a laser had seared its way through my brain.

I couldn't move. I lay there, hand still between my thighs, as my stomach turned. The odd sensation of stepping aside and observing my body came over me. I watched dumbly as my mouth opened and I vomited without feeling it, puke splattering my pillows, all other sensation completely blocked by the all-encompassing horror of my head. I remember thinking obliquely that it was fortunate that I hadn't splattered the book, or I would've had a bit of explaining to do the next time I babysat. Suddenly I was gasping for breath, coughing as I choked slightly on sour-tasting spit and bile. I slammed back into my body, back to the pain, my only thought a frantic prayer that it would stop.

Then a wave of the profoundest, most horrible shame hit me: I had brought this on myself. Masturbating, intentionally getting myself worked up and off by reading what I then thought of as "pornography" (though Alther's novel, however explicit it is at moments, hardly constitutes porn), doing it just for the sheer fun of the sensation, was what had brought on this inexplicable attack.

Just a few months earlier, the teenaged sister of one of my brother's friends had died of a freak aneurysm. Had something similar broken loose inside my skull? Had my brother's friend's sister died by doing the same thing I had been doing? Would it just be a matter of a few minutes before I died?

I tore my hand away from my crotch as if it were on fire, wrenching myself onto my back in a motion so painful that it still remains seared into my memory. As the pain of motion receded slightly, I opened my eyes. The center of my field of vision was black, black, black. All I could see were little glimpses of my peripheral vision. My head hurt worse than anything I could've even imagined, and to top it all off, I was going blind. Was this it, I wondered? Was this what dying was like? I was blind, transfixed by pain, lying on my bed with adolescent pussy juice on my fingers and a dirty book lying open on my vomit-spattered bed, panting from the pain, half-terrified and half-praying that my father (or even my detested stepmother) would come to check on me or nag me about turning out my light and be able, somehow, to help me.

No one came, which in one sense was an enormous relief: I couldn't imagine how I would ever explain what had happened.

I certainly couldn't call for help, for if I was certain of anything in that moment, or during the long night afterward, it was that whatever was happening to me, I'd done it to myself. I had gone blind. I was in horrible pain. I might be dying. With the methodical calmness that comes when you're scared out of your wits but feel as if there's nothing at all you can do, I lay there wondering if what I was feeling really was a burst blood vessel deep in my brain, one that had burst because I had been jerking myself off while reading about Ginny Babcock's dyke lover, Eddie, fucking her with a greased organic cucumber.

Lying there, I cursed desire, lust, sex, and myself. If it weren't for being enthralled by the pleasure of reading about sex, if it weren't for the fact that I had sought out the titillation and indulged in it, none of this would've happened. It was all my fault, and I couldn't tell a soul. Even if I got better (and I lay there whispering silent prayers to God to please let me survive), no one could ever know. But much more important, I could never, ever again do what had caused this nightmare. Ever.

The next morning I woke up and was ecstatic to discover that I could see again. My head still hurt, but it wasn't nearly as severe. Mostly I was embarrassed and convinced I didn't dare tell anyone what had happened. I managed to strip the bed and get my linens into the washing machine before anyone else was up, and aside from telling my father I thought I might be getting the flu, since I needed an excuse for being obviously off my feed, I said nothing to anyone. I returned *Kinflicks* to its rightful owners the next weekend while they were escaping their colicky twins for the evening, and embarked on a zealous campaign of keeping my hands above the sheets and my selection of reading material a lot less inspiring.

For about the next year and a half, I basically did not, would not—with only two or three exceptions—masturbate. It wasn't because I thought it was sinful, or because I genuinely thought it was abnormal or wrong. I'm not sure quite what I thought the connection was between my masturbation and the horrible pain I'd gone through. My father, an anthropologist, taught "Introduction to Human Sexuality" courses at the university where he was on faculty, and I had educated myself reasonably well by reading the textbooks. I knew that masturbation was supposedly common, that even chimpanzees jerked off. I had never felt particular guilt about touching myself. I wasn't poorly educated. I hadn't been beaten over the head with visions of eternal damnation if I was sexually impure. At fourteen I knew more than any of my friends did about sex. I had access to sexuality textbooks, to *Gray's Anatomy*, to my father's stash of *Playboy*, and I knew what masturbation was and that women did it as well as men.

And yet, somehow, it was clear to me that doing it just for the pleasure, just for the thrill, was not merely self-indulgent but an invitation to a kind of pain I never, ever wanted to repeat. Especially if dirty stories were involved. Somehow, in my mind, the fact that I had been jilling off while reading something that turned me on, something as taboo as a scene about two women and a cucumber, was inextricably part of why I had been struck so damned hard by Thor's hammer. And so, for quite a while (a year seems like eternity when you're fourteen) I let the fear of that painful "retribution" erase what was then my primary form of sexual pleasure from my life.

About a year later it happened again. There was the same intense pain, the same blindness in the center of my field of vision, although it was not quite so sudden in its onset. It didn't happen when I was masturbating that time, but it did happen shortly after I'd shared one of my first earnest necking-and-groping sessions with a partner. The boy in question, one of my best male friends, had walked home from school with me, and we'd gone from sitting on my bed and talking to having an all-out kissathon, hands roving over one another's bodies, breath quickening, nipples stiff to the point of aching, bumping and grinding as our teeth clashed and tongues wrestled with the huge energy of new and reciprocated desire.

By the time the sound of my mom's car rolling into the driveway sent us flying apart, hurrying to smooth our hair and get into the living room so it'd look like we'd been doing homework together by the time she got in the door, I'd been fondling his stiffness through the front of his jeans and he'd sneaked a finger all the way down into my panties, sliding in between my labia on a gush of sweet girl-slipperiness. It was the first time another person had run a finger over my clit, and if I close my eyes and think about it, I can still remember how shockingly strong, and how shockingly good, it felt. That night, I jilled off in spite of my usual self-inflicted prohibition, coming hard, burying my face in my pillows as I recalled the taste of my friend's lips, the feel of his hands, the strength of his body against mine, the rough velvet of a finger—*someone else's finger*—on my clit.

The next day I came home from school alone, since my paramour had an orthodontist's appointment. Dutifully plowing through my homework on an overcast afternoon, I turned on an extra lamp when it seemed as if the room had grown a little dim. I wasn't prepared for the pain, or for the blindness, as the thousand-layered curtain of fog and pain lowered gradually into place. By the time I realized it was more than just a headache, it was already to the point of rendering me paralyzed and pukey, and I just staggered into my bedroom and laid down, telling my mom when she came home that I thought I might be coming down with something and I wanted to try to sleep it off.

I might've tried to tell my mother what was going on, but I couldn't bring myself to do it. I was afraid that the pain I was in would tattle on me, was terrified that there was some secret connection between the pleasure and the pain that the grownups didn't want any kid to know about so that they could use it as a way to tell when we did Things We Weren't Supposed To Do. It took another several months before I found out—by sheer coincidence, because a girlfriend of mine was diagnosed with them—that what I had suffered was nothing more exotic than a migraine.

When I finally made the connection between what had happened to me and the symptoms my girlfriend described having every month right before her period, and conjectured that perhaps I too was a migraine sufferer, I began a series of experiments. I masturbated every day, methodically, sometimes five or more sessions of jilling off over the course of the day. The object?

Trying to determine, more or less scientifically, whether masturbation really did cause those headaches, and if so, what kind of masturbation it took to do it. I masturbated while I read Shakespeare for English class. I masturbated in the tub. I jilled while babysitting, having found a cache of skeezy porno mags hidden at the bottom of a big basket of magazines in one family's master bathroom. Another family I babysat for had a huge Panasonic massager in the living room, plugged in and ready for action next to the easy chair. After the kids were in bed, I lay on the couch with it wedged under my pubic bone and massaged myself into another dimension. One day when I was feeling particularly devious, I got a hall pass from my biology teacher and, in the middle of a class period when I was pretty sure no one would walk in, I stuck my hand down my pants and came, silent but hard, in a second-floor high school bathroom with "High School Sucks" and "Denise Is a Bitch Ass HO" scrawled on the dingy tile where I leaned my forehead.

In short, I became an ace masturbator. I did it a lot. Unapologetically. Deliberately. Repeatedly. With erotica, with porn, with an adventurous friend, with shower massages, and even all by myself. And miracle of miracles, nothing happened. My headaches had nothing to do with it after all. They were wildcat things, occurring apparently at random, one or two in a six-month period. I still had to suffer now and then, but at least I had the silent but profound relief of knowing it wasn't me . . . and it wasn't sex, or masturbation, or pleasure, or porn. It had nothing to do with where I stuck my fingers, or even where I did it or how "wrong" it might've been in someone else's eyes that I was there, still very much a virgin, writhing in underaged ecstasy, my fingers doing the walking. Better yet I could read anything I wanted while I did it, because it didn't make a bit of difference.

Sometimes people ask me, friends and interviewers alike, what events and people influenced my choices to write, talk, and teach about sex and sexuality. No matter what I say, I never really feel like I'm giving them a complete answer, perhaps because this story is so much a part of what the answer really is. I often think the experience of literally going blind and insane with pain—and believing it was caused by sexual pleasure—is one of the weirdest, most embarrassing, and yet most formative things that has led me to make writing about sex a part of my life. The moment that I thought I might die because I masturbated, and the moments that followed in which I figured out how to put cause and effect into their proper categories and grab my own pleasure by the handful once again, are at the core of who I am as a sexual being.

As I sit here looking back at the memory of extreme pain and the joy of being released from it, I hope these words, and the rest of this book, help to break the chains of useless self-limitation and restriction of pleasure for my readers. In short, I, like every author, hope you enjoy what I've done here: Unabashedly, aesthetically, intellectually, and yes, one-handedly. I hope not only that my work gives you pleasure, but that it lets you give yourself more pleasure, too.

I get a lot of mail from readers, and a lot of feedback in workshops and seminars that I lead, from people who can't allow themselves the pleasure they want and deserve for a thousand meaningless reasons. They're too old, or too married, or too worried about what their partner will think if they confess to a risqué fantasy. They're too fat, or too bald, or too hung up on their own image of themselves, too busy, too much a pillar of the community, too visible, too out of shape, too freckled or wrinkled or weird.

Or so they think. What they are, what we all are most of the time, I think, is too scared.

We're scared of pleasure, scared of what it represents, scared of not being able to get back to our safe little boxes once we've learned how to open the lid. We get scared of a lot of things, and some of them are good things to be scared of. But among the things that frighten us most, I think, are the subversive, wild, weird powers of desire, pleasure, and joy.

Yes, they can be scary. Our appetites are big sometimes, and they feel hard to control. It seems as if they're liable to take us over, force our hands, run roughshod over our reason.

To which I say: So? Why not learn how to ride that tiger? Why not acknowledge the fear and the risk and learn to grab our pleasure with strength and intelligence, indulge our appetites in ways that are sane and empowering, and transform our lives for the better with the transcendent force of our desires? Our appetites can generate enormous pleasure, growth, understanding, and joy, whether through sex or any other of the venues by which we approach our selves and our souls. All of this is too powerful and too precious, I feel, to squander out of fear. We've got too much to lose.

Within the pages of this book, I hope you find things that help you grab hold of some of that pleasure, some of that joy. I hope it encourages you to seize your own appetites by the handful, sweet and sultry, complex and strange, thick and real. Most of all, I hope it convinces you—even if it's just once in a while—to do something foolish and flagrant and fun. Love hard, live with grace and appetite, forget that you're a grownup now and then. Kiss a lot. Masturbate while you read Shakespeare. Say "I love you" whenever you mean it. Go blindly into your bliss until the startling clarity of a new vision births you, red and hot and naked, into the world you desire.

I look forward to seeing you there.

Baltimore, Maryland
Summer, 2002

Turnabout

S he knocked on the door, short and sharp, once and
once only before she entered, interrupting him in the
middle of a sentence.

His annoyance melted when he saw who it was. She shrugged
her way out of her coat as she walked into the small office, barely
pausing to smear a kiss across his lips, leaving him holding the
snow-dusted weight of her coat in hand. He started to speak,
then bit his lip as she stood between him and his desk, reaching behind her to find the edge of the desk with her hand.
Behind her the window reflected them both against the mirror
of the December evening that lay beyond the panes.

"Isn't this out of your way?" he asked.

"Not if I wanted to see you." She leaned on the desk slightly,
both of her hands behind her hips, her weight settled evenly
against them. The posture made her look almost demure: her
long black skirt forming a seamless line with the ribbed softness of her black turtleneck, her shoulders hunched slightly
forward with her thick braid draped over one shoulder, her
chin tilted up as she held his gaze, hard, with glittering chocolate eyes.

He dropped her coat onto a book-filled chair, not bothering
to look as it slid to the floor, soft felted rumplefall like a sigh.
How odd, he thought, that she would come to the office on a
Sunday, on a cold Sunday like this, particularly knowing that

this was time he needed to work. Dissertations, as he often reminded himself, don't write themselves.

"So . . . ," he ventured. She wasn't like this often. It made him nervous when she was so quiet. An odd tension coiled in her like a watchspring, a muscle twitched in her arm as she shifted her weight. He couldn't decide if she seemed angry.

"I wanted to see you," she explained.

"Here I am."

"Yes."

She reached behind her and pushed his computer keyboard across the desk, a sheaf of papers sliding messily out into a fan-shaped arc as the keyboard dragged them. He began to say something, but the intensity of her look closed his mouth as soon as he had opened it.

"Sit down," she said, her voice low and matter-of-fact as she scooted her butt up onto his desk, sitting just to the right of the monitor as the screensaver went on. Silently, fish flitted through a phosphorescent ocean only to disappear as they swam into her side. He sat in his heavy old desk chair, perplexed.

"So, why'd you come all the way across the river tonight, sweetheart?" He laughed a little, nervously, reaching toward her tentatively. Her stare stopped his hand before it reached her knee. The elderly springs in the old-fashioned chair squeaked tiredly as he sat back again, not sure whether he'd just been scolded.

"You sent me mail this morning," she answered, plainly, gesturing at the monitor on which a fanciful scorpionfish undulated its myriad fins lazily across the screen. She paused. "Put your hands on the arms of the chair. And keep them there."

Sliding his arms onto the oaken armrests, he gripped the forward curves lightly, hooking his thumbs underneath. He didn't understand, but she was strangely forbidding. It was odd for such an effusive sort of woman to be so terse, almost cold, he thought, the falconlike sharpness of her stare making him tingle with anxiety. He tried to remember everything he'd written. Had he written something that offended her, something she found inappropriate despite their various intimacies?

They hadn't been dating long. He hoped he hadn't screwed up. But sometimes it could be hard to know what would piss someone else off. Particularly when your backgrounds were so different. She'd grown up mostly in the States, but from what she'd told him, her parents took their high-caste heritage pretty seriously, and in her upper-class Indian family, you just didn't mention some things. Just the same, she'd always seemed pretty liberal about sex, so he hadn't really thought about it when he wrote her.

"You don't know how that made me feel," she said.

"How what made you feel? Did I say something wrong?"

"You told me that you were thinking of me last night."

"Well, yes, I wa . . . "

She held up her hand. "And you told me that you went into the shower and jacked off, thinking about me, and stroking yourself and remembering how it felt to have me lying against you, and wondering what it would be like to have me there naked in the shower with you."

He nodded dumbly. Fuck, he thought. He'd gone too far. Shit.

"And you told me that you were stroking that cock of yours and thinking of me in the shower and that you came like a rocket. That's what you told me."

He gulped. She reached down as she spoke, unbuttoning one button, then the next, then the third and fourth and fifth, working up from between her calves until only the topmost button at her waistband was still caught in its noose.

"You don't know how that made me feel," she said again, her voice dropping to a sueded alto as she spread her thighs. The black fabric of her skirt shrouded the tops of her legs, but he could see that she was bare beneath, stockingtops giving way to black garters over plump toffee thighs, nothing at all covering the thatch of hair between her legs. Blinking, he tried his best not to stare, to look up at her face, to let her corral him again with that shiveringly intense stare.

"I sat there in my chair and I read your mail and I thought about you coming without me in your shower and I wanted . . ." she drifted off as her fingers slid down, parting her labia, the scent of already wet, already aroused cunt filling the small, still room like the sound of a slap. "I wanted, you know, I wanted to be there to feel you coming for me. I wanted to see you, wanted to see you stroke it for me. Wanted to hear you tell me how much you wanted me. Wanted to watch you gasp and moan for me while I watched you come."

His mouth, he realized, now hung dumbly open. Trying to wrest his gaze from the two fingers that circled and circled her clit, he looked at her face, her lips darkened by arousal, the slight flush at the side of her neck. Absently his right hand slid down from the armrest toward his aching cock, trapped and bent uncomfortably as it swelled precipitously behind the zippered front of his khakis.

"Don't you dare," she snarled, interrupting her litany of desire. "I think you've touched yourself enough for one day without my permission. You made me jealous. I've been thinking about it all day, you know. All day. You in the shower, stroking the length of your shaft. Touching yourself. The way you would arch your back. The look on your face when you were trying so hard to come. I've been thinking about it ever since this morning."

Her voice grew gradually raspy, breath rough in her throat as her fingers continued to circle and rub, the muscles in her arm becoming more tense as she pressed harder against herself. Spreading her legs slightly more, she leaned back on her free hand, extending one leg toward him. At the weight of her booted foot on his knee, he moaned, feeling a slight tickle of meltwater seeping from the hard black grooves of her boot soles into the fabric of his pants. His cock ached and throbbed, straining against the fabric of his briefs as he writhed, hips arching unconsciously in an effort to at least free his erection of its inopportune bondage inside his Fruit of the Looms.

This time, she didn't have to tell him no. Her expression changed, and that was enough. Smiling sharklike, all hunger and no mercy, she slid her fingers into her cunt, surely and slowly sinking them in to the knuckles, and he froze in his seat, hipbones slouched forward, cock making a furious tent of the pleated front of his pants as she fingerfucked herself scant feet from his face.

He could hear it now, the soft obscene slurp of juice as she thrust her fingers in, her thumb flicking her clit like a circuit breaker.

"Yes, you wrote me, you fucker, and you made me ache for you all fucking day with that little story of you jacking off in the shower, you know. I couldn't think without ending up thinking about what your cock would look like sliding through your fist, without wanting to see you squirt hot juice through the water. I couldn't walk without wondering how your hips thrust when you're standing there in the shower like that, or do you stand with your back against the wall, or do you lean into the corner of the shower with your face against the tile and the water pounding down on your back, desperately fucking into your fist . . . because I wanted to see it, you know? I wanted you to show me. I wanted you to have wanted to show me, god-damn it, not just go off and get your jollies and then fucking well think you could just write me about it later and not have to care. I wanted . . . "

She faltered, her fingerfucking and clit-rubbing speeding faster, the muscles of her hips shuddering with the tension as she slid up the banister toward orgasm. A slick slurp accompanied her fingers as she pulled them from her cunt and feverishly mashed her clit against her pubic bone, and he could feel the hard sole of her boot digging into his knee as she worked herself closer and closer to the end. Breathless, he watched her, trans-fixed with lust and jealous fury. He'd never seen her masturbate before. And she had never seen him. He hadn't known she'd wanted to.

"Damn you!" she gasped, "I wanted that so much and you've been making me suffer with it all fucking day." Growling, she bit off each word as if she were snapping its neck. "You weren't home. You weren't answering the phone but your housemate told me you were here. And I . . . . all day . . . five, six times, try-ing to get you the fuck out of my head. But I can't shake the image of you. The one you didn't let me see. And I can't get rid of that thought . . . that hard cock and the hot shower and damn you . . . ohhh you . . . fucker . . . "

For a long moment she caught his gaze, her mouth open in a

startled O of nervous shock as the waves hit her. The force of her coming rippled through him, her foot kicking out, heel gouging into his inner thigh just above the knee as she bit her lip and muffled a short sharp cry. All he could do was watch and murmur her name, soft and low, unable to move or do anything but sit and absorb her ravaged beauty until finally she wrenched her hand away from her clit as if it burned her.

Gently he held her leg, hands cradling her calf just above the top of her boot, not sure whether he dared anything more, wanting to gather her to him but not knowing if he should. Somewhere he was dimly aware that his cock ached and twitched with want, but it seemed somehow less important than her face gradually softening, the right side glowing with the odd blue of the monitor as the fish continued to swim in lazy ellipses across his workstation screen. After a moment she wiped her fingers on the papers on which they'd unthinkingly landed and buttoned her skirt again, the curtain closing over her juice-slicked pussy with dark exactitude.

At the bottom of the row of buttons, she reached for his hand and let her humid digits rest across his knuckles. He shivered, hard, eyes squeezing shut hard enough to drive a single tear onto his cheekbone. Tenderly she slid her fingers into his palm as she brought her foot down from his lap, taking his hand in hers as she slid off of his desk and onto her feet.

He looked up, she looked down. She stood astride his slightly-parted legs, capturing his knees between hers as she raised his hand to her lips. Pressing his knuckles against her lips, she fleetingly licked the cleavage between each pair of fingers, feeling him tense and writhe as he sat trapped and trembling in the heavy wooden chair. His blue eyes met her brown ones, and a slow, pleased smile spread like honey across her face.

"I'll see you tomorrow for dinner at seven, don't forget," she half-whispered, her voice soft and kind now. She stepped away, behind him, picking up her coat and slipping into it as she moved toward the exit. He swiveled in the chair as she turned the doorknob.

"Don't let it happen again, hmm?" she murmured, hand on

doorknob. Wordlessly, he nodded, still dazed, still throbbing, balls feeling leaden, heavy, the dull ache of desire slowly being supplanted by the dull ache of desire unfulfilled. She blew a kiss, then winked as she opened the door and stepped through it. "Or if you must, don't tell me. I'm afraid that I'm the jealous type."

And Early to Rise

To your way of thinking, it isn't morning until the sun comes up. Even then sometimes it isn't, for you are loath to admit the coming of a new day until you've determined that you are ready to be a part of it. I have known you to spend entire mornings, even into the afternoon, lying in bed with your laptop, working on something or other for hours with the curtains still drawn, not even venturing out for a cup of your strong-smelling Russian tea. Eventually you emerge, as bleary as if you'd been sleeping all the while. "Beautiful morning, isn't it, Lilja?" you call cheerfully into my study as you stumble toward the shower, sometimes as late as two o'clock, finally condescending to formally enter the day.

And so for your sake I will say it was the middle of the night, despite the clock on the bedside table that gleamed a red and resolute 5:45 A.M., when I awoke to find you waiting, silently wanting, your back slightly arched, your aureole crinkled, still fast asleep. Thank God you don't dream of sex every night, you have told me, since it always frustrates you when you do. Always the bridesmaid, never the bride, your sex dreams torment you with movie-worthy expanses of perfectly tangible, beautifully detailed arousal, clinches that last for ages, making you confuse your tongue with your clit as your dream-lover's kisses make you buck your hips with want, her (or is it his?) fingers stroking your sides and breasts and belly but never more than grazing the springy soft fur of your cunt, never spreading you open, never going inside where you want them to go. You never do get what you want in those dreams, and you wake frustrated, slippery between the legs, softly grumbling.

I can always tell when you've dreamed of sex. In my study I hear you through the wall when you shower, leaning against the tile with the water pummeling the lush breasts I like so much to tease, your hand between your thighs, unaware that the shower actually does precious little to cover your noises. I listen to you, something deep between my hips quivering at the high, piercing whimper that I know means you're hovering, aching and desperate, at the edge of orgasm.

I wish I weren't such a morning person, wish my body didn't always insist on my being awake so long before you. Morning for me comes when my body says it does, circadian jackboots kicking me rudely awake even if it's December in New England and still dark as the hem of a cassock outside.

This morning I woke yearning to just roll you over and slide between your legs but not daring to rouse you just for that. You slept deeply, though your soft moans made me wonder if your eyes might open at any moment, and in the depths of your slumber you seemed to welcome the caress of my hands, letting me spoon you cozily, palm sleeking the fine full curve of your hip and drifting over the pillowsoft of your belly. Stirring slightly but not waking up, you seemed to know I was there, and for a while that was enough. And so I pressed myself against your spine, my nipples perking slightly at the contact with your skin, slid my arm under the graceful arch of your neck. Unconscious kitten-murmurs came from your throat as my fingers traced the seam where my thigh pressed the back of yours, and as I let my hand meander to the top of your thigh there was a slight, unmistakable shifting of your hip pressing into my fingers.

Wondering whether there were hands caressing you in your dreams, wondering where you were and who she was and whether you could see her face as her hand moved where mine did, I smiled at your reaction, experimentally pushing my knee against the backs of your thighs to see if you'd let me push your legs apart. I flattened my palm against the top of your breastbone to hold you steady, to keep you pressed against me. You arched a little, letting me spread your thighs, those thick gorgeous thighs I love to knead, to stroke, to kiss, to taste, not legs so much as feasts, as succulent and resilient to my bites as grilled sausages, yet as sweet and satiny as ganache or crème caramel against my tongue. Suddenly I could smell the wilderness of your aroused cunt and realized that yes, I was right, you had been dreaming of sex even before I began to touch you. I inhaled you hungrily, delighted to have my suspicion confirmed, wondering how far you'd let me go, how much of this I could enjoy before you woke and shooed me away, protesting *auf Deutsch*, too agitated and too sleepy to remember how to scold me in English.

Hands soft and moving slowly, not wishing to disturb your lust-saturated slumber any more than absolutely necessary, I found a nipple with one hand while the other inched its way between my leg and yours, pushing against the sleek female flesh to either side. Your nipple was crinkly, hard, the tip of it already sensitized to the touch of some imagined seducer's hands. With the pad of a finger I circled it, traced it, outlined it, imagining each ridge and whorl of my fingerprint rasping against it like corduroy, fantasizing that in your sleep, your normal sensitivity would be perhaps enhanced to feel it. Your breathing shifted slightly, deeper now, as my other fingertips barely reached the outermost edges of your cunt.

I love—have always loved, will always love as long as you permit me to touch you this way—entering you from behind. There is an almost illicit thrill in reaching just below the lavish halves of your ripe peasant ass to find the hidden hot-velvet cornucopia of your vulva, lips thick with blood and pouting, poised, waiting to be kissed, parted, spread, entered, filled beyond rational thought. I teased your pussy as we lay together in the almost uterine softness of the pillow-banked bed, two fingertips grazing just inside your lips where the skin is moist to the touch. Your mouth opened, breath still regular and slow, still asleep.

On your breast my fingers rustled, hand flat and fingers straight, letting your nipple rumblebump against each one in turn as I moved my hand to and fro, fanning with my wrist.

When you are awake, you won't often let me tease you like that for long. You become too impatient, begin to urge your hips backward against my fingers, start grabbing at your own breasts, greedy baby, needing the pinch of thumb and forefinger on your hardened tips to sear through your body and spike the need building behind that anxious clit of yours. Not now, though. Did my touches become the touches of the lover in your dream? I hope they did. I wanted you that way for a change, slow and deliberate, the kind of dreamy lovemaking that leaves you so wet and frustrated that you wake up and have to exorcise yourself under an entire water heater's worth of hot shower, not stopping until the water's too cold for you to bring yourself off again.

Would it embarrass you to know that I know how you fuck yourself with the hair conditioner bottle when it's worse than usual, when your dreams have tormented you to the point where you need it deep and hard and relentless but you still can't bear to admit that you need to be fucked so big and so bad? You never ask me to come back to bed when you wake up like that. It makes me jealous that you don't ask me, that you don't invite me to take advantage of the fever inside you. But not this time. This morning, for once, I got to finish what your dreams had started.

Did you notice, in your fevered sleep, that I had begun to push inside you, or that you were slick as egg whites? I wonder at what point it began to register somewhere in your hindbrain that your body was being manipulated not just in dreams but for real, that someone else's hand really was forcing its meaty way inside your clinging, slippery folds. There was no resistance as I entered you, sweet rippling girlflesh opening around my fingers.

A momentary ripple of worry seized me—would you take it as a form of rape, if you woke suddenly to find me coaxing three fingers inside of you without your knowledge or say-so? It troubled me for an instant, but the more I considered it, the more the thought curled in on itself and became redolent with even deeper, redder lust. Would I violate you? Yes, in a manner of speaking, I would, I would take the blame for having wanted this so much that I would do it to you without asking, because I knew it was the only way I would get to. I yearned to plunge into you hard and fast from the second I felt how wet you were, to fuck you hard, to show you no mercy. I ached to feel your body clinging, spasming around my thick fingers. I wanted to lay waste to you, to leave you bruised and spent, to drive away the other lover in your dream with my own undeniable physical presence, to force you to give to me the ache, the need to be fucked that you'd normally take with you into the shower.

Tender violent thoughts circled, tail in mouth, in my brain. Creator and destroyer, I cradled you in the gentle curves of my protecting arms, against the softness of my body, wanting to be as brutal as I was loving, to ruin you with the force of your own desire. My fingers searched within your cunt, trembling, wriggling further into you, almost shaking with the effort not to go too fast, not to wake you too soon. I wanted to bite your shoulder and fuck into you with relentless depth, pushing you into orgasm after orgasm. I wanted a sudden, rough, raw, over-amped fuck like the one we had on the first night we did it, when our bodies screamed for each other like the angst-driven guitars onstage at the club where you backed me up in the corner behind the speaker stack and bit my neck and told me you wanted to take me home with you so you could bend me over in my miniskirt and shove your tongue into me. You told me later that it cost you a good deal to restrain yourself until you'd gotten me into your apartment before you shoved your fingers into me, pinning me against the wall and reaching without preamble under my skirt, shoving past my panties and making me arch and groan out loud with the shivering fulfillment of my outraged desire to feel you there, so rude and yet so pure. It cost me at least as much in the dark hours of this early morning not to do the same to you, not to slam-fuck you into the bed with sharp corkscrewing strokes, not to bite your bubblegum tits until you screamed, not to shake you awake with the rude force of unbounded lust.

With a slow spiraling motion your hips moved, sluggish, the burgeoning energy of the fuck drawing you toward me. Your pussy opened a little to take me in, and I distinctly heard a foggy moan muffled against the pillow. I plucked your nipple: She loves me, she loves me not, she loves me, she loves me not, letting my fingers slip off of the tip before they could pinch hard enough to puncture the bubble of unconscious arousal in which you were still, somehow, sleeping. Twisting my wrist a bit I began to knead the resilient walls of your cunt, a sensation I know you adore, reading the Braille of muscular twitches, the occasional contraction, the opening-up just at the tips of my fingers that made me suddenly wish I could come into you like a man, fill that space with the essence of myself so that it would ooze out of your cunt later and remind you where I'd been.

She loves me. Wrist gliding to the left my fingers arched, stroking up and over, finding the firm nubbled spot where you like to feel my first knuckles rub. *She loves me not.* To the right then, my fingers bent doubly thick, feeling you spread your legs reflexively, opening to me, your cunt stretched full for me because I love the sensation of you wrapped taut around my fingers, almost but not quite a fist. *She loves me.* You rolled back, pressing your ass hard against me, sweet rumbles of sensation having finally woken you a little. *She loves me not.*

I let you turn onto your back, shifting with you so that I didn't have to stop fucking your voluptuous sleepy cunt. The clasp of your pussy around my fingers a crucial connection I refused to relinquish, I slid between your legs as you rolled onto your back, only a soft, slow, hoarse "oh yes, please" telling me that you'd slid, if only a little, over the border between dream and wakefulness. You seemed not to mind, not even to be surprised, that you came to with my fingers inside you. You wanted it as much as I thought you did, my intrusion not only tolerated but desired. Reaching up as I settled on my belly between your sloppily splayed, sleep-limp legs, I plucked your nipple again. *She loves me.*

I straightened my fingers again to reach further into you. You've always liked me to stroke the scallopike slickness of your cervix with my fingertips, the sensation so deep, so intense and primal, that hidden bit of you found out and gently burnished as if such polishing could make it shine like gold. My fingers swimming through a sea of heat that had begun to seep out of you and trickle down along my wrist, you moaned, arching toward me in a slow, agonized rhythm. I looked up at you, your hands on your breasts, fingers splayed, mauling your own soft flesh with the same insensible heartlessness with which your cat, in similar states of bliss, will knead her pin-sharp claws into my thigh. By the faint dawn light seeping in around the draperies I could see your face, eyes closed, radiant, expectant, pure.

It was time to finish your dream the way I'd often wanted to, to be the one to take the place of whoever had begun to seduce you as you slept. I parted your labia with my lips and nose, tongue extended to stroke its way to your clit. At the taste of you my own cunt clenched, and I think I moaned against you as I found your hard little nub and fastened my lips around it, fingers still swirl-kneading the very bottom of your muscular cunt. Your hands abandoned your breasts and made a basket around the back of my head, holding me as I licked you, up and up and up against your clit, the motion I know will get you to come and come again if I keep at it, if I fight you after the first time when you try to push me away. Starving for the taste, the feel, the sound, the clinging grasping arch of you at orgasm, I battered your clit with my tongue, no pretense at subtlety. Mashing my face against your soaked pussy, you ground against me with an agonized sound and I tried to lick faster, wished my mouth into a blur of spit and muscle to please you.

You made your sex noise. My clit throbbed in sympathy. It was *the* noise, not just any noise, not to be mistaken for any lesser sex cry. Long ago they thought the bird of paradise had no legs, that it had to fly the heavens forever in its shocking, extravagant robe. Is that why your cry always sounds like some fantastic bird, because of your desperation to land after flying so hard for so long? Your breath came in gasps, your muscles taut as harp strings. I rammed into you hard, dropping gears suddenly into the kind of all-out fuck I'd wanted to give you all along. You made the noise a second time, and begged me, "please, please."

Your throat went rigid with a soundless scream, an outraged howl of orgasm tearing through you as I fucked you hard and harder, eating your clit with toothscrapes now, knuckles mashing against the entrance of your clasping hole with each stroke. Somehow you caught one enormous gulp of air, but I wasn't ready to let you come down yet. I nudged that infamous spot inside you with my fingertips, Morse code telling you to come for me again, again, again, my tongue lashing at you as insanely as I could make it. You had to come again, my fingers insisted, one more time, for me. Your fingers left my head and I knew, as surely as I knew you would only come for me again if I forced you to, that you were twisting your own nipples far more cruelly than I ever would've, enchanted past the point of pain by merciless need.

Come for me, I willed as I felt you tensing again, a sharp contrast to the momentary lassitude that followed the contractions of your first orgasm. I pistoned my hand in and out of your dripping cunt, jackhammering you well beyond the point you thought you would not reach again. The first one was for the dream. The second was all mine. What came after that was yours and yours alone, until you simply could not do it again, and lay dazed and sweat-damp in my arms.

The sun was just barely up, the day bluish-gray at the corners of the curtains. Pulling the covers back up over you with sticky fingers, I bent and kissed you as you lay there, spent and sleepy, eyes glazed. You stroked the side of my face and smiled a little weary smile. I kissed your palm and you blushed, looking amazingly like the pictures I've seen of you as a little girl.

"You're getting up now?" you mumbled, letting your eyes close again.

"Yes, baby. Time for me to start the day."

"*Nnnpfth. Schrecklich.* Morning people." Your grumbles grew more distant with each syllable.

"Go back to sleep," I replied, "it isn't morning for you yet."

"Mmmmmmphh," you sighed in agreement as you rolled over, cocooning yourself in the eiderdown, practically asleep again. I stood and walked toward the door, licking my lips to savor the taste of you. How pleasantly ironic, I smiled to myself as I walked naked down the narrow hallway to the shower, feeling my clit burning with quiet impatience, on my way to revisit your dreams.

Severine

I t pained her to be so far away. Still, Paris lurked obstinately on another side of the globe no matter how
hard she shut her eyes and imagined the lights from
the distant rooftop where she so often sat and smoked with
one of her lovers.

Alain did not like it when Severine sat on the stone rim of
the roof, furrows in his high forehead betraying his fear of
heights. He never ventured to the ledge, but sat with his back
against the chimney-pot, talking with Severine as she watched
the city the way a sailor's wife watches the sea. The bedtime cigarette on the roof was their ritual regardless of season, and not
merely because they did not dare to smoke indoors. Of course
if they did, Marie-Sophie would pout, and shut herself away in
her room like a petulant schoolgirl. It hurt her lungs, she said,
which a singer should not countenance.

Marie-Sophie, such a little prima donna, such gorgeous platinum
ringlets, such sweet plump lips. At both ends, oh yes, and juicy like a
plum of soft ivory, ripe under the teeth. But such a brat! I am not
immune to her, though. None of us are, no matter what she does. Sophie
is feux d'artifice, our silver baby, the dragonfly that buzzes around our
heads when we try to be serious. She drives Alain crazy, to the point
where he screams, then leaves for a day or two, which shouldn't but
always does make me panic. And yet we all struggled to seduce her to

19

stay, didn't we? Especially Alain. He tried and failed to push her out
of his heart, he said, and so he simply had had to learn to let her have
her way. We should all be so impossible not to love.

Severine ground out her cigarette on the windowsill bricks,
exhaling long and slow into the velvety humidity of the
Vancouver afternoon. Four months more until the contract was
up, just four more.

She thought of them, what they'd be doing nine time zones
away, of sleepy noises drifting through the high-ceilinged spaces
of the old rowhouse. There would be Marie-Sophie and Alain,
curled into one another in Alain's room at the top of the stairs,
at least until Marie-Sophie crept back downstairs to Corinne's
side, taking refuge from the snoring. Corinne would murmur
and shift in her sleep, unruffled, pressing closer to Severine as
she unconsciously made room for the peripatetic Marie-Sophie.
In the morning Corinne's smile was like the sun itself, broad-
casting delight at once more finding herself surrounded by the
people she loved best. Some days, Alain would fumble down the
stairs, unhappy at waking alone, and slip among the three of
them, completing the sleepy family beneath the quilts. Later
there would be coffee and *pain de campagne* and jam and the
ritual bickering over the shower. It was all good, even the tatty
cat-scratched upholstery on the sofa in the front room.

It had been three years, and still Severine marveled that it had
happened at all. She had resisted sharing the house at first. It was
too much, it seemed too much to risk to shift her foundation so
that she had no safety zone, no place to run. But Alain had made
her a small yellow room, just beside his own, and had put
anemones in the vase beside the window, and soon she had
come to stay. It had been her birthday when they kissed her
down to her bed, both of them, and baptized her with semen
and sweat and welcomed her home. Three years ago, the six-
teenth of February, cold and clear and half the world away.

Impossible to think of Alain without Corinne. By comparison I am
merely a satellite, orbiting the gravity of Alain's long fingers and sly

humor, the pull of sweet Corinne's thick hips and calm love. Such patience Alain had with me. Corinne is not patient, she simply does what she does and lets what must happen, happen. Same destination, different journeys.

I miss them together and apart. Alain's sardonic jokes, his long skinny cock, the way he strokes into me to make me squeal and the fact that he loves seeing me in the morning, rumpled and crusted with sleep, so he can tease me. Corinne's voluptuous cruelties, her heavy hand landing again and again on my pale raised ass, her filthy whispers, her silent generosity and enormous thighs, the depths of her drenched hothouse cunt around my hand, over my face. Her serenity. The madonna with a laptop. Her consort in his suit, official, imposing, slicing through the week with carbon-steel words of law. Impossible to imagine either of them without some reference to the other. Between them, they have changed me. I have ceased to exist as I did before. I require their substance to keep me where I need to be.

Severine sighed as she pulled her head back inside. She looked out at Mount Seymour's rain-shrouded flanks, recalling the sounds of Marie-Sophie's sultry giggle over the phone lines, Alain's low-voiced chuckle as he told a joke which he knew would make her blush, Corinne's stern admonitions that she was not to feel too sorry for herself being alone on her birthday. Perhaps she would wait until it was morning in Paris, and call them again.

She stared at the telephone. No, it would not do. Yes, she missed them, but it didn't help to be a baby. Besides, the money on this job was worth it, was it not? She would take them all to Greece for a month when she returned. They would sail, and grill fish over a small fire, and the sounds of water and wind would be quilted with the soft gasps of her lovers. At night they would all sit on the terrace and talk, mending the small inevitable tears in the fabric of a family that come with a member's prolonged absence. In Greece she'd be with them again, on a small island of blues and whites and endless free-roaming cats. Perhaps the travel brochures she had ordered would be in the afternoon mail.

The mailbox door was jammed. The small box was crammed full, the outermost layer consisting of three largish tan envelopes, bent around the other mail in order to fit them in. She wiggled them out, catching sight of Corinne's strongly slanted script on the corner of one of them. In large letters across the bottom of the envelope she read *"Attention Photos! Ne pas plier."* Severine scowled, ironing the envelopes flat with her palm. Weren't Canadian postal workers supposed to be able to read French?

Nonetheless, Severine smiled happily as she ascended the stairs, shuffling the bills to the bottom of the stack and observing, with intensifying excitement, that Corinne, Marie-Sophie, and Alain had each sent something. Birthday cards, she supposed gleefully, happy at the timing of the often undependable international post. But photos—even better! Severine had photos of her three partners elsewhere, of course, but that was not the same as new ones.

Severine took the envelopes with her into the bedroom, nudging the penny loafers from her feet as she leaned back against the pillows. She took Alain's letter first, lifting it to her nose as she opened it. The scent of Lilac Vegetal and black cigarettes met her halfway, bringing tears of longing to her eyes. The paper had been folded around something stiff, and as she unfolded the letter, two Polaroids fell onto the bed at her side. She picked them up and gasped softly, instantly feeling a hot flush creep over her face and down onto her chest as a very similar heat tingled between her legs. Almost unable to believe it, she shook her head and laughed softly, amazedly, feeling dazed.

Sacrebleu. Photographs. I did not know, but how could I have known? I could not see them, and there was enough noise, between that loud little mademoiselle of ours and the sound of my pounding heart and hard breathing that I probably didn't hear the camera whir. Even if I had, would I have known? Even had I known, what would I have done? Nothing. Corinne tied me too tightly for that. The most I could have done was tell them no, beg them to stop. And even that . . . well. Mon Dieu. I had not forgotten this—how could I?—but to live it

*again, in the cold light of distance and not with the comforting blur
of lust . . .*

So disgusting. So beautiful.

Severine, my love—
You will agree, yes, even you must agree that you are a treasure
when you see these photographs. We did not tell you what we
were going to do with you, no, but it was not then your prerog-
ative to know. You had only two duties the night before you flew
away . . . to keep your restless tongue busy, and to open to us as
we took our fill of you. We knew that we would miss you too
badly to let you leave us less than glutted. And we did have your
best interests at heart: Remember, you told me that you, panicky
flier, slept well on the airplane.

I look at these photos, lurid as they are, and remember only
sacredness and love. You, I am sure, do not find that strange, but
you are a benevolent angel of flesh and always have been. It star-
tles me somewhat to see you at this remove, here in my hand, as
lusciously passive as you were between my thighs, to see the
blissful relaxation on your face as my cock slid between your
lips, deeper and deeper into your mouth and throat. I can
almost feel the awed and grateful hum as I slowly drove the
length of myself against the tangling swirl of your ever-agile
tongue. The grace with which you receive me belies the ugliness
of the name of the act each time I straddle your head and fuck
long and solid, as if it were the muter of your mouths into which
I stroked. You have always loved being mouth-fucked that way.
Only Corinne's bites and strong hands make you as wet, as
ready, force you to come as wantonly as does the sensation of
my cock so forcefully invading your elegant mouth.

We all watched you disrobe for us, and when you stood
naked and Marie-Sophie brought your corset, Corinne took
your arms and cuffed them over your head as I stroked your
lovely face. Marie-Sophie laced you in, too tightly, which is to
say just tightly enough. Cori kissed you, do you remember? You
melted against her as she explained to you what you already
knew: that you were ours, that we would take you, each alone

and all together, using your mouth, your cunt, your ass, your breasts, however it pleased us. You clung to her desperately, your lips in a crimson circle against her neck, and my heart leapt impossibly, desperate to keep you with us, horrified to think of letting you go so far.

I could not touch you for several moments, the phantom of impending loss too present, but then they lay you down on the quilts, in Corinne's room, on the mattresses that cover the floor, and you looked up at me with curiously childlike eyes. The other two were busy with you, Marie-Sophie already kneeling down between your legs, Corinne chaining your wrists to the wall (not that you would have resisted us), and yet I felt almost as if you forgot them. "Please, Alain, you mustn't be sad," you said, your voice soft, "I need you, please, in my mouth so I can remember how you use me so well. Fuck my mouth, Alain, please?"

Corinne slipped on your eyeshade and I straddled your head facing Marie-Sophie, whose blonde curls bobbed as her wicked tongue teased you. I looked down at your leather-cinched form, your pretty breasts pushed up and out of the corset, wondering whether Marie-Sophie would bring you to gasping before I could. To my surprise, she did not. As if you had been waiting for me despite the tongue flickering at your submissive clit, it was not until I had sunk myself in your mouth that your body finally shuddered and you began to writhe. But then you have said that you never feel so thoroughly caught up in sex as when your mouth is being ruthlessly used, when a cock crushes your lips against your teeth or when you are within a gasp of smothering from the relentless bucking of cunt against your teeth and tongue.

I used you harder than I meant to. The agony of knowing I was to lose you, if only for a time, pushed my hips against your face harder than I should have let it. Oh, I remember it! No one else, no one, takes a cock like you, *belle Severine*, nothing can compare with the cannibal orchid of your throat. Do you see in this photograph how you lay there, saliva in a stream down your cheek, my cock buried in your throat as you took me in, the raw and open vessel of the fuck?

I used you every way I could, so that when you left, you would have the essence of me in your belly, in your cunt, in your ass, in your skin where Corinne rubbed our mingled juices into your face and breasts. It seemed crucial, somehow, to be inside each part of you, to leave a trace of myself so that you could find me again.

Look at the photos, *mon hirondelle*, do you see the expression on your face? Here, where I was in your pert ass, Marie-Sophie's hand in you to her slim doll's wrist, Cori's quicksilver all over your face, do you see it? Do you see the angelic purity with which you took it all, the way you let us use you? You burned for us from the inside, a cathedral at Christmas.

Yes, *chérie*, we miss you. I miss you. I smoke in the evenings on the rooftop, alone now but for the notebook and pen I take with me when it is dry and clear. It will please you that I sit on the ledge now, and it will probably please you more that, once in a while, when there is an empty space in the air next to me that is shaped particularly like you, I sit down on that old green-gray blanket, there behind the chimney-pot where we once made love, and I watch the stars and stroke myself and think of you.

Bon anniversaire, Severine, *mon amour*.

Lying on the bed, Severine let the hand that held the letter droop to her chest, the paper curling against her breasts. Her small nipples were hard as dart points beneath her sweater. Looking at herself being so deliciously used, tightly clamped nipples so cruelly pulled toward one another by the short chain that connected the clamps, Alain's cock buried in her throat, her hips had begun to undulate as if by themselves, pushing her clit toward the seam of her jeans. She could almost taste Corinne's sweet liquor, feel the meaty bulb of her fat clit mashed against her tongue.

Severine slid her hand under the waistband of her jeans, fingers slipping easily between her puffy lips into the sweet seawater slickness between as she picked up the photos again. Longingly she saw, and remembered, Alain roughly penetrating her bound, helpless body. His cock in her ass, not as thick as the dildo Corinne had forced into her, but longer, so that when he fucked her she felt the forbidden deliciousness in her deepest, most secret of spaces. In the picture all but a few centimeters were buried in between the smooth halves of her ass, and she scissored her clitoris between her fingers, remembering the time that he had made her count— the price for being permitted to indulge her curiosity with a seamstress' measure—as he worked it into her that way, counting one two three four five, all the way to twenty-four centimeters before he was buried in her ass to his balls.

Alain! How dare you write to me like this, how dare you send the photographs and not be here to take me that way again! I am here with one hand in my jeans, fingers slick, remembering that night and the taste of you, remembering the sheer inescapable need each time you lunged into me. Yes, you battered me, you left me bruised. You ground my lips against my teeth so that for a week I looked as if Sophie had sent me off with her bee-stung pout as a parting gift. Your strokes kept me grounded amid the stairways of anguish and delight that rose from Cori's mouth on my nipples, Sophie's on my cunt, the fingers in my pussy, that dildo Corinne drove slowly into my ass to ready me (it was too big, it was, and it hurt, but only for an instant and only as it melted into the thick cream of pleasure).

I did not lie. I needed you to fuck my mouth, to make me necessary, to let me give and not only take. If only there had been three of you instead, so that I could have had you in me, in every hole, simultaneously. If only I could be so replete with you now. If only.

Taking her cunt-scented hand from her crotch, Severine ripped open a second envelope. A single sheet of champagne-colored paper nested inside, folded in half around two more photographs. Circular and swooping, dark green vowel-bubbles rolling across the lines, Marie-Sophie's letter was as short and curvy as the writer herself. The Polaroids wrenched Severine's heart just as ruthlessly as her clit. Corinne. In ecstasy.

> Severine, my sister-love, forgive this bad little girl for not writing or calling as much as you would wish. Forgive me too for not yet having learned to use the computer, but it seems so cold. I am

sometimes thoughtless but I am not heartless, so do not think
that I do not love you just because I do not write.

I picked these because they reminded me of one reason I love
you. You are beautiful because you are endless. You are beautiful
because you satisfy but leave me wanting. You are beautiful
because I can never get enough of the abandon that you achieve
so effortlessly but that I myself cannot ever seem to enter. You
see it, here, in the pictures I made of you.

Corinne bit your breasts, mauled them to make you sing with
lust and agony, while Alain plunged into your cunt, spreading
your legs wide, holding your ankles, slamming to the bottom of
each stroke. He put your legs on his shoulders and reached for
Cori's pussy. As he forced her open, she chewed your little breast
so hard I thought you might bleed, so anguished she was with
her own pleasure. Instead you came, shouting and arching, and
then you came again as Corinne lunged for your other nipple
and bit so sharply, sucking so hard, that I cringed. You screamed
as they claimed you, the two of them, Alain's knuckles disap-
pearing into Cori's impossible cunt and completing the circuit.
Your mouth was open in a scream of purest belonging. I envied
you then, *ma soeur-amie*, but I could not help loving you as well.

Happy Birthday seems pale in comparison, but it is what your
petite blondine who loves you wishes for you, sweet girl. Come
back to us soon.

Severine was grateful for the bits of explanation in the letters, for
she could not clearly remember who had done what to her, or
when, or in what order, the night before she flew away. She knew
only that they had taken her, and did not stop. She had passed out
briefly and had woken to find them still gently loving her, one
mouth at each nipple, one mouth on her clitoris, three soft
tongues calling her back to them. After they had roused her they
had continued, for they were not yet satisfied. She was their whore
that night, after all, a role she cherished, a task she was always
dreadfully afraid she would not be able to fulfill to their satisfaction. It pleased her so deeply that they had continued even when
she could not move, that they simply used her, forcing her to

come, filling her, fucking her. It had felt right that Marie-Sophie and finally Corinne had fucked their sloppy-wet cunts against her mouth, that Alain's cock shot deep into her cunt and was then replaced with fingers, later a fist, and then Alain was in her ass as well and still she remained the center, the fulcrum, the semen-soaked, arching and sobbing delirious animal fulcrum of the fuck.

Marie-Sophie's photographs were agonizing. Shot from the side, they showed Corinne's face contorted with enraged bliss, Alain's hand wedged into her from behind as he fucked hard into Severine's juice-matted cunt. Severine saw her own open mouth, throat taut with the force of her scream. Alain had been caught in mid-stroke, half of his long lean cock pushing into her, Corinne's mouth digging hard, viciously, into Severine's breast. In the second photo Severine could see the dark ring of tooth marks, marks which had taken almost a month to fade. In her first lonely Canadian weeks Severine had often brought herself to a homesick climax, eyes locked on the rings of tooth prints where her sweet Corinne had marked and possessed her.

Corinne, Corinne, so matter-of-fact about the brutal part of love. From the start she simply unleashed her need, seemed to know that my soul required it. Alain understands it perfectly, but he cannot hurt me like she can. He can use me as she cannot, though, with the one-eyed blindness of the male, that selfish possession that leaves me ragged. I marvel that Corinne requires that blindness and force as much as I. No wonder Sophie envied us the mathematics of our linked yielding, the commutative power of alchemical cock-violence opening Corinne's cunt, pushing her teeth into my flesh as I screamed with the obscene freedom of flight. As for Sophie, our gossamer girl with the liquid candlelight voice, I sense she goes there when she sings. She can only go there alone, but wants so much to go with someone—anyone—else. We try, but fail, to take her there. She is one of us, but not one with us, and perhaps that is why we cannot do otherwise than love her as blindly, as unfailingly, as we do.

Tears in her eyes, Severine skimmed her jeans down her thighs, swallowing back the longing that knotted her throat, trying to focus on the shimmering heat that turned within her womb. She flipped her panties across the room with her foot as she tore open Corinne's envelope, aching with longing and lust. The photographs were face down against the letter. On the back of each photograph was a number, and she lay them in order, still face down, on the bedspread beside her, just as she already knew Corinne wished her to do.

My sweet Severine, angel whore, pretty pussy, greedy girl, how I miss you! It is your birthday, almost, and we have decided to remind you of us. I hope you remember how we like to use you, how much we love to make you ours, how much we like to fuck you while we tell you how we violate your pussy, mouth, tight soft ass. Oh, how I miss making you writhe with vicious words and teeth and fingers, and oh, how the bed seems too wide without you to help fill it.

Take the first photograph, Severine. Do you remember that instant? I asked Alain to take at least one picture of me filling your cunt with my fingers while I tortured those lovely little breasts of yours. I wanted to remind you of how it was when we began. It was just you and I then, you so skittish and afraid that you asked me to bind you tightly so that you could abandon yourself to the rapture. Do you recall how I tied you, wrists over your head, and slowly, gently worked you until you were able to let me touch you, not only your body but your heart? Can you remember how it felt to do this for the first time, bound, spread, fucked, used, nipples throbbing? Do you recall how you sobbed uncontrollably when you came, and I pushed you further, held you by nipples and cunt over the fires of your need like a spider being dangled over a candle flame by a thread of its own silk? I remember it well, and I remember your shuddering, sobbing as you begged me to ruin you.

This second photograph of you, I confess, I chose for beauty's sake. My pretty girls together open the innermost reserves of delight in my heart, for I can think of few things more lovely than your body moving with Marie-Sophie's. Look how she rides your face, your tongue and teeth, leaning forward, clawing your breasts, your hips bucking up out of sheer unconscious animal empathy with the nearness of her orgasm. That round little *crème de coeur* of a face gone savage with lust, the dark rose of your nipple just barely visible between two of her greedy fingers, the rolling swoops of her body hovering over the lean pantherine lines of your own! Such a spectacle, the two of you!

And then there is the simple fact that I love what you will take for me, what you will trust. Do you see in the third photo how you arched up for me as I pulled on the chain of the clamps, how you were almost like a marionette, pulled up by your cruelly pinched nipples, your motion forcing you further down on the dildo whose fat head I'd just worked into your ass? I had worked so much lube into you, but still I worried—you'd never taken anything so thick for me, not there. And so I held it in place, braced against my knee, just as you see me, one hand kneading your bubblegum clit, one hand pulling your back up off of the quilts so that you had no choice but to slide down relentlessly onto the cock I'd chosen to violate you. I could feel your clit twitching under my fingers as you began to spasm, though the cock was only halfway inside you. I wish only that you could've seen how much it stretched you, for I know that it arouses you to know how I've forced you to open for me.

I made a puppet of you like that four times, four agonizing, beautiful times, until the cock was buried in you to its base. I can still hear your pleading—"No, no, it is too much!" But oh, Severine, in the next instant you begged me never to stop, to use you, to love you, to ruin you, to tear your sweet body, to fill you and never to let it end. I promised, and I meant it, and ten long slow times I pulled the cock almost out of your ass, and ten long thick wrenching times I plunged it hard back into you. Incoherent, you screamed and could not stop coming, and I yanked the clips from your nipples and sucked at your clit and rammed into you harder with the impossibly thick cock until you arched a final time and then lay limp, beyond yourself, unconscious, truly devastated by what you will accept only from my hands.

How I miss that, Severine, my saucy brilliant love. I miss so

much the way you let me touch you so deeply there, where you
are desperate to be broken. In some ways it is in you, on and
within your body that I become the best and purest version of
my self.

    Bon anniversaire, ma petite. I miss you. I long to have you
again, here, where you belong, at home. Soon. In the meantime,
I hope that you will look at these photos, meager as they are,
and remember that we miss you.

Severine could not bear it. Her cunt and face dripped with different sorts of tears, and there were smears on the pages, on the
glossy surfaces of the photos. Burying her face in the pillows, she
rolled over onto her belly, hand sliding under her hip to her
groin, left hand cupping her breast and pinching the nipple with
a severity that made her gasp out loud. Feverish, heedless,
Severine let present and past collide in a panorama of remembered sensation and the desperate need to be again what she saw
in the Polaroids, to be her lovers' perfect whore. As she came, she
sobbed out loud, though whether more with the force of orgasm
or the brutal longing she could not be sure.

    In time Severine lay quiet, fingers drenched and still tucked
inside her. Softly from the other room she could hear the radio,
CBC news mutter like overhearing the neighbors' cocktail party
through a half-open window. Wiping her hand on the duvet as
she pushed herself up into a sitting position, she looked around
her at the scattered pages, Polaroids lying around her like leaves.
A wistful grin tweaked the corners of her mouth into curves as
she gathered them, ordering the pages, stacking the photos into
three piles face down on the edge of the bedside table, and then
she noticed a few lines on the back of Alain's first photograph, a
note she had not noticed before.

    You are frozen like this in my mind. I am on the roof missing
    you, blowing smoke billows in which I search for your face.
    There is so much I miss. I love you.

She smiled more widely as she reread his words, and the sharp edge of longing suddenly dulled and faded within her, the tightness of her chest easing as the gentle constancy of Alain's words penetrated her core. She missed all of them, yes, but suddenly it was not so unbearable somehow. She would take anything for them, even this, and it was with unashamed lust that she began to reread and review, fingers slipping between her legs, looking anew at the photographs of her truest self, her love-bound self, caught in wondrous abjection, the constant and unflinching bearer of all the terrible weight of love.

What I Wanted
(Cooperstown, New York)

What I wanted was to take you by the hand, pull you to me, and kiss you hard on the mouth, then cling to you for a moment, smelling the fresh sweat on your neck, and whisper in your ear to go and get your things and come with me. What I wanted was your anticipation, loading your baseball gear into the back of my battered, beloved Ford, the bats clanking together with the satisfying sound of solid wood, to see the slightly nervous eager boyish look in your eye as I watched you moving in your uniform with your name stitched across your sweet strong shoulders. I can remember your smell, warm in the back of my nose, knowing how your skin would taste just from smelling you as I held you in my arms or sat beside you, from the shifting veil of musk and malted sun, earth, grass stains, and simple lust that drowsily swam from your body through the late-summer air. It's been almost a year since I had the chance to smell you like that, and my brain and heart still spin like a kid dancing in the rain at the memory.

I wanted to take you into my motel room, where it smelled like the bleach they used on the sheets, not letting you shower first, not letting you change, not letting you protest. I wanted to pull the blinds and turn on the air conditioner with the fan on high, knowing that no fan is going to mask my sex cries, but feeling a little more privacy just the same. I wanted to take you

33

home with me, straight from the ballpark, to that little room, forty dollars a night. I wanted to kiss you, hard and hungry and unapologetic, and dig my fingers into your shoulders and back and slide my hands into your waistband and pull you against me by your hips, greedy and impulsive. I wanted your hands moving over me, touching my chin and hair and neck and breasts, and trying to find a way under my skirt, but then I didn't want to let you. I wanted you to be mine first.

I wanted the chance to savor you and lick the sweat from your collarbones, to marvel at every fresh revelation as I unbuttoned your jersey. I wanted to make you stand until you couldn't bear it anymore, knees too weak, as my hands pushed fabric away from skin, as my mouth swirled little moans and pleased murmurs against your skin. I wanted your fingers knotted in my hair, kneading my skull and neck in rhythmic, restless motions that would tell me *don't stop* and *right there*. I wanted that to be mine, and I wanted to hear and see the half-disbelieving "oh" from your lips as I nuzzled my nose and cheeks and lips against your hip, the top of your thigh, letting my cheek brush against your cock, letting my breath graze your belly and pubic hair. I wanted your voice, hushed and hoarse, telling me, asking me, as I inhaled the potent blend of sweat and skin and fear that came from your vulnerable, longing, masculine thighs. I wanted to hear you, and feel you, and I knew exactly what those words would have sounded like tumbling from your chewable, suckable, endlessly playful lips.

I wanted to look up at you and watch your face as I teased you. I didn't want to let you have it all at once but instead slowly let my lips trail along the length of your cock, tantalizing, deliberate. I wanted the tension of your belly as you watched my tongue curl around the tip of you, watching me take it slow, painting your hardness with lingering stripes, taking that first sweet pearl of honey onto my tongue with a grin and savoring it. I wanted to make you wait, wanted to hear you mumble, to see that handsome face of yours haggard and sublime with need, twitching with the shocks stabbing outward from the tip of my tongue as it flickered along the underside of your sex. And if I wanted to wrap my lips languidly around your cock, knowing that my lips were dark red with my own arousal, and begin to taste and swirl and suck and lick in earnest, I wanted it at least as much for my own sake as for yours.

I wanted to be able to close my eyes and smell you, taste you, feel your cock sliding between my lips, pressing my lips against my teeth, pushing my tongue against the bottom of my mouth as you filled my mouth with such touching hardness, such beautiful agony, that it brought tears to my eyes and it didn't matter that I couldn't say the words to tell you that I loved you. I wanted to reach up, sliding my hands up over your hips, and have you take my hands, sliding your hands down to my wrists as I clasped yours so that there would be no hands in the way of the shaft that filled my mouth and fucked me smooth and true. I wanted to take you there, to be the angel of your release.

I wanted to feel you tremble, to find out how you move and breathe, how your body tenses in the instants before you come, feel the pressure of your fingers on my arms, in my hair, on my head and neck and shoulders. I wanted to feel the truth between my lips, a bubble as inevitable and silver as the moon, shimmying and hurtling upward, faster and faster, until it broke the surface and I drank its tautness down and was satisfied. That, ultimately, was what I wanted, what I wished for, what I finally realized I couldn't have, the desire you shared but said your vows couldn't withstand.

I wanted it, very much.

Hair

"Oh, just because," he answered, flashing her an enigmatic smile.

"No," she countered, puckish. "I don't think that's all of it." She was flattered, and touched. It wasn't every day that someone you were crazy about told you that he loved you. She just wondered if he'd ever admit to the real reason.

"No?"

"No, not entirely," she replied, her fingers finding and slowly spinning the end of one of the long ebony chopsticks that speared the enormous bird's nest of her upswept hair. His eyes followed her fingers, not her lips, and she knew that she was right.

He was older than she. Considerably older. Enough so that more than once, when he had arrived at their restaurant too early, the maitre d' would show him to the usual table and inquire, in his soft Irish accent, "Will your daughter will be joining you this evening?"

He would nod, but he had no daughter. No daughter, and no son, and while he had a wife, they had reached their detente nine years into their marriage. That had been fourteen years ago. Since then, she had her lovers, he had his, and they were fabulous, if geographically distant, friends. With two offices to maintain, it only made sense that one of them stay in New York while the other remained in Chicago. He hated New York.

He wondered what his wife would say if she met her, the younger woman. She'd probably laugh, tell him he was going through a midlife crisis. Shortly after he'd begun seeing the curly-haired cellist, he had browsed through her wallet while she showered. With a wince he discovered that, if her driver's license could be trusted, he had gotten married two years before she was born. She'd never mentioned her age to him. Then again, he'd never asked. He wondered if he'd have been better off not knowing just how many years there were between them.

He hadn't meant to look through her wallet. Sometimes these things just happen. It was sitting open on the nightstand, her phone card still lying next to it from when she'd called her mother back in San Francisco. "Happy birthday, Mom," she'd burbled into the phone before launching into an incomprehensible mixture of English, Armenian, and giggles. She giggled a lot when she talked to her mother, he'd noticed, even more so when he tried to seduce her while she was on the phone.

It had been her mother's fiftieth birthday. She knew he was older than that, older than her mother. It had never occurred to her to ask by how much. His lips on the backs of her knees, applying consecutive kisses up the backs of her chubby, satin-skinned thighs, had eventually drowned out her urge to wish her mother a happy birthday one more time.

It was thickly passionate. It always was. His head nestled between her legs until she gasped and pushed him away, not able to take any more, tears covering her cheeks in sheets as she half-choked for air. And then as she rested, he rubbed himself against her buoyant breasts, tickled himself under the chin with her arrogant nipples. Then he gathered her hair in his hands, fucking his cock into the whorled black nest he'd made for himself as she lay there, indulgent, idly stroking her clit as he worked himself to a quick, spastic release.

Afterward, she showered. He wondered how many people actually sang in the shower like she did, so beautifully and unselfconsciously. The song seemed halfway familiar. He thought it was the same song every time, but he wasn't completely sure.

Fresh out of the shower her hair hung wetly almost to her knees. She bundled it up in two towels. He'd learned to set out an enormous pile of extra towels in the bathroom. It wasn't that the two of them took that many showers, though she did like to shower after sex. She needed them. It was the hair.

He'd mentioned it the first time he'd ever spoken to her, she remembered. She was putting her cello away in the green room after the recital, the rest of her quartet yammering with the friends who had come to congratulate them. Her A string had snapped in the middle of the Schubert, and she was still furious. They'd started again, of course, but new strings never hold tune very well, and now the tape of the recital would be useless.

She fumed under her breath, less wanting reassurance from her friends than to get her money's worth out of a good mad. And then he came up behind her, his tall shadow on the wall the first thing she saw.

She took his breath away. The dark nimbus of hair that surrounded her might've been a thunderhead. "I hate to be so forward," he began, "but I can't think of anything I'd like to do more in this world than walk barefoot through your hair."

The last two latches on her case snapped shut with angry little clicks. "Fuck off," she said, buttoning her coat and shouldering her case, not even pausing to look at him. She bulldozed her way out of the green room, waving sullen goodbyes to her quartet-mates. They rolled their eyes. She was so dramatic.

He pulled up to the curb where she waited for the bus. It wasn't snowing. That would've been too picturesque, and besides, it was too damned cold to snow. She hated Chicago in December.

"Look, I'm sorry I was such an asshole back there," he called, unrolling the passenger-side window. "Can I offer you a lift to the train to make up for it?"

She peered into the car. Leather seats. The heaters had to be on full blast. She could feel the warm air on her face. His cashmere coat fell open, showing a sweater and button-down shirt, a bit of silk necktie just visible. He wore wool trousers, the suppleness of their drape and the richness of their hue betraying not only taste but money. He was probably yuppie scum, she decided, but the vibe that he gave off was harmless enough. It was bitterly cold and there was a nasty little ice breeze sneaking up beneath her skirt.

"Okay, thanks. Let me put Justin in the back seat." He got out and opened the door for her to lay the big, scuffed, black cello case on the broad leather seat.

"Justin? Why'd you name it that?"

"Justin Case," she replied, with the satisfied little grin it always gave her. He rolled his eyes. She arched an eyebrow, watching him stifle a chuckle. Revising her opinion of him slightly, she got into the passenger seat beside him.

She liked him in spite of herself. That was why, when he pulled up to the train station and offered to drive her the rest of the way home rather than making her wait for the train, she said yes. And that was why she let him make her laugh on the way to Rogers Park where she lived. At the end of the ride she let him kiss her. It was a cold night, after all, and the heat of a first kiss felt defiant and good. Besides, she was more than a little attracted.

She had to admit it, if only to herself. She liked older men. Always had. And he turned out to be quite charming, and tall, and his tight black ringlets were spiraled with titanium white, not so unlike her father's as to escape her notice. So she did let him kiss her, but she couldn't very well keep it a secret that she kissed him right back.

She noticed a few things, too, about the way his fingers buried themselves in her hair, and the way that he kissed her neck as a pretense. It wasn't that he didn't want to kiss her neck, not really. It was just that her hair was there, too.

Her hair. That astonishing hair. He felt lucky that she didn't seem repulsed. She gave him her number. It wasn't that he didn't seem interested in her, she explained later to a friend. He had just been very obviously interested in her hair. It was a little odd, but seemed harmless enough. Besides, he almost made the pain in the ass of having so much hair seem worth it. He was her type. She didn't mind.

* * *

The drier her hair became, the shorter it grew. It never did get precisely short, though. No curl could ever be tight enough to shorten her follicular profusion to anything less than ass-length, and that suited her well enough. At that length, at least, it stayed where it was put, a condition that could not be depended on when it was short enough to have a gravity-defying mind of its own.

He lay on the bed, cock stirring against his thigh. He watched as she walked from the bathroom to where her bag lay on the floor, next to the cello case, next to the window. No, he thought to himself, that's not right. She doesn't so much walk as roll, or maybe bounce, or simply undulate. "Walk" sounded too Euclidean, he thought further, too many straight lines. She was thirty pounds of potatoes in a twenty-pound sack, he mused, pleased in a stretchy leonine sort of way that was as much love as possessiveness and as much possessiveness as sheer sensual delight. It would never occur to him to call her fat. It was just that her body matched her hair. That hair, outrageously full, scandalously curly, dark as sin, lush as Aphrodite's undies, and to him at least, hot as hell.

She caught his gaze. "Not now," she complained in a tone that meant she didn't really mean it.

"Yes, now," he said, crossing the room to take her hips in his hands, his body pressing against the still-damp hair that hung in a mass down her back.

"I'll miss class," she sighed as her nipples were suddenly and expertly trapped by two pairs of talented fingers.

"You'll survive," he replied, pressing into her with his hips, the length of his cock nestling into the moss-damp crevice of her just-showered ass, her hair a coarse raw-silk mattress keeping skin from skin. She wriggled back toward him.

"I've already missed three classes this semester," she murmured as he filled both his hands with both her breasts and nipped the edge of her earlobe.

"I'll help you study for the final," he promised, the pressure of his knees against the backs of her thighs pushing her down, three-two-one, toward the bed. She let herself be bent over, sighing as he spread her legs and knelt between them, his tongue probing her cunt, lips suckling her clit until she writhed, almost coming, as he flickered the incredibly sensitive crinkles of her asshole.

She could never resist the quick in-and-out of his tongue in her ass. She knew it. So did he. He knew it would sway her, that she'd yield without hesitation, and she did.

Who was he, he thought to himself, to get to peer like this over the lip of the bowl of creation? Each time he'd ever slid into her he'd been held, transfixed, alarmed, awed. She didn't seem aware of her own raw fecund potential, the quality about her that was so primevally Woman that it made him slightly insane. As his cock drew slowly out from the grip of her sleek wet walls, and the rock-pigeon noises curled out of her throat, he slid back into her from behind and let his fingers wander through the complications of the hair that rippled and shook as she did.

So far away, he mused, his thoughts forming in lucid and much-too-urbane descant to the logical primitive rhythm of his movements. In some moments it didn't seem fair not to be able to enter her with more than just his body. In other moments it was just the inevitable failing of his manhood, and the thing inside him that yawned open with want would wail. His hips would pound her harder. His cock would batter her cervix and make the cat noises rip from her throat, his hands mauling her breasts. His descent into madness matched her descent into rut.

He couldn't seem to come. It often happened like that. That was where the madness came from. He'd almost get there but not quite, stuck forever squinting through the knothole in the outfield fence. He pounded her hard and harder, wishing his way into her womb, into her belly, into the full sweet sweep of her hips. He was furious, and still it wouldn't come. So far away, she whinnied like a mare and her ass slapped his belly, full and fine and fat and glistening with funk as she came full force, her body squeezing him hard, muscles wringing him like a rag.

"I love your stamina," she'd said once, not that she knew that it wasn't stamina, just a peculiar kind of impotence. He figured it was just as well that she thought it was. "I want more," she panted, looking back at him over her shoulder as he shuttled gently, slowly, a few inches in and out of her body. "If you're going to make me miss class, I want another."

She was delighted by it, by him, by his cock and his touch and his smile and the way he wanted her. It was evident in her look, in her voice, even when he made her miss class. Her hungry smile sent a shock through his body as strong as if she'd flipped a switch.

"Where do you want it, then?"

"You know where," she replied, her voice shifting downward to its roots, rumbling as dark as her earth-colored mane. Honest open eyes met his as he smiled. His cock throbbed. Her pussy throbbed around him in reply.

Sometimes he was grateful for the combination of age and inability to come. As a younger man he never would've managed to give her as much as she asked for. In synch he stroked his cock and her asshole, hand on one, tongue on the other. Lube so thick it barely flowed made a layer between his palm and his cock. She shivered and bucked, and he pushed his tongue tip against the pucker of her, parting her just the slightest bit. It was enough to make her say please, and he did.

He'd have thought himself lucky for many reasons, he'd reflected often enough. The hair would have been enough. But then there was the music she made. And there was the way she screamed with his mouth on her clit. And there was the open-eyed awe with which she took him in her ass, opening to him soundlessly as he pushed slowly into her until he was lodged in her to the hilt, staring back over her shoulder at him with her lips in an O. As if it had never happened before. As if it could never happen that way again. As if she had never felt anything truly enter her. At least not the way he could. He believed it even though he knew better.

With his fingers on her clit she never asked him to be slow. Not if she was ready, which she was, almost already on the verge as he crammed into her tightest and tiniest hole. It wasn't that she'd ever refused him. But he preferred it when she craved him. And as he gazed down at his cock, framed and surrounded by the curling tresses that dawdled across her back and over her ass, she moaned and said please again.

One stroke in. All the way. And then all the way out. Two strokes in, all the way in, rocking until his balls made sticky contact with the dripping lips of her cunt. Three.

"Harder." He was only too happy to oblige. She spasmed and whined, her whimpers turning to kitten-mewls when she realized belatedly, as she always seemed to, that he was not yet close to being done. Riding the endorphins, she was almost silent as he built his speed.

"Yes," she said, her voice solemn and throaty. She liked this part of the fuck, where it became raw around the edges, but she wasn't quite there yet. Not quite. And then suddenly she was, bursting with motion and bucking into him with a ferocity that had frightened him the first few times it happened. She called forth his demons and absorbed them, slamming her ass back at him. The challenge was to match her terrible female hunger. They collided like bulls or boars or elk, her need coaxing him until he slammed into her with the entirety of his weight, and she lay pinned, brutalized, beyond herself in the wallowing thrill of it.

"Pull my hair."

It was close. It was not that she couldn't climax from the fuck alone. She came easily, with him. She trusted him. But she needed to trust him to ride her hard, and she needed to trust him not to let her go until he was finished. Sweetly, the reins of conscious thought slipped from his grip as the thick ropes of her hair filled his hands and he pulled her head back taut against her shoulders.

Slamming into her asshole, his cock burgeoned with the force of seed. His balls grew tight. His face was red with furious need and the bliss of being inside her, not merely within her but inside her. Just where he needed to be. Just where she craved him. Pulling her down onto him. Savage. Not letting her go. Handfuls of hair, handful after handful after fistful, knotted in his hands. Desperate. Almost criminal, he lunged as she screamed, deep into the body of the woman whom he could only just admit he loved. He sobbed. They might've drowned in the unforgiving surge.

* * *

In the coffee shop he bought her lunch. She had to go to orchestra and to quartet rehearsal. He had work to do, too. At some point.

"What do you think made you finally decide to tell me that you love me?" she asked. Her coffee cup was almost empty.

"Just because," he answered, flashing her an enigmatic smile.

"No," she countered, puckish. "I don't think that's all of it." She was flattered, and touched. It wasn't every day that someone you were crazy about told you that he loved you. She just wondered if he'd ever admit to the real reason.

"No?"

"No, not entirely," she replied, her fingers finding and slowly spinning the end of one of the long ebony chopsticks that speared the enormous bird's nest of her upswept hair. His eyes followed her fingers, not her lips, and she knew that she was right.

She pulled one chopstick from her hair as she stood up, tucking it into the pocket of her coat as she grabbed her cello case and backpack and turned toward him. He stood up from the table. "It's not that I don't believe you. I just think there are other reasons."

Standing on tiptoes, she stepped toward him and kissed him full on the lips. He kissed back, his lips in a smile. Early March sunlight bleached the side of her face.

"But I do love you," he said quietly, relishing the actinic brilliance the sun lent to the outermost haze of her curls.

His crow's feet only made him more handsome, she thought. Such a lovely man. Smart. Almost a shame that he was already married.

His eyes were clear and strong and they followed her hand again as she pulled the second chopstick from her hair and shook her head, the hair billowing down around her pea coat-clad shoulders. Extending the chopstick, she smiled.

"Pick me up at the bus stop at nine," she instructed. He took the long skinny black stick from her hand. She walked away, not looking back as she hoisted her cello and moved toward the door, the glass opaque with condensation. Her voice wove its way back to him through the clatter of cups and the hissing of steam. "And don't be late. I want you to pull my hair again."

The Cinematographer's Party

C arine didn't look the type.

Delia did look the type, though, and Delia had brought me there, to the cinematographer's party. But Delia wasn't the type, not really. Oh, she dressed it, luscious young curves poured into crazy kitschy getups, cleavage packed like a smoking revolver into a hot pink pushup bra, wearing her filthy, scarlet-lipsticked mouth like a corsage of stinkweed. Underneath it, though, she was Campbell's Cream of Suburbia, slacking through her M.F.A. courtesy of the tastefully upholstered parents for whom she dressed in J. Crew twice a year when she went to see them in a very nice suburb on a very nice coast that wasn't this one. I'd hoped to find a more enthusiastic do-me femme, a little more natchral-born slut behind the fishnets and the leather bustier. Yeah, I know, we butches are supposed to be strong and silent and always be on top, and sometimes I am, but the reality is that I'm at my best when the girl I'm with is just a few steps ahead of me, when she lets me know, in all those fabulous feminine ways, what she wants to let me get away with. Call it a symbiotic relationship.

Delia and I were in the convenience-date stage, that stage where you're not seeing each other any more, but you're not officially seeing anyone else yet. She'd needed a date for a party, so I said I'd go. You know how it is. A lot of dykes around here still believe in U-Haul on the second date, and sometimes it's just no fun to face the marrieds all alone.

Delia's always fun to watch at parties. My voyeur side gets a workout watching the boys try to talk her up. They want her so bad. I think it's the teensy little Catholic-schoolgirl skirts. Of course it never works, but oh, how they try. I like it even better when Delia gets a little tipsy and starts to flirt with other women. They like it, and start to respond, then remember that they saw her come in with me. They keep me in their peripheral vision, and this amazing tension builds as they try to figure out how much they can get away with, how hard they can flirt with "my" girl before I get offended. Delia likes the attention. I suspect the tension, even though it's not precisely relevant anymore since we broke up, is half the reason Delia still invites me to these things.

That was exactly what was happening when I first noticed Carine watching me. At first I couldn't manage to catch her eye. Every time I felt her looking at me, I'd look up only to see her blond bob bobbing and her thick horn-rimmed glasses moving as she talked to someone else.

I started to ask Delia if she'd noticed, but she was busy having her cigarette lit by a tall stone butch in leather jeans who flipped her Zippo open with a James Dean-ish swagger. Delia eats that shit up. Just like I originally ate up Delia's slut-girl drag, the lip-stick, the bravura with which she originally told me—on our first date—to take her home and eat her til she screamed. I wasn't about to speculate whether I'd be driving home solo. I didn't really care. Carine was staring at me again. And damn it all, I couldn't seem to catch her doing it.

After trying to capture Carine's eye for a good ten minutes, I got tired of the cat-and-mouse. Suddenly, she looked right at me, taking me by surprise. Feeling a bit shy, not sure how to respond, I grinned slightly, and she reciprocated with a dazzling grin, immensely warm and just barely predatory, that scrunched up the corners of her eyes. I'm not sure why, but I felt a little thrill when we made eye contact, a little tickle of energy that siz-zled around my solar plexus and echoed softly in my pussy. She wasn't going to stop traffic, short and round and bookish, but there was definitely something about Carine that I liked. I smiled a little more. So did she.

A half-second later she was talking to someone else. Fine, I thought. Whatever. Her place, her party, her friends. I certainly wasn't going to lose any sleep over it. It wasn't like she and I were friends or anything, it was just a second of eye contact. Nothing to write home about. In the meantime I had to pee.

The bathroom door didn't quite close. I hate that, sitting there peeing, thinking that someone might walk in, or worse yet, hear you. But sometimes a girl's gotta do what a girl's gotta do. Which was what I was doing when Carine barged in, slamming the door behind her with a swing of her broad hip. I'd like to say I had something witty to say to that, but my pants were around my ankles and I just stammered.

"Shit," I said, ever the soul of wit as I reached reflexively for my jeans. "I . . . uh . . . what the hell are you doing in here?"

"Taking a bath." Carine winked at me and leaned over the tub, turning on both taps and putting the plug in the drain hole. She kicked off her clogs, reaching down to test the water temperature. "My house, my bathroom, and I want a bath. I'm tired of all those tedious people out there."

"Ah." I wasn't really sure what that meant, or what to do. It was like some kind of nightmare etiquette test: What would Miss Manners say about whether or not to wipe in front of your hostess? Would it depend on whether or not you'd been formally introduced? I decided to wing it. "Well," I said as nonchalantly as possible, reaching for the toilet paper, "guess I'll just finish up and go then."

Carine had just set her eyeglasses down on the top of the hamper, her wristwatch next to them. Unzipping her camel-colored wool slacks, she slid them down, revealing plump, curvy, sleek-looking legs and a pair of slightly overtaxed peach stretch lace panties spanning the generous curves of her hips. "Oh, you don't have to leave."

With one foot, she kicked her pants over toward the bathroom door as she pulled her heavy sweater up over her head. I twitched inwardly. I always love watching women undress. The sight of that soft smooth belly halfway revealed as they pull a shirt or sweater off just does something to me—head hidden, breasts still hidden, tender round intimate tummy visible. I should've, I realized as she tossed her sweater into the pile with her pants, used the chance to wipe and flush and get out of there, but I couldn't stop watching her.

The bathwater gurgled into the huge old claw-footed tub as Carine sat on the edge, peeling off her socks. Then she looked up at me, clad only in those lace panties, a beige underwire bra, and a single sock. "In fact," she said firmly, "Why don't you just stay for a while? Your girlfriend's busy, you don't have anything better to do." With that, she grabbed me with another one of those incredible smiles. The shine in her eyes told me her words weren't a suggestion but a demand, and they sent little half-panicky thrills zinging through me to my fingertips. Suddenly I couldn't remember why I'd been so eager to get out of that bathroom.

I thought about explaining the whole thing about Delia, how she wasn't actually my girlfriend any more, but it didn't matter. Carine was still holding my gaze as if daring me to speak as she reached behind herself and undid her bra hooks, and in spite of myself, in spite of being stuck sitting on the can in a stranger's bathroom, my clit began to swell with anticipation. Braless, Carine's large breasts fell full and sweet down against her ribcage, swinging gently as she stood up, eyes still locked on mine.

On the invisible cables that connected her eyes and mine, shocking little messengers slid back and forth, taking millisecond bursts of fascination and growing lust from her to me to her again as we continued our staring contest. In my peripheral vision I could see her curves, her smoothness, and felt my fingers quiver. She was so lush, with that short round body type that always gets me, and she was there, next to nude in front of me with those incredible eyes issuing their fiercely seductive challenge. "Carine," I whispered, reaching out with one tentative hand.

And then I remembered where I was. Falling down to earth with a thud, I was reminded as I reached out for her that I was still sitting on the toilet and my jeans were still around my ankles. I was sure I looked like an idiot, and I didn't want to look

Carine in the eye. I was damp between the legs, too, but more of it was arousal, at that point, than anything else.

"Come over here," Carine said, just loud enough to be heard over the bathwater. "Don't be embarrassed. I walked in on you on purpose."

My blush went hotter and darker and I felt my nipples crinkle. I looked up just enough to see her thighs, to see the little wisps of dark-blonde that poked out at the edges of those stretch lace panties. "Jesu Maria," I muttered through what I'm sure was a terrifically dorky grin and shaking my head in disbelief.

"I told you to come here." Her tone was serious. Our eyes met, I chuckled, and won the reward of watching the laugh lines around the corners of her eyes crinkle. Pants around my ankles or not, piss-damp or not, it was pretty clear I was going to let Carine get her way.

A drop of wetness hit my calf as I shuffled, shackled by my own 501's, across the bathroom rug. I didn't care. As I reached her, Carine put her foot between mine, stepping firmly on my jeans and boxers. She laughed softly at my awkwardness as I struggled to wriggle my feet out of my shoes and step out of my pants. Then she grabbed my face and kissed me fiercely, tongue finding mine, teeth scraping my lower lip. With some difficulty I managed to step out of my clothes the rest of the way, doing my best to divide my attention between not falling on my ass and returning Carine's kisses. I felt dizzy, standing there half-naked, my hands finally coming to rest on Carine's soft upper arms. Twisting slightly, she swung one leg into the tub, then the next, one hand still on my shoulder as she stood there nearly knee-deep in hot water, still wearing her panties.

"Coming?" she inquired, sliding a hand under my shirt and stopping just at the band of my sports bra.

"Not yet," I grinned.

"We can fix that," Carine purred. "Get in."

And I did. Taller than she as we stood in the tub, I leaned down to kiss her neck, shivering with the sensation of all that compact strength, all that incredibly delicate skin as she arched her neck and wriggled slightly in my arms.

Leaving a trail of red from her collarbone to her jaw, I relished her gasps as I intensified my kisses, adding sharp little bites along the way, feeling her clutch at my hair and hiss encouraging words into my ear. When I reached her lips, she growled into my mouth, one hand immediately heading for my cunt, grabbing me between the legs with a fierceness that made my knees go soft. Together we sank into the water, Carine kneeling between my spread legs as she rolled my slippery clit between her fingers and eased me back against the end of the tub with tooth-crashing famished kisses. Kneading her breasts, rolling her nipples between my thumbs and forefingers, I tried not to moan out loud, knowing that the door didn't quite close and that there was a whole party's worth of people within earshot. I managed to be quiet, but couldn't stop myself from bucking against her hand as she worked me hard beneath the water's surface.

Tongues tangling in the midst of our gasps, we writhed against one another in the hot water, fighting the constraints of the narrow porcelain walls of the tub as we grappled with one another and our lust. The wet lace of Carine's panties was warm and rough against the backs of my fingers as I worked my way inside them, but the drenching slippery wet that greeted my fingertips when I finally parted her lips made the bathwater seem almost cold by comparison. She stiffened as I brushed her clit with my fingertips, and her hand stopped moving between my legs.

"Don't you dare, you bitch," I whisper-snarled into her ear. "You don't corner me in here with my pants around my ankles and then stop fucking me just as soon as I get my hand into this sweet little cunt of yours. If you're gonna do this, you're gonna do this all the way. Just because you're a femme doesn't mean you get to roll over the minute you get your pussy petted."

Her eyes opened, flashing need and playful ferocity. "Fine," she said with another devastating, glittering smile. "Just fine. But two can play at that game. You're gonna have to beg me for it, you uppity cunt."

Fired by her words and by the way she swirled her thumb around my clit, I pinched her slick clit hard, making her bite her lip. Fingers slid inside me, pumping into me to get to my G-spot as her thumb mashed my clit like an elevator button, and I fought the urge to just throw my legs up in the air, to hook my calves over the sides of the huge enameled tub and start begging then and there.

Somehow, in the middle of it all, sloshing and grappling, each of us wanting the upper hand, each of us trying to push the other toward orgasm first, we became aware that there were people on the other side of the door. Knocking on it, in fact. Carine looked up, clearly irritated. "Doyle's is down the block!" she barked, not moving her thumb from my clit.

Our eyes met as she moved to take my nipple between her teeth, and I pinched her clit hard, my free hand cupping the soulful fullness of her breast. Giggling, we ramped rapidly up into a game of chicken, each of us biting and pinching, stroking and kneading, fucking and kissing with greater and greater intensity, trying to be the first to make the other make noise. We didn't know how many people might be in the hallway outside, but we knew there had to be a few, nervous and silent, caught like flies in the ooze of sex that emanated from behind the not-quite-closed door.

Four or five intense minutes passed, thighs tautening, water splashing over the sides of the tub to drench the bathmat as we lay, thighs locked together, hands pressed hard against each other's clits, biting one another on the neck, the shoulder, the lip, free hands stroking, scratching, pinching, caressing, each of us wordlessly daring the other. I can't remember who broke down first, now, though Carine would never admit to it anyway, but suddenly we couldn't contain it a second longer. She growled in my ear, yelped as I thrust fingers deep into her clinging hotness, gasped "please fuck me" as I drilled into her, heel of my hand against her clit.

All I recall of the noise I added was that she made good on her threat. Arching toward her as we lay wedged in the tub, desperate to come, I began to shiver uncontrollably. She lightened her pressure on my clit, and I opened my eyes, silently asking her not to play with me like this, but no. She told me I had to beg for it, and I did, pleading louder and hotter as she goaded me on. I didn't give a damn who was listening. I didn't care if it filled the whole apartment, if it filtered down the block, if it made the crusty Irish barmen down at Doyle's shake their heads and blush. I could feel Carine's cunt responding to the yowls coming from my throat. I wanted to come. I wanted to make her come. And that was all that mattered.

When I came, the only conscious thought I had was that I had to feel her come, too. I wanted blood. I didn't bother to catch my breath, just fucked her harder, trying to crush my orgasm into her through her clit. Sharp and silent, she coiled like a snake, tension building to the bursting point in her muscles, and then it hit her, her free hand clawing trails of fire up my back and over my shoulder as she went rigid, gasping for air.

I didn't stop. As the first spasm subsided, she opened her eyes as she opened her mouth to gulp in air, staring at me, wild-eyed, but I didn't let up. I had found the perfect trill, two fingers, hummingbird-fast, that made her pussy sing, and it was time for an encore.

Brokenly she groaned, trying to roll away, but the tub was too narrow and my free arm too strong around her. "No, Carine," I whispered, my lips brushing her ear as I held her against my sopping T-shirt. "You can run the fuck some other time. But I'm in control now and you're going to come for me until I'm done with you."

I felt her shudder against me. She wanted it this way. She wanted to resist it, too, though. I could tell. It wasn't something she did, not something other people did to someone like her. I wondered how long it had been since she'd had her prey turn the tables, wondered how many times she'd stuck her fingers between her own legs, fantasizing, perhaps half in fear, about what it would feel like to be where she was right now. She groaned, loud and needy, rolling her head to press her mouth against my neck, my fingers still trilling, now faster, now slower, keeping her hanging.

Holding the back of her head, shifting so that she was half on top of me, her head on my shoulder, I took a handful of her hair, gripping it firmly but not tightly as my fingers tapped indecent codes on her clit. "That's it, Carine," I murmured, tightening my grip on her hair ever so slightly as I spoke. "That's right. Ride it for me, slut. You think I'm the only one who can get her brains fucked out in this bathtub? Ride it until I tell you to come." Her breathing was so hard, so heavy, her arms grown limper and heavier as she gave in to me, to the sensations, to the desire to have me fuck her blind and the knowledge that I wasn't going to let her go until I had.

Grasping her hair in my hand, I tugged her head back, exposing her neck in an arch of beautiful tension. She moaned softly, her hips pressing into me, against my hand, a moan that gradually ascended the scale into a keening soft cry, ohs and pleases drifting evanescent into the humid bathroom air like steam. I backed off, then intensified, backed off, and built it up again as I bit her neck, feeling the harshness of her breathing through the thin skin beneath my lips.

Her thighs were vibrating with the strain of not coming, her eyes shut tight. It's so gorgeous to see a woman like that, so ripe, trembling, needing just a word, just a touch. Pulling her head back another fraction of an inch, I kissed her ear tenderly, never stopping the motion of my fingers. "That's right, Carine," I whispered. "Give it to me."

And she did, sobbing and shouting as she curled around my hand, tears washing down her cheeks to mingle with the lukewarm bathwater that soaked my shirt, defenses swept away by the power of several orgasms that came fast and hard. Twice, three times I felt her spasms start anew, and finally I simply held her, amazed, as she clung to me and let her breathing return to normal.

Carine and I toweled off in silence, and I wrung my T-shirt out over the tub before putting it back on. I slipped back into my shorts and jeans, shoved my feet into my shoes as Carine sat on the edge of the tub and watched me. As I moved toward the door, she reached out and touched my wrist. I turned to face her, her wry smile tilted up at me, the ends of her blond hair dripping slow beads of water onto her shoulders.

For a few liquid moments we looked at one another's faces,

relishing the soft pressure of her hand in mine. "I didn't realize this was going to turn into a surprise party," she said in a soft voice.

"Payback's a bitch," I grinned.

"Oh, not so much," Carine smiled. "So. Uh. I know this is a little late, but . . . I'd like to see you again sometime."

"Just throw another party and invite my ex," I said with a wink, moving toward the door. "I, for one, would love to come again."

Waves

I am sleepless in the clear dark eddies of a midsummer night, eyes closed to the paleness of the edges of walls and doors so that I can see the sea that rocks me still, phantom waves lifting me gently in gigantic hands. Beside me he sleeps, so sleek and curled, somehow motionless as I lift and arch, curl and fall into the satin valleys of the Atlantic in which I swam all afternoon until he made me come in. He says he fears losing me to the waves, but he knows how I love to swim.

When I float on the waves, I imagine your hands on me, greedy and rough. I don't see your face. I can never see your face because you don't have one, or if you do it shifts as often as the color and motion of the water as you surround me. I don't have to know what you look like if I know how you feel. And I know precisely how you feel as I imagine you under my hands, my tongue, what it feels like when your cock crushes my lips against my teeth or muscles its way impatiently into my ass or cunt. I know exactly how much fat there is on your belly and how much I like to caress it when I sink down onto you, taking you into me inch by thick exceptional inch. In my ears I am as certain of your voice (it sounds like sand and water rushing through a sluice) as I am certain of its words, and when I imagine the whispered "that's it, take it, take it for me," there is no doubt in my mind that somewhere, somehow, you do exist.

He says "come up for air," and "let me get you a towel," and "aren't you tired yet, you've been swimming all afternoon." I let him rub me with the rough towel—he likes to fuss over me—when it is time to go. But later, when he sleeps, he is gone from me, and I imagine you even though I am dry, back in the city where the shush-rushing of waves is only the mirage of blood pulsing in my ears. He sleeps. I wait for you. Tiredness comes late if it comes at all after the days I spend in the sea. But eventually your waves return and I float again, stretching with anxious joy into the fluid dark.

In the water, in my imagination, I am as slippery as herring beneath your fingers. When you squeeze my flesh, you dig your hands into the sweet thick flesh at my waist like scooping shells into the seabed. Your fingers dive into me, taking without asking, and it hurts. Grabbing handfuls of me, you pull me to you hard and harder, reaching around the swell of hip to clench your fingers into my ass, searching for some way to hold such a slick creature fast. I grapple with you, clutching at your back, to either side of your spine, sinking my fingers into the muscle as your hips rock into mine, insistent, as your belly pushes my belly and your cock prods my hip. The fact that I fight it, even if only as a token gesture, inflames us both. I am a little bitch, yes, you're right. A slut who likes it when it hurts a bit. Your hands like mouths, like suckers on a thousand octopus tentacles, pinching and grasping, kneading and chewing my soft round belly, my breasts, my ass, singing sharp arches of voluptuousness into my flesh.

I float, weightless, at the delta of dream and longing, lying drenched in a pool of moonlight that pours through the window. He shifts by my side, my tether to the shore, and I only barely notice. I remember still being a tadpole in the rich red dark of my mother, and how I loved the water and motion around me. Part of me remembers being so free, not a cripple yet, still able to breathe the waves. I long for that, and for you.

The waves roll through me, over me, with me, my body remembering the rhythmic rise and fall. They lift me and then I sink into you, into the suck-scrape of teeth on my nipples, into need so stubborn and thick. I feel you wanting my salt and slime, my flesh, my sighs, my screams, my struggle, my yielding, my pounding against your chest with furious, impotent blows when you force me to come one more time. I hold you in my body, on my body, as you raise me up and as I curl like the sea foam in your arms, every distant molecule of my lost self cherished.

I feel the sleeping sun stretch himself in the skin of my back. There are memories of the feel of wet torn stockings, my wet dress pushed up when he took me in the fountain. This really happened. I recall the water spray across my face and the cool of night air and the chill cling of wet cloth against the indecent heat of sex-flushed skin. But there were no waves as we stood thigh-deep in the fountain, as he sank inside me, leaning me against a reef of carved marble. He has fucked me in a hot tub, in the shower, in several swimming pools, thinking he is giving me a treat because he knows how much I love the water. I am not sure whether I am glad that he does not trust the waves, the open water, that when we visit you he reads on a towel on the sand.

The snail-whisper of tongue tickles my asshole while you fill me greedy with one two three four fingers and I hardly even know how many it is but your mouth is on my breast one second suckling soft, the next so hard I ache. And you're working your hand into my cunt, and I stroke your arm, your wrist, feel how much of your hand is arching and diving and pushing its way into me, desperately wanting to take it for you, from you. I beg you to fuck me. And you don't, goddamn you. You hesitate, hips pulled back, just the tip of your hardness dipping into the center of me, flickering clownfish immune to anemones. You laugh at my anguish, merry as porpoises. You know I want it, you know I am almost mad with wanting it, but you only arch across my bursting clit, gliding through the mangrove slime I make for you. You make me howl just as I would howl underwater: mouth open, throat taut, and totally silent.

I come, and there are no moments afterward. I will never know what it feels like to linger with you as your cock grows soft inside me. I've never curled by your side in the cool or felt your chest beneath my head, but this is not that kind of love. This is phantom love, the waves of Atlantic summer days that will not stop lifting me even in the quiet of my bed, in the warm dryness of the inland night. Beside me, my man murmurs as he sleeps, utterly unaware that you were here, that you rocked me in your arms. I try to imagine your face, but there is nothing to see. There are only the waves, and the memories of the swells, the wet of my body, and the sea that sings through the night as I dream.

Grenadine

I want to get you a present. What should I bring you from California?" he asked as they talked on the phone.

"Pomegranates," she replied, without the slightest hesitation.

"That's all?" His voice arched like his eyebrow, inquisitive.

She repeated herself slowly, her tone rich, smooth vowels slipping into his ear like lovers slipping into a darkened doorway, their tenancy voluptuously, fabulously transient. "Pom . . . e . . . gran . . . ates."

But the gift had seemed too humble to him, the hard, mottled leather of the dense spheres too graceless. He had had the greengrocer choose them, he hoped that they were good. He wouldn't know. The serrated flaps of pithy tissue at each blossom end seemed to mock his ignorance, weird bottlecaps, corks he wouldn't begin to know how to remove. With the fruit in a plastic bag, he went into a shop that couldn't make up its mind whether it was a boutique or a laboratory, all high white walls and severe glass shelves lit from below, each pristine transparent slab holding a single purse, or a few carefully folded scarves, or a row of sleekly expensive wristwatches isolated as if on a microscope slide. She liked scarves, liked to wear them in her dark hair, or toss them around her throat so their ends dangled down over the translucent skin of her breasts.

He fingered the silk, then picked the one in the middle, as blue as the sky just before the first star.

She had untied it with delight, the heavy, hard orbs inside the silk making her beam with anticipation. "Oh, they're gorgeous!" she gushed, and he felt slightly cheated: The scarf had been expensive, the fruit cheap. She tossed the scarf around her neck without comment and vanished into the kitchen to fetch a bowl.

"Shall we share one now?" she asked as she returned, rather rhetorically he thought. She pulled out a chair for him and he sat, gamely smiling, not sure what to make of the fact that she seemed to be more excited to see the pomegranates than she was to see him. From behind him she leaned down, kissed his cheek, her hands on his shoulders in a firm, affectionate squeeze, warm strong fingers sliding down his arms. He sighed, smiling tiredly, permitting himself to believe for a moment that this was a sign that she really was glad, gladder than perhaps she wanted to show, that he was back. It was so hard to tell with something so new, and hard to tell with someone like her, but perhaps she was. He wasn't sure whether he dared tell her how happy he was to see her again.

He closed his eyes at the feel of her breath on his neck, her cheek against his ear, settling back toward her body, her fine warm body, round and sleek. "Sssh," she said when she pulled his wrists back gently, as if guiding his hands back to touch her. She wrapped the cool silk around his wrists with sensuous simplicity, tying it in a bow. "Just let me."

He did, the pang of separation almost audible when she walked away and left him on his side of the table, a plucked cello string. He waited, watching her choose which fruit she wanted first.

When her fingers split the pomegranate, he almost gasped. She looked up for a moment and smiled, then down again into the dish that lay before her on the table, ruby crystal drops spilling from the cleft pomegranate, raining with a soft purr into the glass bowl. The parchment-colored inner membrane clung to irregular pockets of seeds as she broke off a piece and held it up for him to see. Pale pith connected each seed to the fruit, the walls of each garnet-colored drop shaped by its neighbors, packed in tight.

Precise as a surgeon she peeled away membrane, paper-thin,

shallow dimples making a net to show where each acid-sweet
jewel had hidden. Bending back the peel, her fingers spread the
fruit, seeds fanning to either side of the ridge, the sound of the
fruit's flesh yielding like a spade biting sand. She took her time,
mouth lingering, inhaling the clean, barely bitter breath of its
skin as her tongue flicked droplet after taut droplet from its
moorings. Strange envy flirted with his belly as her eyebrows
lifted, her nostrils flared, her chin lifted just far enough for him
to watch the private motions of her throat as she chewed, as she
swallowed. He had hoped, when he arrived, that he might be the
object of her dedicated hunger, not the fruit.

"So you've never had one?"

"Not yet," he replied.

"You're in for a treat, then."

He cleared his throat quietly, shifting his weight. "So you say."

She leaned toward him, reaching forward, cracking the
remains of the section of pomegranate in two with her fingers,
holding the redness up for him, toward the sunlight that came
in from the window above his head. Ruby prisms caught the
light, her fingertips blushing with reflected glory. He licked his
lips and leaned forward, and then forward still more until the
thick wooden tabletop pressed hard just under his ribs. Licking
her lip thoughtfully, she observed him.

She didn't tease him, didn't move it away as he struggled to
get closer, although he thought she might. He didn't really think
about what he was doing, he just arched awkwardly toward her,
thrusting his head as far forward as he could go, mouth open.

Just to taste the gems in her fingers seemed suddenly the
point of it all, the hidden goal of the long hours of travel, the
days he waited and the messages he left before she finally called
him back at the hotel one night just to say hello. She had made
him laugh, then let him tease her, then told him where her fingers were and whispered buckwheat-honey words into his ear
until he gasped uncontrollably and squirted nine days of work-
filled frustration into the Sheraton's starchy sheets. She did that
to him, made him react without thinking, bypassing his cau-
tions, his roadblocks and checkpoints.

Pushing himself harder against the rim of the table he strained his neck toward her hands. He was aware that his body was pleading for it, eyes wide, imploring, mouth open, tongue reaching but still too far away to taste what she held. Then he faltered, his ears burning as he fell back into his seat, her implacable smile gently mocking. Her dark eyes, impenetrable, fell on his as she plucked one red kernel from the fruit and placed it in her mouth, holding it delicately between her small white teeth, teasing it with her tongue as he watched her. As if her tonguetip caressed his flesh rather than the seed, he breathed in with a hiss, his nostrils flaring as she bit down and crushed the pulp with a satisfied chuckle.

"Try again," she said, still proffering the fruit. Eyes stinging with cross-country fatigue he blinked at her, inwardly chiding himself for his silent and instant agreement, but at the same time leaning again toward her outstretched hand. His smooth shoe soles slipping slightly on the muted tans and greens of the carpet, he tried to raise himself up, to get a better angle, to win the extra inch or two that would close the gap. Useless but straining, his hands hung behind his back, fingers laced tightly together. She could, he realized, see everything: The French doors at his back were a fine mirror.

With a grunt he lurched forward, managing to press his lips against the fruit, startled to feel how smooth and resilient the round seed-tips were against his lips. Somehow he had expected them to be more delicate, more fragile, to burst instantly against his mouth, drenching him in their juice. A soft groan left his throat unbidden, followed by another desperate lunge, his teeth sinking in this time, setting off small, shocking explosions of juice.

Heart pounding, blood rushing, he smiled triumphantly as he chewed, looking into her eyes as he sat back with a heavy thud into the chair. A bead of juice trailed from his lip along his chin, dropping fat and vivid onto his white shirtfront, a purplish-red inkblot near the pocket of his button-down. She rose from her chair, staring at it, at him, her expression an odd mixture of challenge and hunger that made him realize quite suddenly that his cock had become rock-hard.

Slipping between him and the table, leaning into him and pushing him back against the chair, she straddled his thighs, her skirt taut. He thought that she might kiss him, but instead her tongue found the juice on his chin, scouring it off, her cool, stained fingers slipping between the buttons of his shirt, releasing buttons from buttonholes as they moved down his body to his waist. He moaned at the sensation of her inquisitive tongue probing the corner of his mouth for hidden juice, sighed at the feeling of her breasts, her belly pressed against his bared skin. And then the sharp splatter, the instant of resistance followed by a bursting liquid half second, the pressure of her thumb on his chest once, then twice, three times. She'd hidden pomegranate seeds in the palm of her other hand, and now she crushed them, one by one, small bursts of wet against his body.

"You're getting juice all over me," he said softly, slightly shocked, yet helpless.

"So?" she replied. Trickles of red streaked his chest, his belly, their stain dripping down from concentrated bursts where the pulp and the white kernels clung. Juice soaked into his shirt, trailed tickling to his waistband where the dark hairs on his belly became mired in the stuff, slicked with the sweet tartness. She smiled at him, a naughty-girl smile, a knowing smile, the smile of a woman who knows it, does it, and gets away with it anyway. "You don't mind."

She slid off of his lap with a soft shimmy of her hips, smoothing her rumpled skirt back down with her hands. But for the soft, self-satisfied grin that curved her lush, red-stained lips, she might've been alone as she sat back down in her chair, her thumbs hooking into the flesh of the broken-open fruit to liberate more of its succulence. She ate with relish, with the unselfconscious grace of great enthusiasm, pausing periodically to suck juice from her fingers or rescue a fallen seed from the dish or tabletop, taking no notice of her bound, spattered paramour across the room or the way he watched her as she devoured the fruit.

He was speechless, or perhaps not, he thought as he sat in dumb silence. Perhaps it was just that there was nothing to say. He was, after all, quite weary after the long plane ride, the annoyance of the taxi to her apartment, the strange, unbalancing hot-and-cool of her reception, and there was little point in arguing. She would decide what happened next, clearly. As she always did. The thought reassured him, the knowledge that she only appeared to ignore him, that in reality, she was probably monitoring his every move, gauging his reactions, noting the way he winced slightly as the juice dried, sticky and taut, on his skin. He could fight it or give in to it, give in to the knowledge that she thought of him as hers, as her toy to play with, her very own possession, a cross between pet and lover. He was too tired to fight it.

Perhaps she could see it in the way he sat, in the lassitude that let his spine slump and his arms hang limper than they had before. "I imagine you thought I was going to lick that juice off of you," she said plainly, as if speaking to no one in particular. His cock twitched at the sound of her voice, his eyelids flying open to see her studiously peeling membrane from one of the few remaining pockets of seeds. "I suppose you might well be sitting there imagining the hot soft velvet of a tongue on your chest even now. Probably you are, thinking about feeling my breath on your skin, my lips suckling juice off of you. I know it tickles when it dries."

She nibbled a row of pomegranate seeds from their pocket, thoughtfully chewing the nibs for a moment as he shifted his weight, feeling his cock straining against his briefs as he thought—as she knew he would—of her tongue, her lips, her hands on his skin. He could feel the light vapor of her breath on his belly, sense memory of the cool evaporation making tiny goosebumps ripple across his chest, shiver on his arms. Before he had gone away, she had fucked him hard, pinning him ruthlessly and riding his cock to the point of delirium and past it, biting his chest in the midst of some unnumbered cry, half anguish, half delight. He looked down at the spot where the bruise had remained, trying to decide whether he could still see a faint mark or whether it was only pomegranate juice, shivering slightly deep in the core of his body at the recollection of the pleasure and pain, the remembrance of her lust and the way she used him to feed it. Drifting, he let his eyes close, the better to remember the sensations, the better to imagine them.

"Don't think I don't know you well enough to know what you want," she continued after a pause, her voice lower, slightly mocking as it rumbled with the slightest edge of a sharp-clawed purr. He shivered, unexpectedly, embarrassingly, feeling the brittle tugging of hairs trapped in dried juice as the skin of his belly twitched, flinched with desire and tension. And then there was pressure on his thigh, a hand, her hand. Firm, showing him where she wanted him, shifting in his seat without opening his eyes. He wanted to, to look at her bending over him, to see the soft inner curve of her breast, the heartbreakingly sharp cupid's bow of her upper lip, to see if he could divine her next move from the look in her deep brown eyes. But his eyelids seemed heavy, reluctant to open, unwilling to know where or whether he would be touched.

Her tongue was wide and wet and warm as she licked one slow stripe up his stomach, over his solar plexus. A moan dried into a whimper as her saliva dried on his skin, his eagerness for another touch, any other touch, transparent. He could hear his wristwatch ticking, his skin rippling with subtle sensation, phantom brushes with imaginary hands. Then teeth, real and hard, scraped down over his nipple, down the side of his belly, tongue scouring the flesh in rough circles as he yelped, then thanked her, and unthinkingly began to beg. He begged her not to stop, to please keep touching him, not to make him wait any longer, to please let him feel her, to let him please her, to let him do something for her, anything that would make her happy. As she feasted on his skin, her hands roaming beneath his shirt, her nails leaving comet-tails of icy, glittering sensation behind them, he gasped, called her name, shook as if he were having a seizure, back arched, head back, almost in orgasm, torn open by her appetite and his need for it.

And then she was straddling his lap again, his face in her cleavage as she reached down behind him and tugged at the silk. The knot came free, his hands falling toward his sides, helpless and not wanting it otherwise as she stroked his hair, kissed him, licked the stubble on his jaw to relish the salt, the grit of him. Held against her body, he sighed a slow, long sigh, happy just to breathe her in, happy to feel her taking his measure, reacquainting herself, making pleased little noises as she found the spot just in front of his ear that she liked to kiss.

"You'll be here for a while now, yes?"

He mumbled, nodding, incoherent.

"Good," she affirmed, tilting his head up to look at his face. His eyes opened slowly, bleary, bloodshot, searching. Her red-tinged fingernail traced a dark-pink line down his chest from collarbone to nipple, the juice licked clean but the stain still there. He followed her fingertip as it traced other paths, one then the other, down to the waist, looking up from her hand to her eyes as she slid her finger into his waistband. She beamed, slightly, strangely shy, through juice-stained lips, the dark pink of her smile matching the dark pink streaks in his skin, the single tattletale splash on the shirtfront over his heart, the ruddy finger that hooked beneath his belt and pulled him to his feet and tugged him toward her bed, both of them stained by the same fine juice, so indelible, so shocking, so sweet.

The Graduate

She smiled like the sole survivor in a lifeboat, as if she'd come too far and seen too much to even begin to explain. She had, in fact, but I didn't find out about that until later. I'd like to be able to say that we met because we recognized one another as survivors or something like that, something romantic about distant battlefields in one another's eyes, but that wouldn't quite be true. What's more, it would have made her laugh.

No, the truth is less than that, and more than that. I want to make it seem noble because I'm afraid that it won't come across that way. But really, whatever nobility there is in this story lies in whatever nobility there is in rashness, in lust, in the smell of sweat and the shiver of yielding, in youthful stupidity and the fragility of trust. It will have to be whatever nobility there is in clichés, phrases like "our eyes met across a crowded room" and "I will love you forever." Which is, perhaps, not much. Or perhaps it's more than I know.

Our eyes did meet across a crowded room, a loud long room at whose opposite corners we were each separately stranded, eating alone at the edges of a laugh-and-bubble crowd of students and musicians and artists and people who simply wanted to be mistaken for them. She was the only other person eating alone on a cold, rainy Saturday night, and I was drawn to her for that fact

alone. It wasn't until after she caught me looking that I acknowledged, even to myself, that there might be other reasons.

I stared at her long and hard. Of course I did. I was twenty-
one, and like most twenty-one-year-old men I've known, then
and since, I was something of a jackass most of the time. You
can't help it when you're that age. Rather unlike greatness, it is
thrust upon you. Staring at compelling women is hardly the
most serious sin this tired world has seen, I know. But still, I
intruded, and by so doing, helped myself to her attention. She
made sure I was aware of that, later on, and made sure I paid for
it, though the penance seemed a pittance. I would've stared anyway. I couldn't help myself.

I was young and lonely, and it was as nearly impossible to
stop myself from feeling sorry for my solitude as it was for me to
stop looking in the direction of the older woman in the corner
of the restaurant. My circumstances didn't help. I had stayed on
campus for the winter break, claiming that my research required
my presence, but in reality to avoid the mined harbor of home.
I missed my sisters, missed my toddling niece and second-grade
nephew, missed my ditsy, doting, desperate mother despite her
devotion to Wild Turkey "tea" poured straight from her favorite
teapot.

Not that I blamed her. I would've drunk, too, if I'd had to live
with my father as long as she. He was the one I stayed east to
avoid, tall and thin and angry at the world, much more in love
with the army than he'd ever been with his wife. He worked with
heavy artillery, and I never thought it coincidental that he was
similarly prone to explosion. I, his youngest child and only son,
had chosen graduate school over guerrilla warfare in the jungles
of Vietnam. And it had been made clear to me that I was, to say
the least, a disappointment. So I had chosen to be disappointing
at a distance.

Campus was empty, really pretty desolate over Christmas
break. It was also devoid of shouting, the thump of fists and
slamming doors, the soft, shameful, drunken sobs of a woman
whose anger, mingled with booze and frustration, always turned
into a particularly sodden, sorrowful helplessness. The isolation

of being the only one left in the lab, by comparison, seemed almost welcome. I had grown accustomed to being by myself, to spending so much time unseen by others that it seemed odd to be greeted on the rare occasions that I ran into another person on campus. It was as if I were invisible, a slightly pleasant melancholy sensation. Until the woman I was staring at broke my isolation, shattered it like glass with her clear dark gaze and her unapologetically curious expression. She raised her glass, and with an odd sad smile drained it, elegant throat arched back, then went back to her dinner.

I continued to stare, more intrigued now that she'd greeted me, acknowledged me, reached out to me with silent assurance across that crowded babbling room. When she looked up again, I was staring at her high, arched brows, her full lips, the waves of chocolate and silver caught up into a knot on top of her head, wispy curls escaping at her temple, trailing along the crescent of her neck where it met the shoulder. She had been reading, and held open the book with her elbow as she twiddled her fork and stared at me, assessing my youth, my callow, feckless stare, watching the way I watched her. I struggled not to blush. I was flattered, in a way, that she'd looked at me a second time. She seemed from another place and time, improbable, rare. I wondered if she could tell that I thought her beautiful.

I did think she was beautiful, though I'm not sure why. She certainly wasn't a type of woman I'd ever been drawn to previously. Her age, for one thing, would normally have kept me at a distance. And if not her age, then her fierceness, a sturdy upright independence that intimidated at the same time as it attracted. The girls I'd dated up to that point were mostly soft creatures, worried that they'd make the wrong impression, take the wrong step and end up alone, deposed in favor of someone better, cuter, less imposing.

Not Claudia. There was nothing cute about her, nothing merely pretty. Her features were strong, her nose nearly Roman. The lines at the corners of her eyes betrayed depths of endurance and a certain rarefied acquaintance with joy. She was not delicate, nor slim; her bones were sturdy, her hips broad, and I discovered soon enough the intensity of strength of which she was capable. She was old enough to be my mother, a phrase she detested, for she detested children. But she *was* beautiful.

So of course I stammered when she sent the waitress to invite me to her table, and of course I flushed hot red at the unanticipated thrill her voice sent through me. It was throaty, with a slight accent I could not place. From the first instant, Claudia surprised me. The book she'd been reading had not been a novel, as I had assumed, but Kierkegaard. In Danish. She mentioned, in passing, having flown an airplane. Later she quoted Baudelaire at me in French, as the bells tolled the hour and we crossed the campus toward my lab in the cold winter dark, translating on the fly even as she teasingly berated me for being unable to understand the poem in the original. She had asked me to show her the lab where I worked, which surprised me almost more than the way she turned toward me once the lab door had closed behind us, lips slightly parted, and waited until I figured it out and kissed her.

I remember the soft fierceness of her against me, the strength of her body suddenly obvious through the thick wool of our coats, and recall how grateful I was that she saw through my attempts at sophistication, how she made it obvious what she wanted, that she taught me how to give it to her. Claudia kissed as if she owned the patent, raw and masterful, sublime. Her hands were inside my coat, running up my belly, across my chest, sliding up my spine only to drag her nails back down it, making me gasp into her mouth in surprised desire. I swam, disoriented, in a warm sea of sudden possibility and sharp arousal, and reached for her, wanting to feel her under my palms, beneath my fingers, to learn the swells and shapes of her body.

"Don't distract me," she said, and I let my arms hang as she nibbled my jaw line and pushed back my lapels. She shoved my coat over my shoulders and let it fall down my arms, running her hands after it. Powerful fingers encircled my wrists, and I did not resist, but rather let her move my hands behind my back and hold them there as she tasted my Adam's apple, let her teeth skid on the stubble of my beard, each motion of her mouth making my cock twitch in my pants as it swelled.

After a moment she pulled away enough to look at my face; it took me several moments to realize she was watching me. Slowly, dumbly, I opened my eyes and composed my hopeful lips into a smile. "Have you ever done this before?" she asked, her voice soft as sand.

I shook my head and looked down, trying not to look at her breasts beneath the black of her sweater, feeling the blush begin with my ears and spread until my face was on fire. I'd had some dates in college, and one short-lived girlfriend, but I had been shy and they had been shyer. The girls I liked, the smart, bookish ones who could, once they got to know you, really have a conversation, didn't want a reputation and were scared to go too far. High school had been similar: nervous sweet goodnights under the front porch light with anxious blond Baptist girls whose mothers knew my mother, a condition which ensured that nothing more untoward would dare take place than a few chaste smooches and perhaps a slight brushing of fingers along the white-peach curve of tit or ass. There had been nothing like this, nothing like the sudden wave of hunger that rose in me when Claudia's tongue parted my lips, nothing like the gusty groans of pleasure that echoed off the cracked paint on the high old laboratory walls, nothing to prepare me for a force of nature that pulled me into an entirely new world without so much as a by-your-leave.

"Then I will teach you," she replied, nonchalant, pressing herself into me hard, thigh and hip and belly, forcing me to step backward or lose my balance. She slid onto a lab stool and pulled me close, between her spread knees, twining her legs around mine, making me bend down slightly, awkwardly, to reach her. A freezing rain began to spit against the high, drafty windowpanes; the campus bell tower tolled another hour, then two, as she taught me the sly semaphore of tongues and teeth, the eloquent gestures a mouth can make as it opens to another's kiss. Without a word she drilled me in ravishing kisses, teasing kisses, kisses so raw with lust they made me wonder if the throbbing stiffness between my legs would burst then and there. She nibbled my lip, my ear, my neck, all the while keeping one hand lightly on my crossed wrists as they lay at the small of my back.

We kissed an opera of whimpers and gasped, half-formed words, of desperate urging grunts that steamed the cold windows with want. I could smell us. I knew the scent of my own need from countless nights of sleeping with my head on the other side of a pillow I'd humped into oblivion. Her smell, sharper, grassy, came at me each time our bodies parted enough to allow the hot vapors from between her legs to rise toward my nose. My cock hurt like a headache, dull and insistent, my balls pulsed in thick unison with my heart. Nearly feral with lust, I leaned forward and kissed her hard, as hard as I could, hard enough to assume she meant reprisal when she slid off the stool and walked me back until I thumped against the wall and she lifted my hands above my head as far as she could reach, pinning me between her heat and the icy hardness of the plaster. Then she kissed down my neck, teeth sinking into my skin as her thigh spread my legs and she pressed it firm and knowing against my raging cock. I shook, caught between the queer, ecstatic pain of those sharp teeth and the thick, primal pleasure of the pressure against my crotch, groaning so loud that it echoed.

Then Claudia stepped away, and my arms fell to my sides. I clutched at the wall, not sure that I wouldn't slip down to the floor, and watched her as she picked her coat up off of the floor and put it on, winding her muffler around her neck.

"I think you've learned enough for tonight," she said through a glittery, bemused smile. Bending to pick up her handbag, she arched her brow at me and demanded that I take her home.

I had no car, and the hour was too late for the bus I normally took, so I phoned for a cab. In the close darkness of the back seat of the taxi I tried to ignore the insistent throb between my legs and listened to her as she spoke. She explained that she lived alone now, a widow. Her husband had been older, had taught at the university before my time. I tried, and failed, to imagine her as a faculty wife, genteel at some tea or reception, chatting and gossiping with the other wives as their husbands pontificated and stroked their beards at one another. Too soon the cab stopped and she gathered her bag and opened the door, leaning back into the taxi only long enough to leave a kiss on my cheek, a kiss that, though feather-light, lingered in my skin as if she'd branded me.

Distractedly, I gave the driver my own address and he pulled away from the curb. I turned to watch Claudia open her front door and step inside of the brownstone, my fingers on my cheek. Elvis sang on the radio and the cabbie hummed along as I cursed myself for not having asked for her phone number. Then I noticed there on the seat next to me her handkerchief, white and crumpled, as if to remind me of the space she'd filled beside me. I picked it up and realized that the cloth was crumpled around a piece of paper—a calling card. CLAUDIA VAN MEIJERING, it read in small block capitals marching in black ink. I turned it over. A phone number, printed in a neat, small hand, and two words: "call Tuesday."

It was Saturday night, or more accurately, Sunday morning. My cock still twitched, swollen in my pants. Tuesday could not have seemed further away. I forced myself to wait until the afternoon on Tuesday, taunting myself by imagining the sound of Claudia's cruel laugh, a click, the buzz of dead line. But she seemed glad to hear from me, and before the sun was down I was climbing the stairs to her door, clutching a bouquet of expensive hothouse tulips in one sweaty, nervous hand. I hoped they might impress her. She did not hug me, or kiss me, or touch me at all in greeting, merely thanked me for the flowers. She began to trim the stems while I stood nervously in her kitchen and chattered about the lab, not knowing what else to do with myself, until I faltered and fell silent.

"I expect you went home and masturbated?" she asked, not looking up from the flowers, which she was arranging in a squat blue jar.

I turned bright red. I hadn't ever imagined anyone ever asking such a question. I stammered for a moment, and Claudia just glanced at me and adjusted the flowers, waiting for me to get over my shock. How did one answer a question like that?

75

"You mean after I dropped you off the other night?" She nodded. I swallowed hard and felt my ears burning. She was still looking at me, still expectant. I supposed honesty was the best policy. "Well, actually, no," I replied. "I started to. But it wasn't the same."

Claudia looked amused. "The same as what?"

I thought for a moment about how to phrase it. It seemed important that I express myself well, that what I had to say about Claudia would please her. "Anything I could do alone . . . wasn't even close to the way it felt to be with you."

Claudia nodded and smiled as she looked up and met my gaze. "Good," she said, more a statement of fact than opinion. "And since then?"

I shook my head. She picked up the vase and carried it into the living room, setting it down on a small table near the window where the tulips' reds and yellows seemed all the more vivid against the gathering dusk beyond the glass. Like a puppy, I followed several steps behind. Claudia went to the fireplace and put on another log, which crackled as it caught.

"So," she began as she turned, as she began to let her eyes drift slowly up my body. I shifted my weight self-consciously; as soon as she'd asked me whether I'd masturbated, my cock had begun to swell, and it was now an unmistakable presence beneath the fabric of my pants. I hoped that pre-cum hadn't yet begun to ooze through the fabric. Spots on two pairs of pants and stiff splotches on the pajamas that lay in my laundry hamper in the dorm bore testament to the amount of time I'd spent wandering around with my prick full of blood and my head full of turgid memories of the preceding Saturday. I'd thought about just finishing myself off to relieve the lingering suffering of the terrific longing ache Claudia had left behind, but somehow, it hadn't felt right. If I was going to come, I wanted it to be for Claudia. I wanted her to see what she did to me, wanted her to see how much I wanted it, wanted to feel her eyes on me, her hands on me, wanted her to tell me that she wanted me to come for her. Now that I was back in her presence, I wanted it even more, and so did my thickening, straining cock.

Claudia chuckled when she noticed my erection, her gaze immediately locking on mine as she walked toward me. I gasped as her hand cupped my crotch, her body simultaneously pressing into my own, her hip and thigh pressing against me, her breast soft and firm beneath her cardigan as she leaned in to bring her lips almost all the way to my ear. Knowingly, her fingers clenched, making my balls tighten and my penis surge. "Very well then," she whispered into my reddening ear, "since you've been so generous as to offer, I accept. You're mine. As long as I want to keep you. I take it you find that acceptable?"

I nodded. "I can't hear you," Claudia mocked, her nails scraping against the crotch of my pants as she tightened her fingers further.

"Yes, Claudia," I managed to whisper. "I find that acceptable." My heart was hammering in my chest so hard and so loud I thought surely she could hear it; I was only halfway in control of what I was doing, what I was saying. I would've said anything to keep her touching me, to keep her near me, to keep her hand pressed hard against my aching, wanting member.

I'm not sure if I had any idea what it meant when I told her I would give myself to her, though perhaps I had hopes, secret small ones, that it might mean more than simply that I was giving her the go-ahead to seduce me. Not knowing enough to know that it might be possible to want more than that, I just said yes and stood there, looking at her hopefully, waiting, I suppose, for her to kiss me, to spirit me off to a down-comforter bedroom and deflower me. I had fantasized her lying back, letting me touch and kiss her naked velvet self, spreading her legs for my exploring fingers, welcoming me inside her. Instead she stepped back, a soft chuckle in her throat, and sat down on a chaise near the fire.

"Good," she purred, smoothing her skirt. "Then strip. When you're here, I want you naked."

I hastened to comply. Once I was sockless and shoeless, sweaterless and shirtless, when I had finally, embarrassedly, taken off my shorts, she beckoned me to her, patting the chaise beside her.

"I imagine you want very much to come for me," she asked as I tried to ignore the tickling of the velvet upholstery against the bottoms of my hypersensitive balls.

I gushed and babbled as if I couldn't control myself. Perhaps I couldn't. I told her how badly it had ached when I'd dropped her off on Saturday night, told her how many times I'd found myself thinking of her with a cock hard to bursting in my pants, told her how, night after night, I'd willed myself to sleep because I didn't want to come alone without her. Claudia listened for a while, indulgent, then leaned back against the chaise.

"You may come for me if you earn it," she said, lifting her skirt to mid-thigh. "I trust you can find a better use for your busy mouth than all this chatter."

I sat stunned. I had read about it, had heard from some older, more experienced guys that some women wanted you to lick them down there. But I had no more knowledge, at that point in my life, of how to eat pussy than I had of how to read Sanskrit. However, I also knew better than to keep Claudia waiting, or to protest. If this was to be the way I was to gain entrance to paradise, so be it. I knelt on the end of the chaise, positioned myself on my hands and knees, nuzzled my way under her skirt, fervent, kissing her stocking-clad thigh, then the soft bulge of flesh above it, feeling her open her thighs wider as I moved along, searching by feel and intuition and mostly by scent.

The seam of her cunt was already oozing moisture by the time I ran a tentative tongue along the swollen lips. "Lick me," she groaned in response to my mouth's first gentle gesture. I hesitated, trying to place the taste; I had never so much as seen a woman's actual pussy. Where to go? What to do? Was it always so intense? Were women always this wet? The newness of it all was just as staggering, just as overwhelming as Claudia herself. Then a heavy hand was on the back of my head, strong fingers gripping the back of my head, pushing me into her as she thrust her hips up, splaying her cunt lips against my surprised face. She swore under her breath, cursing me in some language I didn't understand as I struggled to lick her, to figure out what I was supposed to be doing. Trying to show some finesse—though I didn't know what finesse really would've been in that case—I lapped delicately at the slick, hot mystery of her, probing little turgid folds and flowery creases, trying not to be too rough, or too abrupt along the way. I had no idea what anything was, where anything was, what to concentrate on, what she might've liked. I was blundering, blind and ignorant, grateful for every rough tug of her fingers, every "higher" and "harder," finally so thankful I almost started to cry when she finally took my head, held it firm between her strong hands, and forced my mouth against her exactly where and how she wanted it.

My nose hurt from being smashed against her and sometimes I couldn't breathe. My poor ignored cock was sore from being wedged between me and the velvet upholstery—I found myself humping against the chaise as I strove to please her with my mouth, reflexive lust pulsing its way through my hips despite the friction. My jaw began to ache and my tongue felt strained, my neck beginning to cramp along the side from the awkward pose. But her fingers were still tense and powerful against the back of my head. And her breath was coming faster, little panting puffs between stretches where she'd hold her breath, waiting, arching against me, hard, hanging at the edge of orgasm. I wanted an orgasm of my own, bad. Hers, however, was in my mouth, on my tongue, and I thrashed the hard bud of her clit as feverishly as I could, sucking as if my life depended on it until finally she made a sobbing noise and arched against me harder, fiercer, than she ever had before.

Claudia fell back, hands limp, her breath coming back to her. Not knowing what I was supposed to do or whether I dared stop, I eased off on my ministrations, suckling her gently, licking my way through the folds and rivulets of her again, exploring gently at my leisure now that she was at hers, tasting her slippery liquids and trying to memorize how she tasted, how she felt. She was my very first. I wanted to be able to recall every bit of her in detail, to capture her that way in my head forever.

"Come here," she said, finally, after letting me bring her to a second, smaller convulsion. I lay next to her on the chaise, wanting to hold her, to protect her, somehow, in the vulnerable lassitude that followed her climax, but it seemed presumptuous, perhaps even preposterous. She kissed me, licking her juice from my face, tasting herself on my tongue as I kissed her back. Chuckling into my mouth, she rolled on top of me, straddling me, slipping the shaft of my burning maleness between the puffy lips of her wet, engulfing sex. I flinched, my body going stiff, riveted to the sensation, quite helpless to react as she bucked her hips, her tongue fucking between my lips as she rode her clit along the length of me, back and forth, there and back, over and yonder and back again, her weight and my position on the chaise making it almost impossible for me to even try to thrust as she frigged her clit against my shaft and coated me with the thick syrup of her seemingly endless lust.

I fought my instincts, then, and fought them hard. I knew it would be wrong to grab her hips, to bring her up just a tiny bit further in her motion so that my cockhead would slip into the wet-silk tunnel whose entrance my tongue had so recently explored. And it would've been even more wrong to flip her and fuck her, no matter how bad I wanted it, no matter how intense the longing, no matter how good she felt against me as she rode the underside of my cock. I wanted her to want me, wanted to give her what she wanted. Whatever she wanted, whatever it was that would erase the sadness from her eyes and leave her with the soft, curious, faraway smile she wore when she pulled me up from between her legs to kiss her. It was the smile I'd seen after I made her gasp and moan so hard on the first night we'd kissed.

And so I managed, somehow, not to try to fuck her. And somehow I managed not to come while she rode against my shaft, and not to cry out and spray my pent-up ecstasy even when she came again, her erection taking its friction from mine until her face contorted in majestic agony. Finally she climbed off of me and stood, her skirt falling down to her calves, smoothing her hair.

"Come for me," she said, pulling up a chair. I am afraid I only stared at her, dumbfounded, as she sat down. Then Claudia laughed, and leaned forward just far enough to lick the head of my upthrust penis, sweeping away the trickle of pre-cum with her sly, soft tongue. I gasped, and she repeated her demand as my overloaded brain finally figured it out and I began to stroke. Her eyes caressed me as I pulled my cock, and I could almost feel her gaze like fingers exploring me, teasing my nipples, stroking my balls, my thighs, tracing my lips and the curve of my earlobe. I watched her face as she watched me, and the pressure of long-overdue release combined with the pleasure I saw in her eyes as my awareness surged into my cock, into my balls, into the slow-motion instant of feeling my cock throb, then spasm, with what felt like oceans of semen rushing up and out of me.

I tried hard to keep my eyes open, to watch her as she watched me come, but in the final instant I closed them, gasping like a landed fish, lost in the release. And I was surprised, when I opened them, to find her sitting with cupped hand poised over my belly as I panted, struggling to catch my breath again. I gasped her name, reached out toward her, touched her knee. Claudia slid to her knees beside the chaise and I pulled her closer, my hand on her side, wordlessly pleading for her to kiss me. She did, and I melted into the kiss, floating in the wake of the most intense orgasm I'd ever had, feeling at once invincible and entirely submissive, ecstatic to have given everything I had to give to this woman, this remarkable creature I wasn't sure I dared think of as my lover.

And then she broke the kiss, and I watched her eyes as she hovered over me, that cupped hand coming between us, forcing my cooling seed against my mouth and between my lips. She smiled then, a searing, predatory smile, a smile I didn't under-stand but that made my half-deflated cock surge, leaping toward hardness. "Lick it up," she demanded, her voice a harsh whisper. "Taste what it means to be mine."

I knew better than to hesitate. And that was the pattern of it, my affair with Claudia. We would meet, sometimes at the restaurant where we'd first met or in some cafe, sometimes in a park, once in a while on campus, but mostly in her second-floor parlor. We might eat together, or share tea, or perhaps it would be one of the times when she wanted to drink: She taught me the skill of cultivating a buzz just heady enough to break down inhibition without compromising ability. We would talk a bit, but usually sooner rather than later there would be no more room for talk beyond the mutters and demands of arousal and the wordless urgencies of sex.

Nothing I had read, nothing I had heard about ever prepared me for what we did together, Claudia and I. I had never come across anything that even hinted that it was possible for a woman to bend me over the edge of a bed and fuck me in the ass with one, then two, then three, finally four fingers slick with greeny-yellow olive oil, her other hand smearing the oil up and down the length of my cock and over my balls until I shot hot and fast and hard, all over her soft lilac-smelling sheets. No magazine I'd ever furtively hidden beneath my mattress ever mentioned what a revelatory pleasure it would be to kneel naked between my lover's legs, hands tied behind my back with a scarf, her knees draped over my shoulders, watching her fingers as she stroked herself to growling, whining orgasm. Certainly nothing I'd seen or heard about prepared me for the shameful pleasure of being forced to beg for it as Claudia taunted me with fleeting strokes of her tongue on my thighs, my balls, the base of my cock . . . or the even more shameful pleasure of being forced to bring myself off as I stood in front of the wide-open living-room windows, watching her as she sat in a chair just beyond the windows and watched, hands moving beneath her light spring dress as she stroked her breasts, her belly, her cunt.

Not in my wildest speculations would I ever have guessed that this composed, fiercely intelligent woman would pull me into a restaurant storeroom and thrust my hand beneath her skirt, whispering to fuck her hard as I slid two fingers into her. Three fingers took her to the edge, four fingers seemed almost impossible, but then she insisted I give her more. Somehow, with Claudia's quiet, sharp commands cutting through my bewilderment, I worked my entire fist into her hungry cunt, twisting within her, fucking her deep and rhythmic, her body stretched around my hand as she bent over a stack of bags of flour. I did come without permission then, embarrassed though I was to admit it later. But I couldn't help it. I'd never felt anything so primal, so unspeakably intimate, had never experienced a sensation as engulfing as the wet, desperate, powerful grip of Claudia's cunt. She bit her hand to keep from crying out and thrust back hard, harder, her cunt mauling my fist, her juices running down my forearm. I didn't even touch my cock, didn't even think about it until suddenly there it was, gushing pulse after pulse of thick heat into my trousers while Claudia came so hard I thought she'd snap her spine in two. Her muscular walls crushed my hand to the point of pain as she came, then contracted in a different sort of way, easily, confidently spitting me out.

Mere moments later Claudia shook her skirts back down and patted her hair into place. She looked cool, composed, as if the flush in her cheeks had come from having done nothing more extraordinary than taking a brisk walk. Her long skirt hid the juices that smeared her inner thighs, the reddened, distended lips of her sex. I fumbled my way to the men's room to clean up as best I could. The wetness of the fabric against my crotch turned cold as she walked me as far as the bus stop, then kept walking, looking back only long enough to offer me a single slow wink as I stood in the dim of early evening and watched her walk away.

No one, even the most sophisticated guys I knew, the ones who talked nonchalantly about getting blowjobs from their cool-gorgeous girlfriends, had ever mentioned being tied to the bedposts by their wrists and ankles and having a kimono-clad seductress lower herself onto them like Claudia did to me, slowly wedging my entire fat, eager cock into the almost painfully tight embrace of her asshole. I watched her, mesmerized by the sensations and by the flutter of silk that eddied down and over my thighs, drifting against my belly, carefully restraining my own progress toward climax as she shuttled up and down, whispering harshly words like *fuck me, split my ass, shove it in me*" as she slammed down onto me harder and harder as her fingers circled on her clit. Only when she finally gasped out that she was coming did I let go of the reins of my careful restraint, bucking up into her as hard as my bonds would let me, helping her shove my cock into her as roughly, as harshly, as she required. She knew by then that I would not let myself come until she did, and our screams mingled as her ass spasmed around my shaft, tugging the seed from my balls until I had nothing left to give.

That afternoon I expected that what we'd done would be it, that I should be preparing to go. When Claudia was done, she was done, and usually she wanted to be left alone. It saddened me that I didn't seem to please her enough to have me stay, but there was little I could do about it. The sadness in her eyes was never far away, and it was never greater than in the quiet that followed a truly galvanic sexual storm. I was young, and yes, a bit naive, but still not enough of an idiot to think I could answer to that huge quiet sadness. I would wash up in her small white bathroom, dress quietly and quickly, kiss her once as tenderly as I could muster, tell her I loved her, and leave her to her thoughts, whatever they were. She seemed to appreciate it. She kept calling me to meet her, which meant at least that I hadn't done anything wrong.

But this time was different. My deflated penis slid with a dull pop from her well-fucked asshole. She untied me and rubbed my wrists, sitting on the edge of the bed. I watched her, searched her face, saw the veil closing across her features, and rolled over, preparing to sit up, to rise, to leave. But she reached across and caught my wrist, held me there, halfway up. "Stay," she said, and I did, laying back down, unsure whether I should try to touch her, not knowing what she wanted. She stood up then and unknotted the sash of her kimono. Shrugging her shoulders, she let it fall down behind her to the Persian rug on the floor, a puddle of plum at her feet.

I gasped and she glared at me, her gaze demanding to know what the gasp meant. I had spent plenty of time unclothed in her presence—enough that it felt quite natural that I should be naked when she was clothed—but had never seen her nude. And now I did not know what to say. She was majestic, sturdy and broad, her heavy breasts set high, the sag of her fleshy belly as heartbreakingly tender as the inner curves of the breasts whose nipples she would occasionally permit me to suck. Finally I managed to whisper that she was beautiful, managed to tell her that I loved her, that I would always love her. She stood there watching me as I looked, as I let my wide eyes canvas every soft inch of her, as I said every foolish thing that came to my mouth to say.

Her face did not change, but slowly she turned around, reaching behind her to pull her hair together and lift it out of the way. Now there was a tension in the air, subtle, sinuous as a viper, lethal as the smell of bitter almonds. At first I did not notice, but as she stood and I looked, I began to see them, the fine silver contrails, hundreds of them, long and straight as well as short and savage, the multitude of scars that crossed her back and drifted down across her voluptuous ass. Hearing me suck in my breath, she turned back around and spread out her arms, her hands low, her palms open as if in supplication.

I looked at her face, at her impassive eyes, at the hands that so expertly stroked me and fucked me, the arms that had restrained me and embraced me. Halfway up her forearm, blurred beyond recognition, there was a blue, fuzzy line of tattoo. Helpless in the face of her past, my brain sluggish, reluctant to acknowledge what I was seeing, I sat up, shaking my head. "Oh, Claudia, oh, no," I whimpered, helpless, unable to look up as my mind inexorably made sense of the scars, the camp tattoo, the asides and veiled references that had never made sense to me before.

"If you're going to love me, you need to know," she said softly, her accent thicker than normal, as if taking off her robe had made it as naked as the rest of her.

"I will always love you," I blurted. "I don't know what else to say. I just . . . Claudia . . . what . . . ?" Fat hot tears spilled over my bottom eyelashes and plopped onto my bare thigh as I turned toward her, wanting desperately to do something, knowing that I was helpless.

"Please," she replied, terse and unapologetic, "don't say anything. You just need to know, that's all. If you love me, then love me hard. That's all I need. That's all I ask."

I nodded and sniffled. She kissed me hard, leaning over me

and pressing me down into the bed, the full weight of her naked-ness stretched along my body. Desperate to do as she'd told me, desperate to chase the memories of agony from her bones, I stroked her and licked her, did whatever she asked, licking and sucking until well after my jaw had gone stiff, every spasm of every orgasm I could bring her a small victory. She shook and writhed, bucking against my face, demanded my fingers inside her. I fingerfucked her as well as I could until my arm protested. Still Claudia wasn't finished: seemingly without effort she tossed me onto my back and straddled my face, grinding her swollen pussy against my open mouth as she leaned forward, letting her hair fall down onto my belly, the strands caressing my stiff, ignored cock.

I had grown accustomed to throbbing alone while Claudia took her pleasure from me, had even grown to relish the sensa-tion of waiting, balls aching, until she was sated before I'd mas-turbate for her to show her how much I loved everything we did, everything I did to her, every orgasm she let me witness. But now I wanted to touch her with more than my hands. I wanted to touch her deeper, differently, than hands or tongue could go. She would not let me express my sorrow in words, would not let me tell her that I would do anything to keep her from harm, would not let me speak my sympathy or my rage. I wanted to hold her to me while I kissed her, while I stroked into her, my cock inside her in the one place she'd never allowed it to go. I wanted the union I'd only read about, wanted to seal myself that way, to consecrate my desire to her and to her secret.

So I begged her to let me fuck her. It wasn't as if she wouldn't have let me come eventually. I knew that. But knowing that you'll eventually get to come and knowing desperately that you want to be deep inside the cunt of the woman you love while it happens are two different things.

She'd never expressed any desire to be fucked that way so I was fairly sure she wasn't interested. Claudia had no qualms about demanding my cock, or any other part of me, anywhere else she wanted it, in any way, at any time. She had never asked for my cock inside her cunt, and my awareness of that fact beat itself against my consciousness like a butterfly battering itself against the jar in which it has been trapped. I knew better than to ask.

I asked anyway. Only later on did I realize that when she made me get down on my knees and beg her for the privilege she was giving me a chance to recant, to admit my mistake. I couldn't see it then, couldn't see a thing except the wounded woman I loved, couldn't feel a thing except the wordless certainty that I could merge with her that way, that I could bear some of what she bore if only she would let me in, let me love her the way I thought a man was supposed to love a woman.

And for some reason she let me. Maybe she let herself believe, if only for a moment or two, in the same facile, hopeful magic. Maybe she was just humoring me. Maybe she was trying to force herself to trust me even further, now that she'd shown me her scars and the number on her arm. Perhaps she thought that doing would make it so, that if she wanted to badly enough, or merely told herself she did, she could let someone else hold the reins and still remain safe, inviolate, that she could let someone else do the plucking and yet still hold tight to the flowers of herself.

Claudia lay back, and she lay still, and she spread her legs and I kissed her as I wedged myself between them, coaxing her with my tongue, with the gentle nips at her collarbone that I knew she loved, teasing her clit with the head of my cock to catch her up again in lust. Claudia sighed, and shifted her hips, languid. She kissed me back, pulled me down on top of her as I pushed my hips just so, cockhead pressing her clit, fucking firm short thrusts against it until she bucked and a slow low moan came, uncensored, from her throat.

Finally I pushed into her, my mouth on hers, one hand stroking her hair away from her face. She groaned into my mouth, a groan I had never heard before in all the months we had been together, all the times she had had my mouth on her or my hands in her, all the times she had so thoroughly impaled herself with my cock deep in her ass. It was sweet and yielding, abject, helpless—far different than the fierce noise I had grown to expect—and it hit me like a burning match hits gasoline.

I had meant it to be a slow, rich fuck, something we both could savor. It was my first time, after all. Yes, I'd fucked Claudia in every other way I could imagine. I had come for her uncounted times, in my hand or hers, on her breasts, in her mouth, in her ass. But she was still my first and because I was young and vain I wanted to be her first, too, in some way or another. Arrogant, I thought that somehow I could manage thrusts so tender and kisses so hot with adoration that it could not help but melt through the thick walls around her heart. But. She groaned that groan and her cunt walls tightened, a short small spasm around my pulsing, granite-hard cock. And I was gone.

I was gone, thrusting, pounding, pummeling, pushing, fucking her, really fucking, no excuses, no feints. I don't think she resisted it. But I don't know if I would've noticed if she had. I was blind with rut, with the atavistic need to fuck the woman beneath me, to drive as deep into her as I could, to fill her with every ounce of myself that I could muster. She met me, rose with me, clawed into my back long red scrapes I would bear for weeks. Under the onslaught of my lust, Claudia writhed and yowled, her eyes tight shut, legs clasped tight around my waist, her fingernails sunk deep into my shoulders as if to drive me further and further into her. I plowed and plunged and pillaged, rocked and pushed and hammered. She came, teeth sinking into my chest as she bit and screamed, and I knocked her back, pinning her to the bed, all my weight on her and in her as I kissed her open, gasping mouth, feeling her fighting to grab me as I drove my cock into her again and again.

The end was close, too close. I slid a hand between us. I pinched her clit and slammed into her, desperate to feel her come around me again as I fucked her across the bed. She reached up, clinging to the headboard rail for resistance. Her eyes opened, pupils wide and molten, her dark lips parted to let the hoarse moans escape.

I looked into her clear dark eyes, not sure whether I could love her any more, or need her any more fiercely, without needing to tear her limb from limb. She was close, tense, her hips jabbing up toward my cock, toward my fingers on her clit. "Come for me, Claudia," I demanded. "Come. Now."

Her eyes dilated further, flashing with a sudden something, an intensity close to fury. Perhaps that's exactly what it was. She groaned again, the same broken groan as before, but louder. And then she came, soundless and savage, her body contracting around my cock as I finally let myself go completely, slamming into her as deep as my body would allow as I soared into the white fire of power and ecstasy.

I lay with her in the quiet afternoon, gently stroking her stomach, her face. Her eyes remained closed. The light that came in from the window bleached her skin, made her paler, softer as she rolled to her side, turning her back to me. I propped myself up on my elbow, spooning her as gently as I could, wishing I could somehow bridge the enormity of the gulf that seemed to lie between the adjacent molecules of our skin.

Finally, Claudia spoke. "You did as I asked," she said, her voice limp. "I can't fault you for that."

Confused, I said nothing, merely nuzzled her shoulder.

"I told you to love me hard," she continued. "And you did."

I nodded, murmured assent. I wanted to tell her again that I loved her, that I would love her any way she asked.

"So tell me," she said, "how did it feel? How did it feel to run things, to be on top?"

I thought for a moment, not sure what the right answer to that question would be, or even whether there was one. "It felt good," I said. "It felt good to be your equal for once."

Without a word she slid out of bed. She snatched her kimono from the floor and wrapped herself in it, pulling the belt tightly, angrily, as she shook her hair free of the collar and walked out, slamming the bedroom door behind her.

On shaky legs I followed her, confused, cold despite the warm late-spring air. The shower was running, a cloud of steam billowing out to greet me as I opened the bathroom door. I called her name, pleading.

"Get out," she said from the shower, her voice flat.

"Claudia, please," I begged, "I don't even know what I did wrong."

She stuck her head out from behind the shower curtain. "No. You wouldn't. And as long as you think getting to stick that cock of yours wherever you want to makes you anyone's equal, you won't. Now get out."

I burst into tears. I begged harder than I'd ever begged her before, my heart in my throat, my stomach threatening to overturn. I told her I loved her. I did love her. I was desperate. No answer came from behind the curtain. Tears running down my face, I apologized again and again. I pleaded, sobbing. And still no answer, even though the water had to be running ice-cold by then. Finally I left, closing the door behind me.

I put on my clothes and waited in the living room, but the bathroom door remained obstinately shut. Finally I let myself out, a hole in my heart and a limp in my soul.

It took five years before I went back to the restaurant where I'd met Claudia. I'd been avoiding it, had been avoiding her neighborhood, the streets where I knew she shopped. And then I found myself walking back along that street, my feet carrying me where my brain would not have permitted them to go had it not been otherwise occupied.

It was a beautiful late-summer evening, but the warm humid embrace of the air was lost on me that night. I was smarting, feeling lonely. I had just broken it off with a young woman who swore she loved me, but whose enthusiasm for things like wedding rings seemed, in some subtle, disturbing way, to outstrip her enthusiasm for me. I had thought about it for days, then took her for a walk and explained that I just couldn't do it, that I wasn't going to give her what I knew she wanted; I was not going to ask her to marry me. She cried and cried, and wiped her nose on my sleeve, and I had patted her on the back and tried as best I could to negotiate the delicate balance required when you're trying to stanch a wound with one hand while holding the knife in the other. Sniffling, she'd asked me to take her home, and I had, then walked away, down the avenue, thinking that I didn't want to be alone, longing for some noise to cut the quiet, wooly sadness that engulfed my heart.

I walked into the restaurant, telling myself Claudia wouldn't be, couldn't be there, but of course she was. She sat at the same corner table, bathed in the seven o'clock glow of the August night. A bit grayer now, she saw me at the same time that I saw her, our gazes entwining as if by instinct across that always crowded room. She smiled at me, and I smiled back, the gesture plucking some deep, resonant string inside my belly as she refilled her glass with the last of the wine in her carafe and raised the cup to me, making a silent toast before she drained it to the dregs. There was a certain wry gleam to her eye as she did, a slight twist to her smile, and in the soft but real joy that for a moment inhabited her features I saw that same lambent smile I'd learned to relish in the moments after her climax. My cock stirred, fattening against my thigh beneath my faded jeans, and my mouth went dry. I wondered what she felt, whether I would get to find out.

I knew my lines, knew the steps of the dance. I sat at my table, ordered my supper, waited for the invitation. But it did not come, and did not come, and finally I looked up, eyes searching the room. There was Claudia's table, empty carafe next to empty glass next to empty plate. And there was the door, swinging lazily closed. And then there was Claudia, turning just for an instant as she crossed in front of the restaurant window, blowing a kiss my way through the glass and across a crowded room.

"Wait," I mouthed, holding up a finger. She paused, her eyebrow arched, quizzical. Her eyes on mine, feeling the strength of her gaze intimately entwined into my own once more, I raised my own wineglass and tilted it in her direction, then drank it down, savoring the sweet tang of the grape, the dark bitter of the tannins, the heady bloom in the back of my nose reminding me of nothing so much as the way her breath had tasted in my mouth the very first night we met.

By the time the wine was gone, so was she. I smiled, and turned back to my dinner. And I understood, perfectly.

Downtown

Adult Books flickered the neon sign behind grimy glass. Katie hung back a little bit as her lover strode purposefully into the shop. An even five feet of fireplug-stocky, red-haired freckle-faced stone butch, Mick looked a lot like Opie Taylor. Opie Taylor with D cups and a strap-on, and a reckless swagger that was probably the thing Katie liked best about her.

The shoppers inside were few and uniformly male. Mick's presence seemed not to trip their radar, but then again, Mick passed more often than not. She usually used the men's room.

Katie was another story. You just don't walk into a porn shop when you're an expensive-looking five-eight brunette and expect heads not to turn. The boys don't know, and don't care, that you sleep with girls when you look like that . . . in fact, if they knew, they'd think it was the answer to a prayer. The hungry glances that strafed Katie's body made her nervous as hell. Eyes down, she walked past the racks of cheap plastic dildos and grubby-looking magazines, watching Mick's short, firm legs, feeling a little tingle of excitement smoldering somewhere below her belly button. She would've sworn that she didn't know how she'd let Mick talk her into this, but her swelling clit would've called her a liar.

Katie liked sleaze. Secretly. She never came right out and said it. Not even to Mick. But it didn't matter. Mick knew how to read between the lines. And Katie liked it dirty, and rowdy, with a scintillating edge of danger. She wasn't about to cop to it, but that's just not something one does. Not when one wears pearls from Tiffany, carries a briefcase from Coach, and boasts a birth certificate that says "Grosse Pointe, Michigan," a law diploma that says "Harvard," and a business card that says "Junior Partner, Hunting, Daniels, and Smith." It was the unspoken contract of Katie and Mick's relationship: Don't ask, don't tell. Just pursue.

And pursue Katie did, following in Mick's footsteps past the Swedish penis enlargers, past the copies of *Shaved Pregnant Oriental Twat* and *Barely Legal Lesbo Teens*, past the rows and rows of video covers that showed every conceivable orifice and every conceivable thing with which an orifice might be stuffed. They walked straight to the back and turned right, Katie catching up with Mick as she paused before the doors.

Booth number three was small and dark and barely big enough for the two of them when they closed the door and slid the bolt home. The dim light overhead reminded Katie of the light in Mick's beat-up old Toyota, yellowish and wan. Without preamble Mick's hands were under Katie's blouse, silk tugged from her waistband, breasts spilled from underwires, rough thumbs pinching nipples, rolling them over and over. Katie whimpered, kittenish, into her lover's mouth, already telegraphing her urgency though they'd hardly begun.

The booth wasn't comfortable, but that wasn't the point. Fortunately the floor wasn't sticky. Katie breathed a sigh, then shivered and sucked in her breath, her long, red-tipped fingers anxiously fondling the short soft fuzz of her lover's brush cut as Mick's tongue and lips and teeth fastened onto one already-hard nipple. The tinny whine and thud of the disco music coming through the wall accompanied their grinding embrace, doing nothing to mask the raspy groans that limped out of Katie's throat as Mick bit and chewed and licked and sucked.

"Whaddaya want, little slut? You sound like there's something you want," Mick coaxed as Katie squirmed.

Katie blushed, the scarlet in her cheeks as obvious as the

unconscious grinding of her hips. Mick slid her hand down, sneaking it under Katie's hem, and stroked the soft skin just above her stocking top.

"Good girl, Katie," Mick growled smokily. "Hose, not pantyhose, just the way your Micky told you to. Did you do the other thing Daddy told you you had to do if he was going to bring you to the peeps?"

Katie nodded shyly.

"What's the matter, girl? Cat got your tongue? Did you do what I asked you to do or not?"

Katie's voice was a hoarse whisper. "Yes, Daddy. I did what you asked me to."

"Show me."

Her cheeks and ears red, conservative pageboy falling forward to cover only some of her embarrassment, Katie leaned forward and pulled up her skirt, hitching it up slowly. Black garters descended to tan stocking tops, and between her thighs . . . nothing. Not even a scrap of pubic hair remained to hide the puffy cleft of her pussy. But that was the way it was supposed to be. Daddy told her she should be bare. So she was.

"Oooh, Katie. What a nasty little girl you are, no panties on, getting felt up in a peepshow booth like some trailer-trash slut," Mick snarled, stroking one fingertip up and over the arch of Kate's silken-smooth mons. "I think you should reach in Daddy's pocket and find out what he's got in there for you."

"For me, Daddy?" Katie asked, her voice more little-girlish as she slipped further into role. Mick could feel how hot she was, could already feel the slip of girl-juice as she stroked the edges of Katie's cunt.

Mick nodded as Katie's long fingers slipped into the pocket of her 501's, withdrawing the roll of shrink-wrapped quarters. "What are the quarters for, Daddy?"

"Well, we are at the peeps," Mick said, leaning Katie back against the wall and teasing her nipple with her thumb and forefinger as she nudged her knees apart. Katie's eyes were wide. "But these quarters are for you."

With that, Mick grinned wickedly and slid a finger into Katie's cunt. Her wetness, gratifyingly copious, let her slide right in, all the way to the knuckle as Katie's eyes closed reflexively.

"That's right, baby," coaxed Mick, "you love the way your Daddy fucks you, don't you?" Working her fingers in and out several times, Mick waited until Katie's hips were rocking in anticipation of the next stroke. In slid the plastic-wrapped quarters, ragged ends and all, right alongside two of Mick's fingers, and Katie's eyes flew open again.

"Don't worry, baby," Mick soothed, "I brought more quarters for the booth. Don't you worry. Daddy's gonna take care of everything."

With that, Mick fumbled in her pocket with her free hand, then slapped two coins into the slot in the wall. The rickety creak of the metal shade accompanied the arch of Mick's hand as she ground her fingers and the quarters deep into Katie's sopping cunt, forcing her to arch and muffle a squeal.

The gel-covered lights that surrounded the peepshow stage lent an odd bluish-purple cast to the light in the booth, like a television screen. Katie could see the reflections of eyeglasses behind other windows. Men were watching. Could they see her and Mick? Or were they watching the dancer? She could see them, if indistinctly. Were they looking at her? What if . . . ?

And then Mick was biting her nipple. And then Mick was grinding the roll of quarters in and out of her sopping cunt, mashing her clit with her thumb. And then Mick's mouth opened wide and she tried her hardest to take Katie's entire breast inside, and Katie gasped and Mick moaned and thrust into her with four fingers, the cunt-juiced roll of quarters hitting the floor of the booth with a thud.

"Tell me how good it feels to have your greedy little pussy full of Daddy's hand, Katie," Mick demanded, grinding Katie's G-spot as her thumb relentlessly circled her clit. "Tell Daddy how much you like being his peepshow whore."

Faltering—partly from embarrassment, partly from desire, and partly from the searing knowledge that she did like having Mick's hand in her to the knuckles as she bucked and moaned like a porn star in booth number three of a sleazy peepshow in a sleazy porn store in a part of town she would've never been caught dead in—Katie did, spilling out the words interspersed with the sharp sweet noises of impending orgasm. And Katie forgot to try to figure out whether anyone could see her, or Mick, or not.

Blouse tucked in, hair hastily combed, Katie followed Mick back out of the store, pausing for a moment or two to look at the magazine rack, tall and cool and femme next to short and butch and boyish.

"God, that's so fake," Katie laughed, pointing at a typical girl-girl spread: the teased hair and fake nails, silicone tits and neon-painted lips frozen in the industry standard blowjob pucker. Considerably less anxious now, neither Katie nor Mick noticed the few glances of the few men who lurked in the store as they stood, backs to the counter, pointing and giggling.

Suddenly a male voice boomed from the counter, half the length of the store back. "Hey, lady!" it shouted, and Katie turned around, alarmed. Mick, of course, never responded to being referred to as "lady."

"Hey, lady," the cashier repeated, his voice a perfect match to his burly, stocky, hairy-armed Sicilian frame, "you can't bring that kid in here."

"Kid?" Katie murmured, looking at Mick, then at the shopkeeper.

"You can't bring the kid in here, lady," the shopkeeper yelled, gesturing at the short, boyish Mick. "You gotta leave. I don't care if you come in here, but you can't bring kids. It's against the law."

Katie looked at Mick, who arched an eyebrow eloquently. Lifting her hand to her mouth, she licked one finger, smiling at the lingering taste of Katie's juice on her skin as she looked into Katie's eyes, tugging her toward the door.

"C'mon, little girl," Mick purred. "You heard the nice man."

Sauce for the Gander

I hardly heard the first ring, and I certainly wasn't getting up to answer it. It was a Saturday morning, and I was busy violating sodomy laws. Dan noticed it more than I did, pausing momentarily, halting the exquisitely rough-edged glide of his sweet cock slowly pumping in and out of my aching-to-be-fucked asshole. I wriggled my butt backward toward him, wordlessly reminding him of what he had been doing, grinning silently to myself at his office-conditioned Pavlovian response to the electronic chirp of the telephone.

Dan murmured, pleased to feel me moving against him. The phone rang again, and as it did he pushed in slowly, burying himself slowly to the hilt in between the soft round halves of my ass, his thickness prying me open at both ends as it coaxed a gravelly moan from my throat. The third ring came, and he backed out the same way, rhythmic and measured, making me whimper as my flesh clung to the smooth tender skin of his shaft, lingering like goodbye kisses at the train station. I gasped out loud when the head popped free. My hips bucked backward reflexively, anxious that he not leave my body. His fingers dug into my hips, keeping me from fucking backward against him, and as the phone rang a fourth time, I let my cunt muscles contract against themselves, feeling in a sudden overwhelming wave the need to be fucked, and fucked hard. But no, no such luck. He slid into me with a lackadaisical corkscrewing motion of his

99

hips, sighing as he pushed into me, forcing my well-lubed and eager ass to yield to his hardness with an unhurried glide. It was nowhere near enough. Clit throbbing, I tightened my muscles around him, milking the base of his cock.

"Please, just fuck me," I begged hoarsely, burying my face into the pillows in frustration. "Hard, please, please?"

The phone rang a fifth time, and I prayed like hell I had remembered to turn the answering machine on as he reversed the process, withdrawing from me with gentle deliberateness, almost completely dislodging himself from the tight, almost unbearably sensitive confines of my ass. There was only so much of that I could bear.

"So, just how many rings do you have that machine set for?" my lover asked with a sardonic leer in his tone, his cock dragging out of my ass, feeling as if it were dragging my clit along with it. I groaned, pulling a pillow over my head, simultaneously loving and hating the tease, the wait, the thrilling slow satin-rasp of his motions. He had about two more seconds before I would pass that threshold where I couldn't sustain the arousal without consistent help. I needed more from him. Without something to sustain it, my lust would vanish out from under me like a magician's tablecloth.

With a click like a marble falling into a metal dish, the answering machine clicked into action. Mercifully, his fingers clawed my ass cheeks, pulling up and apart as if he wanted to split me like a sweet tangerine. I cried out with a high, keening whine of want, feeling his tugging at my buttocks pull the floor of my ass all that much more firmly against the fat head of his cock. Oh, fuck me, please, I thought as he teased me with little hummingbird-like thrusts, a fraction of an inch in and out and in and out, making my nerves shriek and my muscles tense reflexively, sweet hard male flesh tormenting me in the most intense possible way. I arched back, trying to press into him, wanting to take him deeper.

The answering machine motor whirred. The volume was turned almost all the way down, and all I could hear from down the hall was a faraway murmur. I wanted Dan to reach around and stroke my clit, wanted him to slam into me, craved the feeling of his hands on my breasts. Whoever was leaving the message talked long enough that I found myself wondering who it could be. I'd already learned that she who answers the phone during sex gets what she deserves: By the time one has hung up, the juicy rare meat of lust has often become a cold fried egg, rubbery and tasteless when forced to be reheated.

Daniel, of course, noticed my distraction. A cold glob of lube slipping down the cleft of my ass from where he squeezed it onto my tailbone brought me back into the moment, sliding down over increasingly sensitive skin to coat his shaft, paused two inches into my buzzing sphincter. My attention was riveted to that sensation, those precise bits of hot flushed flesh that felt as if they were steaming the lube into clouds. I love the sensation, tawdry and sleazy, messy and primal, gorged and sluttish, of feeling someone fucking gooey liquid into me. Lube dripped off his cock, down my crack toward my cunt, oozed in rivulets onto the towel he'd slid under us before we'd begun. Too perfect. I bit into the pillowcase, an almost-agonized wordless cry ripping out of my lungs as I was forced inescapably back into my own deep need.

My fingers clawed at the pillow when he stopped halfway into me, desperate to get it out of the way of my mouth so that I could beg him to let me have it plead with him to pound his cock all the way into me, split me open, slam me through the futon frame and down to the floor, anything, as long as I could feel him all the way into me, balls-deep, promising the incandescent rush of thick hot viscosity yet to come. Incoherent, lube still dripping down my ass and making me insane with need, I sobbed out a heartfelt "please," only to have him stroke my hair gently, calmly.

"Unh-unh, Anna," he whispered, maddeningly in control of himself and relishing my lack of it, "Better keep that pillow right where it is. You know how loud you scream when I give you what you're beggin' for and rape that greedy little cum-slut ass of yours."

His words, the parody of a threat sugarcoated by the loving rasp in his voice, caused a sudden trembling, radioactive bubbles carbonating my engorged pussy lips, my nipples, my clit, my cunt feeling cavernous and craving something to fill it with weight and force. I heard the footsteps of a thousand soldiers in my ears as my heart hammered. Every neuron in my ass and pussy felt like a naked wire, alive and threatening a short circuit as the rest of my body melted away, muscles going limp, unimportant. It was the instant of want he waited for, the sudden lassitude that told him to take me over, hard and fierce, driving into me as he collapsed onto my back, his weight driving me down onto the bed, cock like a butterfly pin nailing me, going through me, unstoppable. I sobbed with the intensity and the pleasure, my body quaking, trying not to come yet, not yet, not quite yet. Powerful fingers with short sharp nails slid under me, found my nipples, pinched hard as his hips drove into my upturned grateful buttocks, fingers kneading my tits roughly, hurting me just enough to provide spontaneous-combustion counterpoint to the thick pleasure of his cock driving in and in and further into my hungry asshole.

I reared up against him, meeting his thrust, feeling myself caught on an updraft of pleasure so thick that I could barely breathe. With a slam our bodies met, hard enough to have knocked us over had we not been locked so desperately together, and I floated away, my body hammered into the bed by the torrential, relentless, pistoning fuck, my tiny tender butthole so pristinely, so roughly, so sweetly opened by that candy apple of meat and muscle that it ripped scream after scream of pleasure out of my unthinking throat. Somewhere else a part of me soared, serene and freed, clean and immaculate in the acid bath of that coruscating, perfect ass-fucking. Nirvana. Nerve-ana. The jewel is in the lotus. *Om mani padme cum.*

Slowly, muzzily, I opened my eyes, pushing the corner of the pillow off of my face. My throat hurt. Panting softly, almost recovered, he lay on top of me, his weight as reassuring to me as the fact that his cock was still nestled inside me and still halfway hard. Gently I tightened my muscles and gave his cock a squeeze, enough to make him gasp and scold me, telling me he was too sensitive.

"Don't tell me you want more?" he asked with mock incredulity.

"Fuck it into me," I whispered, a shy, greedy little smile on my lips. "Give me one more. Let me feel you fuck your cum into me, just a little."

He knew full well what I wanted; I knew full well he just wanted to hear me say it. Pulling out to let me savor the tip of his cock slipping out of me, I felt a small trickle of semen leaking out of my battered ass, warm, the consistency of honey. With a soft moan, he pressed his cockhead back up against the doubly-lubed ring of my ass and pushed against me. After all these years he's never confessed that he loves this part as much as I do, but I know better.

"You like that, don't you, baby?" he purred in a loving tease as the head of his cock slipped back inside me and he began to fuck me quickly, pulling completely out of me with each stroke, words and sensations instantaneously putting me on the verge of another release. "You just love feeling me fucking all that cum up into your gorgeous tight little hole, don't you?"

Convulsing with the sharp suddenness of orgasm, I didn't need to answer. I felt my sphincter gripping his cock, milking it with hard inward strokes, and heard his amazed groan as he felt an encore of his own searing its way up and out of his almost-empty balls. "God, how luscious," I gasped, the words spurting as fast as his seed, savoring the clarity with which my overtaxed nerve endings could feel the few short jets of semen he pumped deep into my rear end. We both collapsed as the orgasms rolled away, giggling and panting, careful to be still below the waist, both his cock and my hard-used but pleasantly tingling anus too tender, too sensitive to bear even the motion of uncoupling.

Showered and shaved, buttoning the shirt my mother had given him last year for Hanukkah, he stood in the bathroom doorway. "That was your other sweetie," he said, a twinkle in his eye. "She says she needs to talk to you, hopes you have the afternoon free. She's horny as hell, she says, and she was purring like a kitten the whole time she left the message."

"Never rains but it pours, does it?" I asked rhetorically, walking to the phone. "Why do I even bother to shower in between?" I gave him a wink as I dialed Jill's number, enjoying the gentle throbbing of my backside, a lovely reminder of how well he'd fucked me.

"Jill, it's poor manners to answer the phone when you have your fingers in your twat," I teased. Her "hello" had been so breathy, so transparently aroused that I could very nearly smell the sweet aroma of her slippery, bare-naked cunt. She had a little-girl voice at the best of times, and when she was aroused it went from Betty Boop to breathless waif, a strong contrast to the powerful, tall, well-curved solidity of her body.

She stammered a hello, the redness in her cheeks seeping into her voice so thickly that I could tell she was blushing clear down to her gumdrop nipples. In short order I discovered that I had been spot on the money with my opening salvo. She had been masturbating, fantasizing, and wishing I would call her back when the phone rang.

"I crave you," she whispered in my ear. "Inside me."

"You want to be fucked, do you?" I replied, trying to sound cool as my clit tingled between my demurely crossed thighs.

"Oh, yes, Anna," she sighed, a boa constrictor of anticipation squeezing breathless words out of her.

"Is it okay with you that Dan is here?" I asked, smiling slyly up at my partner, who stood watching me, his arms folded across his chest and a knowing grin on his face.

"Oh, of course," my lover agreed. She was fond of Dan, and he was fond of her. They shared their fondness for me with remarkably little friction, a fact that pleased me afresh almost every day. It wouldn't be the first time, and it certainly wouldn't be the last, that Dan was around when Jill came over with sex on her mind. I wanted something specific, though, something rather different than anything that had ever happened before when Jill came over to our house to make love with me.

"Is it okay with you if Dan is with us this time?" I ventured, less sure of her response. For a few instants I was caught between my partners, suspended in silence. Dan's eyes had gone wide, and he pointed to himself, index finger on his chest, incredulous. Impressively, for the straight boyfriend of a bi woman, he'd never even asked me for a threesome, and he seemed to be suffering advanced mindboggle at the prospect of having one offered to him out of the blue.

When she spoke, Jill had a chuckle in her voice. "You've got something up your sleeve, don't you?"

"Sort of," I admitted. "Is that a yes?" Dan was shaking his head disbelievingly, wearing a goofy anticipatory grin. "I cannot believe this," I heard him mutter. "Un-fucking-believable."

Jill murmured agreement with a silky light purr, about as close to a growl as a soprano that high can get. "I'll be over shortly to help you with Daniel," she agreed with a luscious little chirp. "But I want you to fuck me."

The line went dead, and I hung up. A triumphant smile plastered across my face, I looked up at my lover. "She said yes."

"Holy Mother of God at the Tastee-Freez," he replied, genuinely taken aback. "You're serious?" He'd often told me how he envied me fucking Jill, not jealous, just envious and intensely attracted to her muscular rugby-girl thighs and long-fingered hands, her small olive-skinned breasts with their almost ludicrously large nipples, her quirky half-Lebanese, half-Japanese features. I still savored the memory of his defenseless, guttural croak when I told him that she kept her pussy shaved and that she wore a small titanium hoop in one naked inner labia. Dan was far too respectful of my bisexuality and far too aware of how seriously I took my polyamory—to say nothing of my very genuine love for Jill—to importune me to let him watch, but he was far from immune to my beloved girlfriend's charms. I found his discreet, utterly politic lustfulness endearing.

"Of course I'm serious," I said as I walked toward the kitchen. "But you've never . . . " he trailed, following me. "She's never . . . was it her idea?"

"Doesn't matter, Dannyboy, and it's none of your business anyway. We have plans for you." I smiled like a tabby with a mouthful of canary feathers.

"Plans?" he questioned, gesturing to me with a poppyseed bagel. "What do you mean, plans?"

"You've told me that you want to know what it feels like for me when you fuck me like you did this morning," I answered as matter-of-factly as possible.

"You want to have Jill watch you fuck me?"

With a wry grin, I looked up at Dan, shaking my head. "My word, you're quick to jump to conclusions. Who said anything about Jill watching?"

"Well, color me slow, but wasn't that what you had in mind?" Now he was slightly defensive, unable to figure out what I intended to spring on him, no longer sure that this threesome was going to be what he'd thought.

"Nope, not really." I reached across the table and brushed my fingertips against his jaw affectionately. "I want to watch *her* fuck you. You told me once that you thought she was so hot you'd let her do almost anything to you if only she were willing."

"You want to watch *Jill* fuck *me?*" Dan echoed, sounding entirely stunned by the idea. I could see in his eyes that the notion of my tall, strong, slightly butch lover bending him over and making him take it for her was not entirely unattractive. He squirmed in his chair a little, his eyes a little unfocused.

Silently, I chuckled into my mug. "Of course I want to watch Jill fuck you. You told me you'd let her." He stared at me, swallowing hard, but not saying a word. "Or were you just whistlin' Dixie, Danno?"

"God, Anna, I don't know if I can take it . . . I've never . . . ." He liked it when I fingerfucked him, in recent times working him up to taking three of my fingers inside him. Still, he'd always balked at letting me fuck him the way I really wanted to, with the long slim silicone dildo that I loved to work into my own asshole when I was desperately horny and he was out of town.

Dan's eyes locked on mine with an astonishing look of terrified, fierce arousal. I stroked my toes up the inside of his thigh, letting them brush against his chino-clad crotch. As I suspected, he was ragingly stiff. "Ta, ta, ta," I clucked, stroking my toenail along the length of his fly as his face turned a bright embarrassed pink. "If I didn't know better, Daniel my love, I might accuse you of looking forward to this."

Dan lay on the bed, right hand idly stroking his massively stiff cock, pre-cum dripping over his fingers like a caramel glaze over ice cream. He'd been given strict instructions not to come, and not to disturb Jill and me until we were ready for him.

She had opened to me with her usual silent completeness, our kiss in the foyer of the house immediately wringing-wet with overtones of desire. She'd ridden to the house on her bicycle, and the slight fresh dampness of her T-shirt pleased me. I loved the grassy, woody smell of her, rubbing my face between her persimmon-half breasts, savoring the distinctly female way she made my heart beat faster, so different than what I felt with Dan. We hardly ever spoke while we made love to one another, sly games of Mother-May-I played with butterfly tongues and ravenous hands on bodies so eloquent that words are clumsy by comparison.

Her mouth found my right nipple almost immediately, pushing the lapel of my robe aside, latching on like a nursling. I unbuttoned her skirt and let it fall onto the tile floor, unsurprised to find her nude beneath. "Naughty Jillian," I chided teasingly, my lips brushing her ear through her storm system of curls. "No panties? Only tramps go around without panties." My right pinky tip parted her labia to find her little titanium hoop, tugging her pussy slightly open. I hissed with pleasure to find her already wet, my hiss resolving itself into a coo as I tugged harder on her labia ring and she gave the softest of moans, relinquishing her hold on my breast.

"Let me take my boots off," she murmured, and I let her go. Before she could straighten up, I moved behind her and slid my thumb into her cunt. The sensation of being so quickly and unexpectedly penetrated made her clutch at the doorframe to keep from falling over. It was as though I could hear her in my mind, hear her whispering, begging me to fuck her, telling me that this was exactly what she'd been wanting all day. Jill's back arched slightly, her hips pressing back against me, trying to get more of me into her, wanting so obviously just to be fucked, without fuss or fanfare or even foreplay. Immediately I pulled out of her, pulling her around by the waist to smear her own lubrication across her mouth. I kissed her, hard, and when she smiled and her mouth opened under mine, I tonguefucked between her lips just enough to make her shudder.

"I love you, Jill," I said, taking her by the hand as I looked into her pale green eyes. Jill beamed, her lipstick-tip nipples hard as erasers and poking out under her thin yellow T-shirt, and squeezed my hand, not quite able to talk. She tugged at my arm and pulled me after her, sprinting down the hallway toward the master bedroom, naked but for her shirt.

"Hi, Dan," she said jauntily as she pulled off her shirt and grabbed me by the ends of the bathrobe sash. I could feel Dan watching as Jill and I kissed, but my attention to his presence in the room faded into the remote background as my body tuned itself in to the wavelengths of Jill's response. Standing by the foot of the bed, I grabbed her wrists and held them tightly in the small of her back, bending down to take her left nipple between my lips. Jill's nipples, so disproportionately large on her tiny breasts, always responded so well to a combination of tongue and sharp-edged nipping. Switching from left to right, back and forth, I intensified the pressure until I actually succeeded in getting her to moan out loud, a rarity for her. Letting go of her wrists, I ran my fingertips along the seam between her newly shaven, eiderdown-soft cunt lips.

Gently I turned her to face the bed and bent her over, enjoying the sleekness of her strong body under my hands as I stroked her back, her hips, her thighs. Dan moaned softly, watching, as I spread her firm, sherbet-scoop ass cheeks with my hands. I loved looking at her like that, bent over, spread wide, totally open and totally vulnerable, knowing how much it was making her tremble. When I bent her over like this, she was utterly mine, just the way she wanted to be.

Holding her light-tan thighs in both hands, I gave her ten of the long, agonizingly wide licks she adored, tongue painting a broad stripe from her bursting clit up and over her cunt—she contracted reflexively as I flicked the tip of my tongue just barely inside—then over her perineum to her swirling plum-blossom of an asshole. Her breath was growing ragged, more so with each swipe of my tongue. I pushed my tongue into her cunt as far as it would go, and she ground backward against my face, hard and needful. My hand flat against her belly, I slid my palm toward her breast and clawed at it, her reactionary writhing against my tongue tattling that she was more than ready to take whatever I dished out. I snatched a latex glove from the bureau top and put it on my right hand, teasing her labia with slick rubber fingertips as I once more found her endlessly pinchable nipple with my bare hand. I tweaked it hard, and she sucked in her breath as I slid three fingers into her, filling her to the knuckles with one simple push.

Inarticulate, preverbal gasps punctuated her panting as I kneaded the walls of her cunt just the way I knew she liked it best. Slipping my pinkie into her, she shoved back against my hand so forcefully I worried that she would hurt herself, but instead she stopped, dead still. I arched my wrist and twisted my hand inside her, just enough to push her entirely over the edge. With a high-pitched squeal she shuddered and came, cunt clutching at my fingers, sweet girl-juice dripping down my forearm as I resumed fucking my hand into her.

I'd done it to her enough times that I knew I didn't need to ask what she wanted next. I tucked my thumb into my palm and began to slowly rock my hand in and out of her, fingers forming a cone, knuckles rubbing in and out, in and out against her entrance. She began to push against my hand, soft powder puffs of sound floating from her throat as she fucked backward into me, and I slowly, gently twisted my arm inside her until the instant came when she opened that tiny bit more and my fist slid, fingers curling in on themselves, wrist-deep into her impossibly lush cunt. The smell of her heat was overpowering, the sensation of her body wrapped around my arm so hot and wet and tight and yet so yielding that I felt lightheaded. No matter how many times I'd fucked her this way, it still seemed holy, in extremis, so rarefied and sweet as she started to come and come and did not stop until that sudden last spasm that always seemed to take her by surprise, cunt mauling my hand with contractions, and squeezed my fist completely out.

I lowered her to the bed, stripping the glove off and throwing it over my shoulder, not really caring where it went. Cradling her against me, stroking her hair back from her ruined, exhausted face, I kissed her softly. Looking up I saw Daniel, sheer awe on his face, his cock standing stiff but unheeded. I smiled at him, and he smiled back slowly, his eyes never leaving mine, amazed by this side of me that he was just now getting to see.

As Jill recovered I sank down between her thighs, tongue slipping easily between her hairless lips to find her clit. The taste and feel of her in my mouth would have been enough to have kept me there a long time, ordinarily, but we had things to do. Somewhere in my peripheral vision, I noticed Jill and Dan making eye contact. A fuse of jealousy sizzling in the pit of my stomach, I wrested her attention back where it belonged, trilling my tongue against the tender hood of her clit. I wanted my girlfriend eager, ready, aroused again, her own hunger blunted just enough that she could give my other lover the kind of unstinting fucking he so richly deserved.

Wrapping my arms around her waist, I looked up into Jill's glowing face. We held one another's gaze for a moment, and I buried my face against her breastbone, her fingers lovingly stroking my neck, my hair. She curled around me, whispering gentle words into my ear. We kissed, and she held me to her as I whispered in her ear what I wanted her to do to Daniel, who lay at the head of the bed, transfixed by our little show.

The slow, liquid smile I love so much flowed across her eccentrically lovely face. She cleared her throat, looking directly at Daniel with suddenly predatory eyes. Dan gazed at Jill, taking in the sight of the bald-crotched temptation he'd so often imagined from the far side of a closed door while I was on the other side of it fucking her.

"I hope you're ready for me, Dan," she rasped, her voice still high but remarkably sexy from the postcoital grittiness in her throat. "I'm really looking forward to being inside your sweet little man-cunt. I love giving someone a good ass-fucking."

• • •

I had to fight the urge to cut to the head of the line. Jill in the leather harness, eight-inch black silicone cock jutting out from her mons was a sight that infallibly reduced me to a twitching mess of estrogen and yearning. I could tell by the Mona Lisa lines of her smile that she was looking forward to this at least as much as I. All I had to do was to keep from throwing myself between the two of them and begging to be first. I sat next to Dan, stroking his side as he knelt on all fours, Jill's long hands caressing his ass and hips. He was nervous, but he couldn't resist the fact that he had two women's hands caressing his body, and gradually he began to wriggle slightly under our palms, soft little groans floating into the air whenever Jill reached down far enough to caress the undersides of his balls.

Jill leaned down to kiss me, and I opened my mouth to her as I cupped her breast in one hand and took Dan's cock in the other. Clasping Dan's shaft in my fingers and finding Jill's nipple with a gentle, rolling pinch, I shuddered happily as I got them both to moan at the same time, Jill's baby-doll murmur like cotton candy in my mouth. I cupped his balls in my hand, jostling them gently like dice before the throw, and he pressed forward to thrust his cock against my forearm, then back, pressing his ass against the sleek length of the cock that Jill wore so well. Jill's tongue was in my mouth, playful, teasing the tender spot on my lower lip, wearing her toppishness at a rakish angle. She was eager, quite aware that she held both Dan and me in the palm of her hand. Not just because she was about to fuck Dan, and I found it unbearably hot, but for reasons she couldn't have known, couldn't have seen.

I loved Jill, loved the way she moved inside me, loved to look up when she fucked me, my legs hugging her waist, my feet on her ass pushing her cock into me further and further. I loved to let her torment my cunt with her tongue, her fingers, with dexterous, unending fucking until my system couldn't withstand it anymore and I would just start coming, enormous waves of orgasms rendering me incoherent for five, ten, fifteen minutes at a stretch. I was desperately envious, and had to laugh at my own envy—of all the people in the world that I could want to allow to have the kind of pleasure I knew Jill could bring, Dan was the one I wanted to share her with. But try telling that to the stupid reptilian part of me that kept shrieking at me to grab her for myself. As much as I yearned to watch my lover working her cock into my other lover's tight, untested ass, I also wanted to take her off somewhere, mine and no one else's. As Jill straightened, she began rhythmically to rub against Dan's ass, her eyes locked on mine, and I shivered with the empathetic knowledge of exactly how suavely, precisely how skillfully, she was capable of stroking with her silicone member. I was scalding hot, yes, but at least part of that heat came directly from the surly flames of sexual jealousy.

Jill's expertise was by no means lost on Dan, who groaned a soft "Oh God" as he dropped his shoulders to the bed, clutching a pillow under his head, ass in the air. A wolfish conquistador smile spread across Jill's face, and she stroked his sides, fucking her hips toward his ass, letting the shaft of her cock rub up and down his buttcrack. My pussy quivered as I watched him beginning to lose control, and I thought momentarily about sliding underneath Dan and slipping his cock into my cunt as Jill slipped hers into his ass.

I couldn't bring myself to do it. I wanted Dan to experience being fucked as purely, as whitely hot, as he possibly could. Being inside me at the same time would be too much of a distraction, the cock in his ass demoted to a sideshow attraction, and I didn't want that. Jill's expert cocksman skills deserved all his attention. And mine. Incapable of forming words, Dan just groaned and arched backward into Jill the way he wriggled against my hands when I teased his asshole during a blowjob and he wanted me to penetrate him.

"Are you trying to tell me that you want girl cock in your boypussy, Dan?" I asked coaxingly, "Is that what you want? You want Jill to shove that great big tool of hers into your tight little ass?"

Jill's eyes flashed with lust, Dan's groan broke in the middle and descended two octaves into rough gravel at the bottom. Squeezing Dan's cock, letting my fingers ripple around it rhythmically, I picked up the bottle of lube from the corner of the bed and handed it to Jill with a conspiratorial smile, sharing a moment of tenderness with her as our eyes stroked one another's faces. She lubed her cock and resumed sliding it up and down between the halves of Daniel's slim-hipped ass, making him shudder so hard I thought he might convulse.

"So hot, baby," I half-purred, half-growled, my nipples starting to tingle, speaking to both of my lovers as they moved against one another. To Jill I said, "Lube him up good for that nice long cock, sugar girl. He's virgin pussy." To my surprise, Dan moaned at being called pussy, his hardness twitching in my hand. Jill opened the flip-top on the lube bottle and held it high above Dan's ass, letting a long thin ribbon of clear sticky liquid spill down onto his waiting skin. Jill wore a beatific smile, meditatively stroking lube all over my boyfriend's ass with her cock-tip, squeezing out more in an extravagant stream.

"I hope you've got more lube," she intoned seriously. "If he's anything like you are, he's going to soak it up and beg for more, and I do want to hear him beg."

"Oh, there's more where that came from," I grinned, watching the side of Dan's face. His eyes were closed, his lips slack, as he let himself be manipulated by my hands and Jill's, abandoning himself to the sensation of being painted with lube by a thick, hard cock. I stroked gooey pre-cum up and down his shaft with my hand, encouraging and rewarding his willingness. "Plenty more lube for that pretty little boy-cunt whenever you want it. Lube him up just like you lube me up, Jill. He'll like that. What's sauce for the goose . . ."

". . . is sauce for the gander," my girlfriend finished, catching my drift as she took three fingersful of lube and brought them directly against Dan's tight muscled ring. "Breathe," she told him, and he did, breathing deeply in, then out. On his outbreath she slid two fingers into his ass, smooth and sure. He yelped, but then groaned as I gave his ragingly hard cock a few firm strokes. Two fingers inside him, she squirted lube into the groove between her fingers, letting me watch, my cunt oozing as she used her fingers to channel the lube into my boyfriend's ass, slowly working him open for her. The fires of my jealousy raged in competition with the flames of deep, unreconstructed lust. I knew precisely how it felt to have her working all that slickness into my own ass, and the thought made me shiver. It was all I could do to remember to keep gently stroking his shaft.

Without telling him she was doing it, Jill worked a third finger into Dan's butthole, her fingertips doing invisible things inside him that had him moaning almost nonstop. Soon he was pressing back against her, pushing himself down onto fingers well versed at making me beg her to shove her cock into me, until she was in him up to her knuckles. Dan was beyond words. He had shut down the part of him that would've told him he couldn't do it, couldn't take it, and was letting his body be taken over by sensation, by lust, by the almost incomprehensible idea that two women, one whom he loved, one about whom he had long fantasized, were working together to fuck him in a way he'd never been fucked before. I got onto my knees, right hand still encircling Dan's dripping member, left hand caressing Jill's satiny ass, looking into her eyes.

"Give it to him, baby," I whispered. "I want to watch you just destroy that ass."

Jill's eyes were bright, her smile devilish and voluptuous at the same time. Pulling her fingers out halfway, she squirted another good shot of lube into him. With a long slow firm shove, she slid her fingers back in, extra lube oozing out of his butt and down his ass, over her fingers. His moans were soft and vulnerable, his cock occasionally jerking gently in my grip. My lover squeezed lube onto her cock and I reached down to smear it all over the condomed surface, eager to feel the firm weight and thickness of the shaft, altogether too well aware of how good it had felt all the times it had entered me. I positioned the tip of the phallus against Dan's sphincter, waiting for Jill to pull her fingers out, but she merely winked at me and grinned. She opened her fingers like a scissors and wedged the head of her cock between them, forcing a keening wail out of Dan, whose face was still half-buried in the pillow he held under him. I clenched my fingers around his cock, thumb stroking the sweet spot just below the cleft of his cockhead.

"Kiss me, Anna," Jill croaked, hoarse with lust, and I did, twining lube-sticky fingers in her hair as she slowly began to push her way into Dan's body, fingers coming out as her cock went in. Dan's cock swelled in my hand and I pumped him long and slow, reassuring and firm, rhythmic and constant as his body went rigid, trying to cope with the invasion. Kissing Jill, I was floored by the force of her lust and the exquisite control that she kept, somehow managing not to slam her cock all the way in to the hilt, even though I could tell she wanted to. Slowly, inexorably, she worked into my boyfriend's ass, until her hips pressed against his lube-painted buttocks. Only then did she break the kiss.

"Let me have his cock," she said, sliding her arm down my forearm and replacing my fingers with hers. "He's mine now. I'm going to ride him until he screams. I want you to fuck me while I fuck him."

Relinquishing my hold on my boyfriend's aching, oozing penis, I could tell that her words had somehow penetrated his half-consciousness. Dan wriggled his ass against her, inviting her to take him. I grabbed a glove from the bureau and moved behind Jill, the split peach of her ass and cunt open to me as she knelt spread-legged behind Dan. My own cunt spasmed, aching, yearning to be fucked. Later, I told myself, later. Right now, my girl wanted me in her pussy while she fucked Dan's round narrow boy-butt, and that was all that mattered. She bent over Dan's body, supporting herself on her left arm while her right hand teased his prick, slowly building her strokes into his ass until he was groaning ecstatically to take her in from tip to base in slow, liquid strokes. I was amazed at her, amazed at him, amazed at what I was seeing, tender, intimate, and scaldingly familiar.

It was almost difficult to intrude. My jealousy had suddenly, mysteriously vanished, perhaps overwhelmed by the erotic magic of watching my girlfriend fucking my boyfriend and my boyfriend loving every last millimeter of the cock that slid into his ass. Tentatively I pressed my knuckles against her slit.

"Bitch, I thought I told you to fuck me now," she play-snarled, looking back over her shoulder at me with sheer lust in her eyes. "I hate it when you keep me waiting. I've been fucking away for five minutes here, wondering why those fingers weren't in my pussy."

"I'm sorry, Jill," I breathed, kissing her shoulder as I slid two fingers into her sopping-wet hotness. "I promise I'll make it up to you."

"You won't make it up to me, Anna," she rasped, as much for Dan's benefit as mine, her thrusts into Dan's ass picking up speed. "You'll pay for it. And so will he."

I let her thrusts time the movements I made, her withdrawals from Dan's body pushing her back onto my fingers as I wriggled them within the tight clinging walls of her cunt. Absorbed by the rhythm, by the wetness around my gloved fingers, by the mesmerizing tense and push of the muscles of her ass as she fucked, it took me several minutes to notice that Dan's moans had turned into a torrent of words.

"Anna, fuck me, Jill, Anna, please," he pleaded, lust slurring his words. "Take my ass, fuck my ass, break me open, fuck me, Jill, fuck me, Anna, please dear God don't stop fucking me take me oh Jill Anna Anna God . . . fuck . . ."

"Listen to him sing," Jill marveled, letting go of his cock and squeezing another helping of lube onto her cock without a pause in her stroke. I corkscrewed my fingers into her again and again, reaching up to pinch her nipple as she hunched with concentration over Dan's body and started to fuck him in earnest. I slipped my thumb into her asshole and she squealed, the added sensation spurring her on. Trying hard just to keep from having her wrench herself off of my fingers, I pressed closer and did my best to hang on for the ride, feeling the thudding smack of her hips as she barreled into Dan's ass in an all-out fuck that I never would've dreamed he could've taken.

Dan sobbed, pleading with her to fuck him, to break him, to split him open, to tear him apart, his knees sliding apart and his body lowering down onto the bed, cock mashed between his belly and the bedspread. It seemed as if she was trying to do just that, sweat beading on the smooth damask of her back, eight inches violating his boy-pussy with exceptional, exquisite brutality as he arched, close to the end.

Down the hall, the phone rang. I was the only one to notice, Jill grunting savagely as she clawed at Dan's shoulder, ramming herself into him as his entire body tensed. With one final plunge Dan came, his harsh sharp scream echoing off the walls in between the annoying rings of the telephone. Jill lay on top of him, not moving, letting him shake off the aftershocks, panting as I slid my fingers back into her. I'd lost her as she finished Dan off, her movements too frenzied for me to manage to stay inside, but she groaned with appreciative need when I reached two then three fingers under the harness straps and into her, filling her in time with the fourth ring of the phone. I quickly found her G-spot with my fingertips, letting my fingers dance against it until she became caught up in her own urgency and spasmed against my hand with a motion that drove her cock deep into Daniel one last punishing time. He gasped out loud, then almost immediately began laughing, his chuckling jostling Jill as she collapsed on top of him.

I heard it, too. Down the hall, tinny through the answering machine's tiny speaker, we could clearly hear a woman's voice, chatty and high-pitched. All three of us now held our breath, trying not to laugh.

". . . so I was at your Aunt Cheryl's," my mother's voice continued, disembodied, slightly adenoidal, "and what she found when she was cleaning out the attic you would never guess. Now we've got all your bat mitzvah pictures all in the same album! Anyway, Anna, give your mama a call when you get a chance, and make sure you give Daniel a kiss from me. Love you, bubeleh." The machine clicked off and we lost it, caught in a gale of laughter. Dan gasped in between giggles, short and sharp, as Jill rolled off of him, her cock sliding out of his well-used ass. Lying there together on the bed, Dan on my left and Jill cozied up on my right, the three of us basked, laughter trailing off into a satisfied, comfortable silence. Jill arched her back, lifting her hips as she slipped out of her dildo harness, her motions breaking the quiet.

Dan raised himself up on his elbow to watch Jill removing the apparatus with which she'd given him such a thorough dose of his own medicine. He shook his head at the thud it made as it hit the floor, then reached across me to stroke Jill's arm as he kissed my cheek. "One of these days, Anna," he chuckled into my ear as Jill cuddled back up to my other side, "we're going to remember to unplug the phone before we have sex."

"Don't be silly, Daniel," I smiled, reveling in the feeling of being sandwiched between my lovers' warm luxuriant bodies. "Where on earth would I be then?"

Lust, Debt, and a
Practical Education

W hen it comes to love, the confessional is one of the most difficult edifices to inhabit. It's so much easier to stick to the present tense of the slippery rooms that my lovers and I create together, to remain in those palaces of moaning and biting and glad-hearted fucking, licking the salt and the come off of one another's bodies, than to set myself apart like this to try to recall the old, the long-broken, the shameful, the glorious, the once-upon-a-times and the might-have-beens.

For the sake of memory, though, and for the sake of love, it is sometimes good to spend time in confession—and if not for love, then at least for clarity. It is difficult to gain clarity where love is involved, and more difficult still when the matter at hand is lust, but sometimes the attempt at writing them down proves, in the end, the most fruitful part of the love itself.

I once wrote that lists were the pornography of history, so I cannot be so banal as to simply list my lovers. I've done it when asked, but people's reactions to the litany make me feel too much like Leporello, narrating Don Giovanni's *mille e tre* with his cruel, titillated leer. People are altogether too pleased by such impersonal epics of seduction. Instead, I will write about the first man who took me to bed, and what I found there.

I was eighteen then. A bit more than half my life ago, I was a virgin, whatever that really means. I wasn't in a particular rush to get laid, but then, I was (then as now, no?) fairly content to take advantage of what life might throw my way. So life threw me a Frenchman in his mid-thirties . . . but I begin to precede myself.

I had left home young and moved to Europe, studying and traveling when I could, existing in a charmed bubble of stolen time, great art, and fabulous bread, unconscious of my good fortune. How heady it was to be able to come and go as I pleased, no parents breathing down my neck, to be able to hop on a train and go to Paris, to Amsterdam, to Nuremburg or Nice.

It was a spring day in Nuremburg, the sun lambent and gently yellow on the old stone. I remember the walk down the river and across town to the museum of toys where I first met him. He noticed that my backpack was a Jansport, not a European make, and he struck up a conversation by asking me where I was from. I was looking into a case of little pull-toys at the time, the kind with a number of wheeled toy animals on a string, perhaps a mama duck and a line of baby ducklets following her, antiques or something, though I hardly remember anymore. When I looked up to see who was speaking to me, I met a glittering pair of hazel eyes framed by curls just starting to turn silver in places, and a cautious but warmly gorgeous smile that made me want to smile back. As genial and as much older as he was, he probably tripped every little Electra-complex switch in my psyche, not that I would've known what to call it then. At the time I was a lot flustered and not a little intrigued by the flattering attention of this handsome older man in the museum.

I remember his clothes quite vividly, for some reason, though I don't often notice such things now. Over a blue denim work shirt he wore a soft chamois leather hunting jacket with great big scoop-shaped pockets, dark-green trousers, and a braided leather belt. He carried a small knapsack, but I remember his jacket best. I can smell it still, in my memory. (Why is it that we have phrases like "the mind's eye" but not "the mind's nose" or "the mind's ear"? Such a stupid omission: More of my sensual memories are sounds and smells than sights.) His jacket smelled of Gauloises and leather and whatever the slightly grassy cologne he wore was, with an undercurrent of his skin, his sweat. If I smelled him again, I would know him instantly.

We'd gone to lunch, and then we spent the afternoon walking through the city, looking at churches, shops, galleries, alternately shy and gushing, trying to maneuver conversation without really having any single language in common. I didn't speak much French, he didn't speak much English and he seemed shaky in German, or at any rate uncomfortable. We eventually taught one another fairly well, a phrase here, a phrase there, much of it in bed. I learned French in the Horizontal School of Gallic Studies.

His name was Paul. I remember that. He told me his family name once, but I, never one to remember names, have to confess that I forgot it quite a while ago. Does that make me a tramp, not knowing the last name of the man who took my virginity? It can hardly matter now, I suppose. It isn't as important as the fact that we kissed for the first time in the doorway of a church, ducking in out of a rain shower, or that I can still remember how it felt to have the hot red flush of half-embarrassed arousal spreading over my cheeks and down my neck when he reached across the dinner table and caressed the side of my face.

I was so scared by it all, trembly and with no idea what was going to happen, but light-headedly high on the exhilaration. He kissed me shortly after we left the restaurant where we'd eaten supper, a for-real kiss, a kiss that left me literally breathless, holding on to his shoulders with both hands and shaking. I was eighteen, and though it sounds unbearably young to me now— if I had an eighteen-year-old daughter I certainly wouldn't want her doing what I was doing at eighteen, but I suspect that most mothers feel that way—I think in retrospect that it was the perfect age for me to have been introduced to the erotic.

I never told him that I was a virgin. I was too proud, I suppose, or else too afraid to admit I didn't really know what I was doing. I lied about my age, told him I was twenty-one, and I remember so clearly the way he held me then, the way his hand tightened around my upper arm when he kissed me, and his other hand flattened between my shoulder blades, his fingers fanning out, supporting me, strong, pulling me to him with an extraordinary guttural sigh.

It's never like that again, never quite the same. The first time, when it's all so shatteringly new, everything is so scaldingly vivid, searing you like a flare whose afterimage you see long afterward on the backs of your eyelids. Yes, of course, it is delicious later. Exquisite, even, with its own delights and pleasures that a first time can't hope to match. But still, that first time is something unto itself. Sometimes I wish I could have just one more first time, now that I know what to do with it.

But I digress.

He offered to walk me back to my hostel, and we walked along in tense erotic silence, the almost-embarrassed stillness that comes after the first physical confession of desire and before one knows how, or really whether, that confession will be received. What a scholar of minutiae one becomes in those moments when every gesture is analyzed, every word, every breath is feverishly turned over for significance, weighed for its density, judged.

I was shivering in my light skirt and sweater, my teeth chattering. He gently lifted my backpack off my shoulders and draped his jacket over them, carrying my bag for me as we walked on in the beginnings of a cold drizzle. When we reached the hostel, I turned to him, not sure how to say goodnight or thank you, not sure I wanted to leave and go inside, not sure whether I dared imagine anything else.

I gave him back his jacket as we stood at the hostel door, feeling somehow more lost when I lifted its reassuring weight off my shoulders. I embraced him as he put it back on, sliding my arms between his back and the lining of the jacket, still warm with the heat of my body. I have never been able to embrace anyone like that since—slipping my arms between a person and his coat, huddling into that deliciously intimate orbit of body warmth— without having that person turn (if only for a second and only in my mind) into my first lover. I remember pressing close to him, operating on instinct, the length of my body against him, and I remember the urgent gratitude of his arms enfolding me, his voice whispering something incomprehensible into my hair as he clasped me closer still. Somehow it was clear to me then that I wasn't going to spend the night in the youth hostel at all.

The bed in his room upstairs at the small *Gasthaus* creaked. It rocked a little, too, the joints obviously well worn and perhaps no longer as strong as they had once been, maternally cradling us while we rocked into one another under the thin duvets, on the starched, darned sheets. I remember bright, shocking instants of that night: Technicolor glimpses of ass and thigh, hair and belly, more than half a life ago and almost fresh enough to smell.

I remember his hands knotting in the hair at the nape of my neck, pulling my head back, my neck stretching and arching backward for his hungry kisses, his teeth sharp on my skin but careful not to hurt. Moaning softly, unthinking, I was shocked and tremendously aroused when he pulled my head back like that, shocked by my own noise and the lava blossom between my thighs that threatened to burst when he held my head that way, pulling my hair just enough to show me.

Why did I just write "show me"? Show me what? Show me that he wanted me, I suppose, or perhaps show me that I was his now, that he was taking what he desired? Show me that I was desired, show me that he knew how to make my body arch and sing with sensation and need? Show me, on some level, how to acquiesce, how to yield while at the same time making my own insistent demands? Yes, all those things and probably more as well, things it took me many more lovers to learn thoroughly, things I only now seem to have the latitude and perspective to begin to articulate. But he began, at any rate, to show me.

I remember how his hands felt against my sides when he started to push my sweater up, over my belly, uncovering my breasts. We didn't speak except for soft murmurs, encouraging noises, sounds of pleasure and surprise. He had long fingers, I recall, and they were smooth as they brushed my sides, grazing over my teen-pudge tummy and the elastic band of my bra. Eager to seem like I knew what I was doing, I raised my arms and he pulled my sweater over my head, dropping it on the floor. His eyes widened and he looked at me in my blue skirt and prim white bra. The bra embarrassed me, ugly white cotton with a stupid little ribbon bow between the cups, a bra my mother had bought me. I whipped it off, ashamed of it, and pitched it into the corner, where it remained when we left the hotel together a day or so later.

We stood between the bureau and the bed, kissing ferociously, nipping and purring, undressing one another: his shirt, my skirt, his shoes and socks, my tights. I remember gasping out loud and shivering hard enough to make him chuckle and stroke my back the first time my breasts pressed his bare chest, our bellies touching, the sleek warmth of his skin against mine. Shortly thereafter, I ventured to touch his cock, and that was another thing again. I had felt erections before, prodding me insistently in the hip or belly as I kissed a high-school boyfriend, but I hadn't touched one. To be honest, I hadn't really wanted to until then, but things change.

I was bold for a virgin, I think. I stepped back from him slightly and unbuckled his belt. He smiled, stroked my hands with his, then put his hands on my shoulders and watched my hands as I unfastened his trousers, slid the zipper down its track. I looked at him as if asking his permission, flattening my hand against his belly just above the waistband of his underwear. He wore blue briefs, bikini-cut, and it seemed almost as if his cock were trying to tear them off, pressing so hard into the waistband and against the fabric that I was astonished. The muscles of his belly tensed, and he nodded, his eyes meeting mine with a look I still don't know how to characterize—perhaps he was as panicked, and as eager, as I.

The next instant I had encircled his shaft with my fingers, unsure what to do, what to say, intensely aroused by the feel of the alien creature in my hand, perhaps somewhat afraid of its amplitude, its rigidity, definitely somewhat seduced already by the impossibly fine satin of the taut-skinned cylinder. He moaned, leaning into me, burrowing his face into the crook of my neck, one arm around my shoulders, the other hand sliding from my shoulder to my breast, covering and cupping it in the basket of his fingers.

I'm not sure how I knew what to do, how to move and touch. All I remember is trying to listen to his gasps, his bass-growl moaning, his strained, breathy mutters. I wanted more of that, and kept doing whatever made him moan and whisper, basking with unrestrained delight in the sable-furred flow of his dark, basso purr. With the vibrations of his moans against my neck, then against my lips as our mouths met again, with every press of his body against mine, I smoldered hotter. I fought my moans for a little while, worried they would be somehow unseemly. But I also know I cried out in spite of myself when his head descended to my breast and his lips found my nipple, because I remember how loud it seemed in my own ears. I remember that, and I remember the way his cock thickened and throbbed in my hand at the sound.

His cock was large. Not monstrous, but big. I suppose anything would've seemed big to me at that point, given my lack of anything to compare it to, but I remember it in my hand so well that I have been able to compare it, albeit retrospectively. Longer than my hand from the heel of my palm to the tip of my middle finger, by an inch, perhaps, and thick enough that I could just touch my thumb and index finger around his shaft as I stroked it. It seemed formidable. I remember thinking to myself quite clearly, succinctly, *I know that technically it's supposed to go in there, but I can't imagine how it'll fit.* I didn't think about it in terms of pain. I wasn't afraid of it so much as I simply couldn't fathom it happening.

It did hurt some, when he began to enter me. I was wet, soakingly so. He had slipped his fingers into me with great delight, cooing delightedly at the juices that had already begun to mat my pubic hair by the time he had me out of my skirt and panties and lying back on the bed, one of his arms under me holding me to him, the other hand stroking my thighs, my mound, parting the puffy, swollen lips of my pussy. The touches of his fingers were extraordinary, shimmering and electric, gleaming bolts of sensation making me sigh and arch into his hand, clinging with my arms around his shoulders. I remember kissing him feverishly, unable to get enough of his lips on mine and the density and weight of his body against me. It was more than new, and more than terrifying, and still I was so unbearably aroused by him, by the situation, by the seduction, by the knowledge of what was about to happen (Oh, all the whispered gossip at the cafeteria lunch table when we saw Tiffany Chamberlain, our high school's "town pump," passing by with her latest boyfriend! Oh, the pilfered copy of *The Joy of Sex* that my friend Andrea and I used to point at, half-aroused and half-horrified, in her frilly suburban bedroom!), that in those bed-bound, breathless moments I couldn't imagine ever having wanted anything more.

I trusted him more than I should have. He didn't use a condom with me, not that night or during the remaining days we spent together, and I suppose I am lucky that I neither got myself knocked up nor infected with something either embarrassing or potentially fatal. This was, after all, after AIDS had made its ghastly debut, little that I thought or knew about it at that age. They say God looks out for drunks, little children, and animals, and though I'm less than comfortable trying to surmise into which of those three categories God must think I fall, it often seems that He looks out for me as well.

I trusted Paul, though, and I looked into his eyes, utterly open, waiting, as he stroked up and down my pussy with the tip of his cock. I remember thinking only that, yes, it was what I wanted—I wanted with such desperation to be filled, to feel him inside me. That's the sensation that has always floored me, left me gasping and watching myself, almost as if I were a bystander viewing my desire to be fucked as almost an independent force, a creature unto itself. I grew impatient when he kept teasing my clit with the head of his cock, slipsliding through my wetness, no doubt trying to tease me close to orgasm before pushing inside. I remember instinctively pressing my hips toward him, my ass lifting up off the bed, my thighs clasping his hips. I wonder whether I winced when he pushed inside my cunt. It did hurt, a little, a thick, marrow-deep sensation of something yielding, perhaps tearing a bit, inside me.

I can remember that sensation vividly, and I have remembered it often since then when other lovers have entered me. As profound as prayer, and much the same, opening myself and inviting something into me, being blessed to have it be something so precisely right. It's that letting-in, not so much giving something up as reclaiming something, a barrier I no longer want or need finally being broken. I want to be filled. Do I dare say that it's a desire to be completed, in some primal, unspeakable way? I may as well be honest and say it is; when my arousal takes me to that point, being penetrated completes the circuitry of my psyche and my agitated nerves, and finally I can abandon myself and be ecstatically lost in the repetition and sensation of being fucked. No, I don't have to be fucked to come, but I do have to be fucked to be released into the place where I no longer know who I am, and I no longer care that I don't know.

I wonder where he is now, my Frenchman, the one who taught me what it was like to be loved that way. I wonder whether he is still alive or whether he has died. I wonder if, when he left me, several days and a few cities later, he went back to France and to a wife, a family. Did he ever wonder if he might have had a child by me? Might he have felt guilty for leaving me, eighteen years old and collapsing with loss, my cunt freshly full of his ecstasy from our last—not that I knew it was the last— wild-eyed fuck in the tiny train bathroom, an hour before he got off the train in Braunschweig and left me on board, bound for Hanover? I will never know.

I smelled of his body for days afterward. I was so saturated with him and his juices that he was embedded in my body, physically penetrating me long after he left, stinging olfactory reminders of him where I could not escape them. We had fucked each other hard and long, again and again, and every time I smelled him on me, in me, it reminded me who he was.

He was an opportunist. Maybe he was a bastard too. Still, Paul taught me more than I realized then. From him I learned how to take insane sweet plunges, how to say "I love you" with a heart full enough of passion that there's not much room for regret. It's a good thing; there hasn't been much space in my life for second guesses.

He fed me blood oranges and bittersweet chocolate in bed.

He licked his own cum from my cunt, driving his tongue into my pussy to hear me gasp and sigh, suckling my clit between his lips as if it were my nipple and he my nursing baby. He kissed me with our juices mixed on his lips, on his tongue. We listened to the radiator pipes clanking and we laughed at our dishevelment, our sweat-matted hair and the stains on the sheets and the dried white on our bellies and thighs, until suddenly we were doing it again, me on top of him, his hands holding my hips as I moved against him with his cock buried deep inside my body, crazy-drunk on the joy of it.

We fucked literally all night that first night, his fingers stroking in and out of me when his cock couldn't, his lips and tongue teaching me that I had many different shades of climax; his arms around me, tender and sheltering, when I lay there, so drained and raw from repeated climax that when he forced one more orgasm out of me I just lay there and wept. He held me, sweet and silent and strong, until it passed, and as it passed, he stroked me slowly and deliberately to orgasm again with his fingers and told me he loved me.

Did I believe him when he said he loved me? Of course I did. I believed him and never once thought beyond it, didn't think about the future or all the romantic claptrap I might have expected from myself at that age. I was too overwhelmed, too busy just trying to react to the newness of it all and the strange sacredness of reciprocated lust. As far as I was capable, I loved him, too.

The sun came up on us still going at it, his fingers lightly flickering over my clit as he bent me over the edge of the bed and slowly, slowly—with Nivea cream as lube, the thick white kind that comes in a squat round tin—working his cock into my asshole with such gentle persistence that I cannot remember a single instant of pain, only a deep if unfamiliar pleasure. By the time we slept that morning, we had fucked in every way we could have. He oozed from my pussy and ass, and I could still taste the slightly bitter saltiness that lingered in my mouth as I drifted off to sleep curled in his arms. I remember waking up, slightly sore, and stretching alongside his still-sleeping body, thinking smugly, *Well, I certainly did a thorough job of* that.

He and I stayed together for a week, traveling, fucking, loving, until one day he said he had to go home and told me goodbye. No phone number, no address, no lingering adieu. I cried, of course. God, how I cried, bereft the way I think only a teenager can be. For the first and last time in my life, I cried over a lover and cried him completely out in one fell swoop.

When I finally stopped crying, I felt strangely serene, somehow satisfied, just as I did the morning after he took my virginity. I loved him, he left, I suffered, and it was done. There's a certain pristine quality to that kind of love affair—cause and effect clearly delineated, neatly defined, devoid of all the messy strings of breaking the news to your friends and deciding who keeps the couch—that I instinctively find satisfying. If there was a lesson in my relationship with Paul, I think it was the lesson of how to go to the end of my strength, to the point of collapse and tears, and go on. He was, after all is said and done, only the first, and there are many debts one can only repay by passing them on to someone else.

The Princess and the Tiger

I just can't sodding well believe she gets to and we don't," Daniel growled as he piloted the rugged, squat little six-wheeled mover back into sight of the Wall. "That's all. You and me, we're spending our lives trying to work by Monkeyvision, and this rich weirdo just coughs up enough cash and *bam*, she's in. The PM's a fucking sellout and so is Chakrayaborti."

"Chakrayaborti knows that what she paid for this will finance the Preserve for a long time," Lata replied mildly, scanning the infrared and radar screens for signs of any nearby wildlife that might not be visible among the greenery. The mover rolled slowly, almost waddling through the undergrowth on overly wide tires that distributed its weight evenly to avoid creating tracks or ruts. Designed for minimum ecosystem impact, the mover emitted ultrasonic beeps that helped keep animals clear of its path, but even so, it was rarely driven within the perimeter of the Wall. "That's an enormous amount of money. And that's the primary concern. I frankly agree with her, though: What's it to us whether she survives? She signed the authorizations for the transfer of funds, she signed the releases. Her lawyers agree with the Preserve's. What do you call one human—"her voice halted abruptly as she manually overrode the autopilot. "Snake ahead. Let me vibe it out of the way."

The mover shimmied momentarily, pulsing several times,

vibrating the ground on which it stood until the zoologists watched the thick reptilian body slide into the underbrush to the left of the path. "Pretty," Daniel remarked admiringly. "Pity we couldn't see it better."

"We can check logs later," Lata noted, putting the mover back on autopilot. "I'm sure Dian and Paulo's team caught it. Anyway, as I was saying about the Princess back there—it's like what Britten and Spiers tell the undergrads back at Harvard: What do you call an untrained human in the Preserve? Dinner."

She had longed for it all her life. There were no more of them in the zoo where she had first seen them as a small child, of course, but she could still recall their astonishing striped pelts, their powerful haunches, their huge blocky heads, the mouths with their unthinkably deadly teeth and jaws. Most of all, Iona loved their muscle, their power, the sleek effortlessness with which the huge cats moved. She owned thousands of books, holovideos, photographs, and spools about them, ancient and modern. She had studied their habits, their vocalizations, their history, their anatomy. The countless hours she had spent working on conservation efforts had been fueled by nothing short of raw passion. When things had become truly critical and they finally put the Wall up and created the Preserve, she had rejoiced—the simple fact that there was now a multinational effort to protect endangered wildlife, that they'd managed the feat of political and physical engineering necessary to cordon off nearly half of the Indian subcontinent, was reassuring. At least they wouldn't all be killed off or forced to live in concrete cages. At least they had jungle again. Not just the tigers, but all of the animals, of course. But especially the tigers.

When her father died, she was finally free to do what she wanted with the money. There was more of it than she could ever spend, she discovered. Even having been raised among the thinnest upper crust of the monetary elite, she had been unprepared for the sheer scale of her inheritance. She found the situation almost ludicrous: No matter what she did, the money kept making more money, as if it couldn't help itself. It seemed only proper to give the bulk of it away. The Preserve, or more properly, the nation-state of the World Wildlife Protectorate, had been able to implement most of its ambitious visual and sound surveillance thanks to her. The microminiaturized Eyes and Ears, satellite-linked, had enabled the humans to withdraw almost entirely from within the Preserve and monitor the animal populations from outside. Research could still be conducted but at a respectful distance. It was, or so the scientists said, a near-perfect solution to the problem of studying endangered species, even entire ecosystems, while protecting them at the same time.

Lakshmi Chakrayaborti, the director of research of the Preserve, had been opposed at first to the notion of Iona Sternhagen going inside at all. Certainly Iona, of all people, would understand the need to maintain distance from the animals. After all, she was the one who had largely made it possible to do so for the past twelve years. But when Iona had put her hand on the director's arm, as she looked into Iona's eyes and saw the vertical slits of her surgically altered pupils and simultaneously felt the tips she realized were implanted titanium claws, razor-sharp and retractable, the director simply shuddered and said she'd have the lawyers draw up a release.

The heat was thick and oppressive. Flies buzzed around Iona's head and settled on her belongings as she waited in the clearing. She was pleased, and somewhat amazed, to notice that she really couldn't figure out where the Eyes were, though she knew full well that they were all around. There wasn't much of the Preserve that the researchers couldn't observe if they wanted to, at least with sound if not visually. She felt more acutely watched there in the jungle than she ever had in the city, though logic told her that the level of actual surveillance was probably considerably less. Just the same, her skin crawled. The knowledge that she was being watched while so very alone among the forest's dense green seemed, incongruously and suddenly, completely obscene.

They had dropped her off in the middle of the known territory of a large Bengal male. She had been advised to sling her hammock high: otherwise, territorialism might end her foray into tiger turf sooner than she anticipated. "Miss Sternhagen," the plump, dark zoologist had said, her voice stern but her English turned up at the corners by her accent, "with all due respect, as a senior fellow in the study of the large cats in the Preserve, I have to warn you to be very careful. You are a day and a half by mover from the nearest medical attention. If you are badly injured, bitten by a snake, or mauled by a cat, you will probably die before we can get to you and get you out of the Preserve."

To this, Iona had merely shrugged and sauntered into the bush, the curves of her hips swaying as she ignored the sotto-voce curses of the scientists who were left to unload her belongings. She had walked a little ways, perhaps a quarter-mile, until she found the stream she'd seen on the mapscreen in the mover, and near it, reasonably fresh-looking scat. Picking up a chunk with a fallen leaf, she returned to the mover and handed the excrement to the researchers. "Is it what I think it is?" she asked.

"Yes. Tiger," Lata confirmed, "and quite large."

"Good," Iona replied, with a strange, faraway smile. "You can both go, then."

There was nothing to do but wait until the hottest part of the day was over, and Iona sat with her back to a tree, fanning herself with her hat to keep away the flies as the mover rumbled quietly away. Then she was alone, and there was little to do but set up camp and wait.

"Miss Sternhagen, I suppose you realize that there are quite a few people who would regard it as an abomination? I mean, not just something unusual, but evil and wrong?" In the confines of his laboratory the geneticist's words, meant to sound reasonable and cautionary, took on a classic mad-scientist aura.

Iona chuckled. "I've been funding you for years, Frank. Don't tell me that you're going to back out now that you have the chance to find out if it works. Isn't the point of advanced genetics research to try to advance the species?"

The geneticist closed his eyes and put his head in his hands, elbows propped on the edge of the lab table. "Miss Sternhagen, as grateful as I am to you for all your loyal support, I can't let one successful dry run push me into something so premature. Just because I've managed to get live young from one primate-feline cross doesn't mean . . ."

"The fuck it doesn't. You can try. It might not work, but you can try, can't you?" Iona's voice was no longer quite so cocky, the sass replaced by a note of something more anxious, possibly even approaching desperation.

"I don't know. The ethical problems are stagger—"

"You don't understand, do you? Ethics have nothing to do with it. I am asking you a personal favor. Personal, do you understand?" He looked up, lifting his head to look at her face. Tears sifted slowly down her cheeks. "I'm going to get to go inside the Preserve. I'm going to get to be with the tigers. It's all I've ever wanted. I just want the chance, the ghost of a chance, that I might be able to take something away from it. I just want to be able to believe that it might, just maybe, be possible."

The geneticist pushed his palms against his forehead, smoothing his skin and dark chestnut hair vigorously down against his skull. He stared at Iona, her sky-blue eyes ringed with moist red from her sudden burst of tears, her stylishly round form clothed in a close-fitting dress that bore subtle gold-on-gold stripes in an ingenious brocade. Her hair, a tawny blond, framed her distraught face in thick curls as she bit her lip and tried to quiet herself, but at her throat the large yellow diamond pendant she wore still bobbed occasionally as she swallowed a little too hard. Despite her evident upset, though, her lips were dark red and as swollen as the nipples that were clearly visible through the fabric of her dress, her lips and breasts tangibly engorged with an arousal that even her distress didn't much dampen.

"You really want this?" he whispered brokenly. "It could kill you. Even if you survive the Preserve, the . . . you know. If it worked it could kill you."

Iona nodded sadly. "I know what happened when Zika had the cubs," she said hoarsely. "I have to try. You have to help me try. I need to do this."

"You're insane."

"That may be," the heiress replied, smoothing the sleekly clinging fabric across her ample, well-toned thighs with both bejeweled hands as she regained her composure. "But you can't afford to find out what might happen to you if word gets out about the unsuccessful crosses, Frank. Like you said, there are people who just think this kind of thing is an abomination. You might find yourself inconveniently dead. The lab would be destroyed. Remember Wilhelm Muhlhausen."

Muhlhausen. The syllables fell to the floor like a shot duck. The mob hadn't left much for the coroner. All the animals had been killed, indiscriminately, even the ones who had never learned to speak. Even Muhlhausen's wolfhounds, Fasolt and Fafner, the first true successes of his efforts to expand animal intelligence to human levels, had committed suicide, drinking pesticide when the videotank in Muhlhausen's home, where they lived, brought them news of the massacre. "We know the so-called 'people' will come to kill us too," Fasolt had spoken into the recorder in the now infamous sound bite, as his brother canine frothed and died in the background, "and we are not dumb animals, not willing to wait like lambs for the slaughter." Frank shuddered and felt his stomach lurch. God, no, that couldn't happen, not to Zika's cubs. Almost anything but that.

"You wouldn't," he said, aghast.

"Don't bet on it." Her tone was low, menacing.

"You're insane."

"You're repeating yourself," Iona said crisply, her habitual air of power returning with palpable force. "I believe you meant to say, 'I'll do my best, Miss Sternhagen.'"

Frank Capek, his brain choking on the idea of agreeing to her suggestion, then choking just as hard on the notion of not agreeing, nodded mutely. Helplessly, his eyes surveyed the enticing curves of her lower lip, her grandly swelling bustline, her sweetly padded belly. For her it was the tigers. For him it was her, golden and impassive, fashionably fat and traffic-stoppingly gorgeous, fiercely intelligent and completely insane. She smiled her slow, glittery smile, her eyes shone with her inimitable sense of presence, and he felt his heart melt and his cock throb in spite of himself. Even without the threat, and even without the money, he would eventually have been powerless to say no.

"Well, well, well," Daniel said, leaning back in his swivel chair and folding his hands across his midsection, "take a look at *that.*" Lata walked into Observation 4 from the outer office carrying a pile of charts, the log spools from the past week, and a bottle of her favorite mango drink. Looking at the largest of the many screens that covered the wall in front of them, she immediately saw what Daniel meant.

In the months since the two lead feline zoologists had dropped the woman they referred to as "the Princess" into the wilds of the inner Preserve, they'd been fairly astonished by how well she'd adapted. Having expected her to lose it and simply go crazy, or else do something stupid and end up dinner for some opportunistic carnivore—of which the tigers were merely the largest and most impressive of those the Preserve had to offer—they'd been impressed at her ability to keep her cool and to survive reasonably well on the supplies she'd brought in and what she was able to forage with the aid of her field guides. She had surprised them, but what truly impressed them, what they hadn't counted on at all, was the fact that she had actually been able to achieve contact with a tiger.

It had been slow going, of course. The Princess probably hadn't even known about the first few contacts: tigers, more often than not the big male whose favorite den was on the other side of the rise from her camp, would sniff her presence from a few dozen yards, huff, and stalk silently away. But eventually they had come to investigate her. She left food for them near her camp each day, trapping birds, small rodents, and monkeys, gutting them, and leaving them for the tigers to find. Only after several months of this did the big male actually approach the Princess herself, sniffing her hair while she slept on a mat on the ground under a neem tree. The visits had become more frequent, and, perhaps because she never spoke but only imitated tiger chuffs and other sounds, the big Bengal had eventually warmed to her and had begun to permit her to touch him and groom his pelt.

And now, as Daniel and Lata watched from monkey's-eye height, they could just see the back of the Bengal's head as he licked the Princess's hair. "He's grooming her. My God," Lata whispered, astonished, setting down her pile without really looking at what she was doing. "I wouldn't believe it if I wasn't seeing it."

The naturalists watched, their eyes glued to the screen, as the human and tiger took turns pressing their heads against one another's necks. Never mind the fact that the tiger was at least three times her size and much stronger, the Princess did her best to press her face into his hide with the same heavy meatiness as he did hers. He was scenting her, marking her as part of his territory, something that tigers normally only did with mates. Clearly the Princess knew it. The resolution wasn't fabulous given the low light, but the speakers in Observation 4 resonated with expressive noises that made it perfectly clear just how positively the Princess was responding to the Bengal's interest.

"Damn, Lata, she's going to come in her pants." Daniel was too stunned to blink, and could scarcely breathe. Low, throaty moans of sensual excitement mingled with the purr-chuffs and low feline grunts coming out of the speakers as the Princess's arms encircled the Bengal's enormously powerful neck, biped and quadruped muscling against one another happily.

Lata couldn't tear her eyes away, either. For several moments she simply stared, feeling her clit hardening, buzzing between her thighs, her nipples coming to attention beneath her regulation green Preserve uniform blouse as her breath grew ragged. Suddenly she stood up straight, her face turning an intense and sudden red as she realized that watching the woman and the tiger, hearing their sounds of mutual pleasure, was turning her on enormously.

"That's disgusting, Daniel," Lata snapped acidly. "You're as much of a pervert as she is. I can't believe Chakrayaborti let her in to do that. Revolting. Turn the sound off. We've got it on spool, we can log it later. Under 'anomalous.' Come on, I need to get to these logs."

The two scientists glared at one another, embarrassed and furious, neither of them knowing what to say. From where he had been sitting tilted slightly back in his chair, Daniel lurched forward suddenly to snap the sound control down to zero. Neither one of them would say anything, but neither had missed noticing the raging erection that had made an obvious tent of his dark green Preserve uniform.

Iona had developed a strange craving for privacy, a sensation that had never plagued her before. Before the Preserve—where Eyes were necessary so that autosurfaces and servants could respond to unspoken needs, where surveillance was a means of being safe in public and well-catered-to in private—she had never worried about the Eyes or the computers and people that monitored them. Somehow it was different here. Perhaps it was just the knowledge that the surveillance was only for the researchers, only for human—and prying—eyes, but she found herself seeking out odd corners, places where it seemed highly unlikely that the cameras could see.

The researchers who implemented the visual surveillance system, placing Eyes among the forest's branches, had nicknamed it Monkeyvision. Iona figured that if she couldn't see the trees, chances were good that the Eyes couldn't see her, and so she had arranged a lean-to against the overhang of rock that kept her dry when it rained. In the shady privacy it afforded her, she was checking herself, making sure that the implants still worked and opening one of the several containers she had never, and would never, open in a place where the Eyes might see.

Her steel and titanium claws flexed easily, gracefully emerging from and retracting into their sheaths as she worked them. Almost an inch long, she hadn't really learned to use them for hunting, but perhaps they'd serve her well enough in a time of need. They were, she satisfied herself as she used one claw-tip to slit open the shrinkseal on a transdermic, certainly sharp enough. Hiking up her skirt, she slapped the 'dermic onto her full, bare ass cheek and winced only slightly as she felt the hundreds of needles, each thinner than a human hair, penetrate the outermost layers of her skin. One of the only side effects of the stuff seemed to be that it made her skin a bit more sensitive, but that was nothing to worry about.

There it was, then. The last dose of a full month of Frank's serum, and if the timing was all correct, perhaps it would even work as planned.

She hadn't started administering the serum until she was sure He wouldn't spook at being touched. No sense wasting it. There was only a three-month supply, and besides, she might need to try again. She might get to try again, she thought, a shiver of intense arousal running through her body. The thought of trying even once was almost too much to bear. Every time He came and permitted a grooming, every time He groomed her, and pressed his cheek glands against her, she trembled and moaned uncontrollably. He seemed to like it, and sometimes licked her neck with broad, heavy stripes of his enormous rough tongue. She wondered if He had known that when He did that for the first time, she orgasmed. It had been the most powerful climax she'd ever had, effortless and enormous, leaving her wide-eyed and gasping with her cunt clenching rhythmically for minutes afterward.

After that, she had given up wearing blouses and dresses and had begun to dress simply in skirts or sarongs, letting her large, heavy breasts swing freely as she went about her days. It might've been more comfortable to wear something, but the fewer clothes she wore meant that whenever He came to visit, she could feel his muscled, furry, powerfully virile body against more of her breasts and body. It was well worth it. It was all worth it, she thought to herself as she readied the ampoules and cracked off the tips. She spread her thighs and fit the tip of one ampoule into the tiny aperture the surgeon had left just inside the entrance of her vagina, and squeezed, her clit throbbing with excitement as she imagined she could feel the pheromone filling the makeshift scent gland that had been constructed inside her body. It would all be worth it. The second ampoule tip slid home into the other ersatz glandular opening, and she could feel a vague warm sensation inside her cunt, the sensation, perhaps, of a little pocket being filled with the thick, powerful scent of tigress in heat.

She needed to lie flat for a few minutes, she knew, to let the valves in the "glands" reset, so that later she could squeeze her muscles tight to force slow droplets of the pheromone out of her "glands," just as the surgeon had designed. She lay there imagining his bulk above her, stroking her clit with two fingers, her other hand finding her left nipple and tugging insistently at the stiff nub of flesh. She could smell him on herself now, remembered how He felt when she embraced him, knew the power of his body when He rubbed against her. Shivering with arousal and fear, Iona knew as she masturbated that He might injure her, might inadvertently tear her or bite her, might be too much for her, might leave her bleeding and dying on the jungle floor. What's more, she knew that back outside the Wall, they would see it all. Once, the thought had given her pause, but not anymore. She didn't care, and with the image of his enormous feline cock unsheathing as she had glimpsed it doing once before as He preened in front of her, she came, sharp and sudden and severe.

The Princess, they had noted without surprise, had taken to going nude. It was logical enough given the climate, but to Lata there was still something slightly unsettling about seeing the woman she knew to be one of the world's wealthiest running around naked, as if she didn't know any better. Perhaps it was just that she got a little jealous. Daniel, after all, was not the only one in the big cats research unit who had remarked lustfully about the eccentric heiress's extraordinarily bountiful, beautiful body, made all the more attractive by the slight sheen of the oils she rubbed into it daily. Certainly they'd all seen enough of it to know: For the past three days, since the last time the Bengal had visited her, she hadn't worn a stitch.

Daniel was typing up a log summary and Lata was dictating set-point scans for their major observation points when the Princess came into view late that afternoon. She sat near the edge of the view from the camera in the clearing, doing nothing unusual but seeming extraordinarily happy and expectant. Aside from flicking the feed up to the main screen, they ignored her and continued to work.

When the Bengal appeared, Daniel looked up. Something was different, but it took Daniel a moment to figure out what it was. In contrast to his usual cautious dallying five or ten feet away, the tiger walked directly up to the Princess and began to sniff her all over, which the Princess seemed to encourage, spreading her arms and legs as she sat on a large log. The whuffling grunts of excitable giant feline could be heard in the clearing, but the Princess was silent.

"Lata, look!" Daniel said, gesturing to the screen. In fascinated silence the two zoologists watched with increasing intrigue as the Princess spread her legs wider and slid a finger into her pussy. She presented it to the Bengal, who sniffed and huffed, his upper lip curled in the snarling face of a cat recirculating air between mouth and nose, and suddenly the tiger's eyes seemed to widen and intensify at once. Nearly knocking her over, He battered her belly with the top of his head, his broad powerful tongue rasping rudely over the Princess's cunt. She caught herself and arched up against the big cat's tongue, seemingly unafraid of the Bengal's enormous, lethal teeth, and her cry of delight was so loud and unmistakable that Lata winced and clapped her hands to her ears as Daniel reflexively snatched the volume control down.

"This can't be happening! It can't be! Look, Daniel . . ." Lata breathed as she saw the Bengal's penis beginning to unsheath. The Princess was watching it, too, seemingly frozen or transfixed by the massive member that hung below the huge cat's bulk. The tiger's growl was low, dangerous, and intense. The sound seemed to wake the Princess from her trance, and she moved as if dreaming, arranging herself on top of the broad log she'd been sitting on, her knees to either side of the log, her chest against it, her broad, fleshy, heart-shaped ass in the air. Even in Monkeyvision they could see the slick shine of the Princess's cunt, spread open as the Bengal circled her, sniffing her relentlessly, trying desperately to figure out what to do.

Daniel's cock was enormously hard, throbbing painfully as it pushed the folds of his uniform away from his body. His balls ached as he glanced at his colleague. She stood raptly by the console, her mouth open in an O of arousal and shock, the nipples of her small high breasts visibly hard. Lata looked at him. "Do you think she managed . . .?"

"Pheromones, maybe urine, of an estrous tigress," Dan whispered. "I don't know how and I don't know why, but it has to be. It's the only way. My God, Lata, look at him."

On the screen the Bengal had paced around so that He stood behind the Princess's upturned ass. He looked at it quizzically, angling his head as if trying to understand what was happening to him as his muscles filled with the irresistible energy of rut. His cock was dangling threads of liquid below him, glistening in the late-day sun, and He took a long experimental lick of the Princess's exposed cunt. Her scream when the enormous feline tongue raked her most sensitive tissues was somewhere between agony and ecstasy, and Lata's hand moved, unthinkingly, below the waistband of her skirt to her own sympathetically aching cunt.

Daniel's hand stroked his cock through his dhoti as the two colleagues moved closer together for a better view. Nothing they'd ever heard of, nothing they'd ever seen had prepared them for what they were seeing in Observation 4. They were both almost too shocked and terrified to speak, and too aroused to stop watching as the Bengal made his first attempt at mounting the Princess. Her body, by no means frail, all but disappeared beneath the tiger's enormous, striped, muscled frame.

Discretion forgotten, Daniel undid his dhoti and let it fall to the floor, his thick cock jutting out from under his shirttails in the gray-blue light of the screens. Lata pinched her nipples and gasped with animalistic pleasure as Daniel moved behind her, moving her directly in front of the screen. His cock rubbed against the cleft of her ass, and she wriggled backward unthinkingly as the tiger attempted to make contact but failed. In the observation booth both Lata and Daniel moaned in a unison of disappointment and frustration, mingling with the frantic noises of feminine and feline need that emanated from the speakers.

"Oh, God, Dan, he's going to kill her," Lata whimpered, violently unsnapping her skirt and letting it fall so that she could more easily reach her engorged clit. "He's huge. And it's got to be as big as my arm. He'll never get it inside her. He'll crush her. He'll maul her to death."

Dan said nothing, eyes fixed on the screen, hands on his colleague's hips as his cock butted blindly against her ass and the puffed cleft of her labia, seeking entrance. The Bengal lurched and bucked, and they could hear the Princess crying out, as clearly as if she were in the room: "Fuck me, yes, fuck me, tear me open! Fuck me, you magnificent beast, fuck me." The words were nearly incoherent, mixed with sobs of need and desire. Dan took his cock in his hand and nestled the head in between Lata's pouty nether lips as Lata wriggled backward against him, letting out a sucking gasp of satisfaction as she encouraged his thickness to open her, never once taking her eyes from the screen.

The Bengal stopped in midmotion, as if He had suddenly figured the whole thing out. Dan plunged forward, slamming himself to the balls in Lata's desperate wetness as a scream tore out of the speakers. Even with the volume lowered, they could hear the growling Bengal and the screaming Princess as the long, thick, barbed penis of the enormous cat finally filled her cunt with ecstasy and pain, six hundred pounds of feral muscle forcing her to accept a cock so large, so dangerous, that even in her most extreme fantasies of the tiger she had never imagined anything like it. Blinded by lust, Daniel bucked and thrust into Lata's superheated cunt as she arched backward again and again onto his cock, caught up in the wild and uncontrollable lust on the screen.

Coming over and over, tears running down her face as the orgasms ripped through her body, Lata struggled to hold herself up as Daniel thrust relentlessly into her, tugging hard on her plum-colored nipples. She watched in a haze of orgiastic disbelief as the Bengal continued his brutal assault on the now sobbing Princess, whose crazed gasps and whimpers could occasionally be heard, via speaker, above her own. Every few moments the tiger would stop, and Lata knew that He had just shot an enormous load of thick, gelatinous, feline semen into the woman's battered cunt. That was the way cats were: The male's sharply barbed penis kept the penis embedded, kept the fuck from ending until the male was completely finished and could come no more. It could take a while. Brutal, yes, but that was the way it was.

Daniel and Lata kept watching the screen, Daniel fighting hard not to come yet, not quite yet, as the Bengal fucked and came, fucked and came. Finally, as the frighteningly powerful animal paused a third time to let the seed erupt from his huge, heavy, furred balls, they again heard the Princess. Fumbling, Lata slapped at the control to raise the volume as Daniel slowed the pace at which his cock slid in and out of her trembling pussy. Watching and listening with acute care, the humans paused, waiting, terrified and expectant. Blood dripped from the Princess's shoulders where the Bengal had tried, instinctively, to grab at her neck with his teeth in the place where a female tiger would have a ruff of loose skin and fur. Lata thought she could see blood, or more probably a mixture of blood and semen and the Princess's own juices, on the ground below the spot where the Bengal's penis was viciously locked into his human mate's woefully inadequate cunt.

As if from miles away, they heard her voice, trembling and childlike. The faraway "Fuck me, yes . . . oh yes . . . oh the pain oh Jesus oh how it hurts oh so good so good yes oh it hurts . . ." was cut off by the tiger's belly-deep growl as He lurched into another round of thrusts, turning the Princess's pleas into full-throated screams, equal parts terrible ecstasy and horrifying agony.

"Fuck me, Daniel, please, just fuck me," Lata sobbed, unable to bear it any longer, closing her eyes to block out the sight of the orange-and-black-striped back and sinewy haunches hunched over the juicy curves of the blonde's bloodied body. Hammering into her harder than he remembered ever doing to anyone, Daniel fucked ruthlessly into Lata's creamy depths, again and again, fingers digging into her generous hips and still watching the Bengal, imagining the power of those muscles behind his own thrusts as he bit down instinctively on the curve of his colleague's smooth shoulder.

Lata screamed and came one last torrential time, cunt tightening spastically around Daniel as she arched and shook. The blinding whiteness of his own orgasm hit, and he lost his grip on Lata, who slumped against the console, her limp arm brushing the volume control, pushing the gain to its limit. In the tremendous vortex of orgasm, on the verge of blacking out, all Daniel could hear was the Princess, accompanied by the virile yowls of her unhuman lover, screaming the unmistakable bliss of the impossible.

Debutante

"U ndress," I say softly, knowing she is doing more than just listening, that she is praying hard for each syllable I utter, hoping silently that they'll form the right words, the longed-for words, the dangerous words. Or at least the words that will keep the threads of promise spinning, send skeins of want and fear and expectation flying in nets as fine and deadly as the ones that enmesh songbirds unawares. She stands still for an instant before her fingers move to the button at the top of her blouse, caught in the chaos of desire, lust's staticky snow fuzzing out everything but the throb of want.

There's no lust like the first lust, no yearning as sharp-toothed as the abstract longing that exists in the spaces spun by desire. We dread it even as we crave it, this longing that floats us into the elongated moment between stumbling and falling. I look at her, watching it shimmer in her eyes, knowing that the desire crackles in her skin so sharply that she'd jump if I so much as reached out and touched her hand. She's waited a long time for this, wanted a long time for this, the first time with me.

Her lips tremble as if she is about to cry, and my own butterflies rustle against my ribs. "I want to fuck you so bad," she whispers, barely able to force herself to look at me as I slide the backs of my fingers up her arm.

"I'm aware," I reply, firm and quiet. She doesn't move to

unbutton another button. It wasn't what she wanted to hear. I almost feel the knotting in her gut as I deliberately disappoint her, throw her off her bearings. She's the kind of girl who's used to a degree of certainty, accustomed to either getting what she wants or at least knowing straight out that she won't. Her dark eyes land on mine tentatively and, after a long indrawn breath, find only reactionless freefall. I feel her shiver a tiny bit, then straighten, but do not let myself smile.

You never learn to fly if you don't learn to fall, I muse to myself, and sense her plummeting into the space without borders, waiting for me to stop her, give her her bearings. I examine her face, caress the candy drop of her lower lip with my eyes as I lick my own lips, delicate but ravenous. She breathes in slowly, almost managing to hide the tremor that makes the air catch in two or three subtle, tiny hiccups as she nears the end of her inhalation. Pink floods her face, but my own shows nothing. I heard her: I know, she knows, but she gets nothing in return, nothing except the knowledge that I now hold one more piece of her.

A gift, I lift my hand to her face, fingernails stroking soft as grass along the underside of her cheekbone. The pink in her skin grows pinker, her ears glowing like the glossy hidden vulvas of seashells. Her eyelids close heavily as she hides the only way she can, unable to look me in the eye as she reels with the dangerous strength of a new hand touching her skin. I pause, wondering if she knows how gorgeous she is.

Turning my hand, dragging one fingernail down along her jaw line, I admire the way the burgundy of my nail polish contrasts with the delicate pinks of her skin. I tilt her chin up toward me: She is small, like so many of the other women who've wanted me, who've come wanting that helpless tossed-like-a-rag-doll sensation, wanting my strong large arms to make them gasp, overtaken, overwhelmed. Maybe, I muse to myself, I'll give it to her later. But not now. Now I am holding her on the tip of a finger, showing her exactly how she must force her own head back for me as my nail-tip impresses a slender arch into the skin of her jaw. Just as I am about to instruct her to open her eyes she does, and finds me hovering right above her, as close as possible without our bodies touching, my lips mere inches away from hers. She bites her lip.

Then I kiss her lightly, holding my head high enough that she has to work to kiss me back. But she does, immediately, kisses raw as carrion bursting as our lips slide against one another, contrails of lipstick smearing as lust erodes artifice. I teach her that size has its privileges: I make her fight to reach my lips, make her stretch and angle herself so that she can open to me as I lick her tongue, as I trace the inner edge of her lip. It is not so simple a thing to kiss me, she discovers, gasping into my mouth with breath sweet and strange as violets. Lifting an arm to try to grab me, to pull my head closer to hers, she finds her hand returned to her side, my fingers staying on her wrist only long enough to remind her of her place.

Pulling back, I look at her, drink her in, her wide eyes and her want, the red corona around her glistening mouth. The penalty for rushing is to begin again, to show that you have learned from your mistakes. I lick the bottom-most curve of her lower lip as she stands there motionless. Her fingers are shaky, her breath uneven as she lets her mouth fall open gently, no longer trying to kiss me back. She knows she's been warned.

Leaning in, I make her arch backward for my mouth. She leans with me, head falling back almost to her shoulders, mouth open, silent, hopeful, almost pleading. I feel a soft molten shift in her body, a sudden warm pliability in the air between us just before my hip brushes her belly and the weight of my kiss comes down and crushes her, hard. She staggers, off-balance, knees yielding to the warm wobble in her belly and the clench of torrid wetness between her thighs. She grabs for me, panicking as her legs give out, red-faced for real now as she slumps against me, fingers digging desperately into the backs of my shoulders. I don't move, somehow stilling the involuntary urge to catch her.

Her eyes are open now, wide, a little scared. I shake my head. "Oh, Christ," she whimpers, feeling my solid strength under her hands and knowing neither it nor I will help her. I let her use me to keep from falling too fast as she slides down my body to the floor, but even that, she knows, is a privilege, not a right.

Straightening my dress, I stand over her, leaning toward her just enough so that she leans back, realizes that the edge of the sofa is just behind her. Gratefully she leans back, slouched against the firm upholstered front, watching me watch her.

"I thought I told you to undress," I remind her gently, my tone carefully not quite warm. The top button of her blouse is undone, so her fingers find the next one, fumbling only a little. I sit down in the armchair opposite her, appraising the plump lines of her thighs and the point at which they vanish beneath the rumpled skirt pushed high, the skewed hemline hitting just low enough that I can't see whether she's wearing underwear. I pretend to ignore her, wiping her lipstick from my chin and cheek with my fingers as her buttercream curves begin to emerge from her clothes. Under the soft ivory of her blouse lie the softer, barely pink slopes of her breasts, packed into an embroidered pushup bra so clearly intended to impress that I almost crack a smile.

"Pretty," I opine coolly, crossing my legs and sitting back. "Let me see the matching panties. They *do* match, don't they?"

She lowers her eyes, the apples of her cheeks turning the same rosy hue of the embroidered flowers that festoon the lace froth confining her heavy, luscious breasts. She blushes so easily, growing redder as I watch, fingers of pink streaking down her throat to her voluptuous décolletage, and she gets up on her knees, preparing to stand so she can take off her skirt. Just before she does, I catch her eye and shake my head.

"I like you on your knees, girl," I tell her, holding her gaze to let her savor my light smile. The pounding of her heart is almost audible, and she straightens her bearing, shoulders settling down and back, chest high as she smiles back at me with pleasure and pride. I cock my head toward her, arching my eyebrows, needing nothing more than gesture to remind her that she has yet to show me her panties. Her hands behind her back, I hear the zipper of her skirt, and then I see her panties do match her bra, skinny strips of flowered lace making finger-wide indentations in the hills of her hips as she pushes her skirt down to her knees.

She's beautiful, partly because she simply is, and partly

because she wants so badly to be exactly what I want to see, which she is: shoulders barely draped by her blouse, cleavage so deep I already know my tongue won't touch bottom, presented to me in lovely lace that strains with the effort. The hint of darkness behind the sheer cloth of her panties makes the hairs on the back of my neck stand at attention, the roundness of her hips curving my hands into reflexive arches already ready to mold to her curves.

I tell her to give me my bag. I dropped it by the end of the couch when we came in, still flirting, laughing, tossing it casually so that it would not be out of reach, though she has to shuffle on her knees several feet to get it. She is relieved to be given a task, happy to have something she can do, to be back in a universe where effects have causes and causes have effects. She could resist me now, and though she doesn't, I can tell that this alone is enough to reassure her.

She's pert, consciously cute as she hands me my bag, which I disregard, her face falling when no praise follows. Extracting a compact, I remove the remainders of lipstick from my face before applying new paint, feeling her stunned, still-expectant gaze as she watches me line my lips then filling the outline with dark, shimmering color. Finally I look up into her pout, snapping my compact closed and dropping it back into my handbag after the barest instant of meeting her eyes.

"Service is its own reward, girl. It had better be, or you shouldn't do it." She bites her lip, then nods shyly. Closing her eyes, she waits and I watch, the airless feeling of effect no longer being in synch with cause taking hold of her again. I fish in the bottom of my bag until I find what I want, then set the bag down, reaching out with my other hand to graze her solar plexus with the backs of my fingers.

She flinches, but only for an instant. Moments later she is purring and gasping, murmurs rising lazily from her arched-back throat as I stroke her neck with the nails of one hand, knuckles of the other rumblebumping against the nipple that has begun to harden beneath the lace of one brassiere cup. I whisper to her, and her hands go behind her back without question or hesitation, shoulders back, breasts thrust forward. My ass on the edge of my chair, I sit with her between my knees, blowing a cool stream of air down her throat, between her breasts, watching the tiny bumps of gooseflesh appear as arousal flashfloods her skin. She whimpers through puffy lips, eyes still closed when the back of my hand grazes the hillock of her belly, hips writhing one involuntary time as she presses toward me, then stops cold, stiff with effort.

I lean over her, my breath on her face, feeling the heat of her body rising up against me as I shift the still-closed knife in my hand. Pressing it against her belly, I feel her muscles tense against the unfamiliar hardness, the chill of the metal handle. Rhythmically, suggestively, I tease it toward her groin, letting it skate over her panties until it slides neatly along the groove between her swollen cunt lips. She groans out loud at this, grabbing her heels and leaning back on her arms to spread herself wider for me, the scent of her excitement rushing up into my face as she kneels before me.

Fingers outstretched along the length of the knife's handle—the knife is folded shut, the handle a sheath for the blade's mirrorlike sharpness—I rock it from side to side, gently parting her cunt lips with the seductive smooth hardness of metal. Nudging her clit with the curved back of the handle, lust thickens her throat, and I listen to her breathing growing fast and rough. She's wet enough now to make the metal shiny with it when I take it away from her crotch. Hard nipples poke at the lace that encases her breasts, and she looks up at me, curious to know why I've stopped.

"You want this bad, don't you, girl?" My question is somewhat rhetorical, but the simplicity with which I flick the knife open with my thumb is not. Four scalpel-sharp inches of steel gleam in my hand, the knife's edge catching the gold of the lamp in the corner. I feel her swallow hard through the air that separates us, and then she is still, looking into my eyes, afraid of the knife, afraid of how much she wants whatever I might do with it.

"Yes," she breathes, words all but inaudible. "God help me."

She bites her lip, tears in her eyes, overwhelmed by excitement, anticipation, and plain panic.

The flat of my blade slides delicately beneath the strap of her bra, thin dangerous metal gliding harmlessly against her delicate skin. With a twist of my wrist, I pull the edge against the fabric, watching it part as if rigged by a magician, neatly severed ends dangling, brushing her skin as I let her shiver for a second or two. Looking into her eyes, I allow her to calm herself, girding herself for wherever the blade might go next, holding her secure with the force of the intent I hope she can see in my eyes. Finally she breathes, and as she inhales, I slip the knife under her other bra strap, slicing it almost before she knows I'm about to. Her head nearly spins with shock and sheer desire.

"I told you to undress for me," I remind her, my voice calm and cool and low in spite of the flush that flutters my body, the rush that speeds my pulse. I pause, drawing an infinitely light, infinitely tiny circle with the point of the knife, right between her breasts. The silence as her breathing stops is crystalline. I let it settle over us like snowfall before I continue. "And you didn't finish. So I'm afraid I'm just going to have to finish for you."

Hooking a finger under the band of her bra, I cut through the strong elastic, then let the knife glide upward through the double layer of lace that connects the two underwire cups. Gasping and red-faced, panting and shaking, she stares deep into my eyes as I pull the destroyed remnants of the bra from her body. Sticking the tip of the knife through the lace of one of the empty cups, I hold it up for her to see.

"This is mine now. And so are you."

Her body shakes when I say it, the quake of flesh making her heavy breasts jiggle as they lie against her torso, her chest suddenly heaving with the feverishly rhythmic breaths that lead to orgasm. I shake my head once, then twice. Somehow she battles her body to a stop. Her eyes close as tightly as she holds herself, every muscle tense, fighting her instincts, focusing inward to stop the swell of desire. When she is still, I slice through the lace band at the top of each hip, then silently close the knife and tuck it behind me on the chair as I wait for her to open her eyes.

Finally she does, a tear of effort escaping from the corner of one of them. I lean over her and lick it gently away as it rolls down her cheek, feeling her catch her breath at the touch of my mouth, the scent and warmth of my body and breath, so close, so longed-for. I can feel how much she wants me to wrap her in my arms, but for a moment I leave her to her hunger, to look into its jaws alone.

Finally, I cover her lips with mine, catching her grateful sob in my mouth as I begin to pull her panties out from between her legs, tugging slowly, pulling the fabric up and between her drenched labia, doing my best to drag it against her burning clit. Again her body shakes as she drinks in the taste of my mouth and the rasp of fabric on her pussy, trembling harder and harder until suddenly the slick, wet fabric dangles impotently from my hand, the sensation instantly gone.

Sitting back, I bunch her panties in my hand and press them to my lips and nose, inhaling the concentrate of pungently female scent that seems to fill the room. She stares at me, the tense arch of her body collapsing so that she sits on her haunches, exhaustion beginning to show at the corners of her eyes and mouth as she watches me savor her scent.

"Oh my," I beam, the heady scent of her cunt making my own pulse thick and deep inside me, "you smell so pretty when I treat you like that."

She is so beautiful there on the floor at my feet, slick with her own juice and the rapidly cooling thin skin of sweat that coats her body. Slowly, she smiles, then laughs gently, her body relaxing as she leans back against the couch again, stretching.

"Earlier tonight you told me you wanted to fuck me." I nudge the pumps off of my feet with my toes, shoving them to the side. "Is that still the case?"

"More than ever," she whispers, nodding, damp hair falling into her eyes. Her voice is hoarse but somehow still soft, the timbre so rough-edged and yet yielding that it makes my clit twitch. Her voice mirrors the way she gives herself over, raw as a fresh scar, soft as sand.

I watch her for a moment, temporarily holding back the urge

to throw her back and dive between her thighs even though I can practically taste her clit. Before I let her do anything, I'm going to make her come for me, get her to give me the orgasm she was so close to before but I wouldn't let her have. That much, at least, is mine.

Finally I stand up, towering over her petite frame, stepping just past her as I shrug off my cardigan.

"Get your juicy ass up on that couch, then, girl. You've earned it."

Reasonable and Prudent

H e knew I liked it fast. That was the point of this particular exercise, the reason we'd decided a road trip was in order. He did, too, and he didn't bat an eyelash, not even when I snapped around the bend of a hairpin turn that had nothing but freefall beyond a lick-and-promise of guardrail.

"I love the way you drive," Mark smiled, unbuttoning his 501's. "You drive like you fuck, you know that?"

I smiled slowly. "What do you mean?"

"Intrepid."

"Tell me," I said.

He did, his elegant voice dripping, just like his cock, with liquid lust. I breathed deeply, as if I could inhale the Porsche's effortless speed, noting how the musk of him filled the small space between us. Stroking the gearshift with purposeful fingers, I caressed the curves of highway, foot instinctively nudging the accelerator a little closer to the floor in parallel with his growing excitement. I couldn't take my eyes off the road enough to really look at him, but the glimpses I could catch in my peripheral vision made my cunt throb.

Dazed by speed, as aroused by the rush of it as we were by one another, we could only smile when we noticed the blue and white lights in the rear-view mirror. Coming down out of Missoula we'd decided to glide for a while, but the creamy

157

smoothness of a hundred miles an hour had gradually increased to something sharper, harder-edged, well beyond cruising speed. It seemed somehow right for the land, for the space and endless sky. It also felt right, my clit thrumming in response to the lunge and purr of the engine and the arch of my boyfriend's cock as he stroked it for me in the passenger seat.

"Coitus interruptus," I said as the lights drew closer. He buttoned his fly. "So much for no speed limit."

My nipples were still hard when the state trooper wrote out the ticket. We hadn't anticipated getting one, but it seemed almost welcome. "Reasonable and prudent" was the speed limit dictated by the brand-new law. In spite of ourselves, we had to agree with the trooper that 122 miles an hour, on that road, was neither.

Darkness fell as we pulled off of the ramp into Livingston, the trooper's blocky, childlike capitals marching across our badge of honor as it lay on the dashboard. In the middle of the old main street, bars and neon and soundstage-worthy Old West facades lined the few short blocks of downtown. We parked down the block from the Murray Hotel.

In the lobby the glowering heads of several ex-bison observed as we registered, monitoring our progress as we ascended in the hand-cranked cage elevator. Little about the place was modern, which suited us both. The tub was old and lavish, the floorboards worn, the brass bed heavy, antique, and nearly shoulder-high. The satisfying thump of bass from the band in the bar filtered up through the floor, and I shook down my hair as I carried my bag to the closet.

Hanging up the spare dress I'd crammed into my overnight bag, I felt his hands on my hips. "It's nice here," Mark whispered into my ear as he gathered me in his arms, pulling me back against his chest. I nodded, closing my eyes and letting my head fall back. It's rare that a lover is as much taller than I as he was, rare that I get to enjoy the sensation of being held so fully, so well-encompassed by a man's body. Kissing the side of my neck, short beard rustling against my skin, a raw heat surfaced precipitously to the skin of my breasts, the insides of my thighs. Scant seconds sufficed to bring back all the arousal of the drive. I shivered at the sweet low rumble of his voice in my ear as he asked me whether I was ready to be his slut now. I nodded, relished the delicious anticipatory chill in my bones—fiercely aroused to feel, and to know I could not stop, his desire and my yearning to be crushed by it.

I was already gone, and he knew it. The barest edges of his teeth stroked the tender skin of my throat, and I shivered, soundless, atypically incapable of forming even the smallest word as his hands slid down my arms and his strong fingers encircled my wrists. "Very nice," he purred, reminding me how fast he could take me over, body and soul, and my psyche yawned open in a rude chasm of need. I didn't know exactly what was coming, but I knew I needed it, to be the vessel, the object, the abject, the fucked.

His voice was lower now, and rougher, filling my ears with sable and the faintest razor's edge of amused sneer. My breath caught in my throat, my knees buckling as his tongue found the crease behind my ear, pinning my arms to my sides as he forced me to stand upright. "Nice dress you've got on, you hot little slut. Almost as nice as the way you drive my car."

Like a sugar cube in coffee, my ability to think grew soft, crumbling, sliding down with inexorable logic to the sweet, sticky pool between my legs.

"You like it when I call you a slut, don't you?"

I didn't say anything. I did, and he knew that, too. Moving slowly, he walked backward and I moved with him, careful not to step on his feet as we swayed our way across the room. At the edge of the bed we stopped, and I stood there trying to calm my ragged breaths, grateful to have his chest to lean against.

"I didn't say you could close your eyes." I opened them and saw him reflected in the mirror, his commanding height behind me. My nipples poked indiscreetly at the chocolate-and-cream print of my long button-front dress. "Such a sophisticated girl, and such an old-fashioned dress," he mused, his breath warm on my ear as he let go of my wrist and unsnapped the holster on his belt. "You're the big tech queen, you drive like a race car driver, you take no shit from anyone, but you get up in the morning and you put on this long, girly dress with all these buttons. My little bundle of contradictions."

I chuckled, but my tongue turned to cotton as I watched the blade of his buck knife caress the thin fabric over the curve of my breast, my eyes wide with panic as I felt the coolness of the metal against my nipple. My mouth opened, then closed, then opened slightly again as he popped the topmost button off, holding the blade briefly against the threads, then flicking it away.

I looked stupidly down as the second button fell to the floor, transfixed as the silver traced its way between my breasts. "No, Mark . . . don't . . . please . . . ," I whispered, but I only half meant it.

"Oh, please. Don't bullshit me," he growled, his tone glossy with the shimmer of power as he flicked off a third button. He knew I was terrified of knives. He also knew that I would let him scare me, that I even wanted him to, though the adrenaline made me tremble and my eyes never wavered from the blade. "You know you've been wanting this all damned day. Don't try to pretend your panties weren't soaking back before we got stopped. And don't try to tell me you're not wet now. Don't forget, slut, I know you pretty well."

He was right. He did. And I was.

The knife mesmerized me, frightened me, but Mark wouldn't hurt me. Of that I was sure. At least not in any way I didn't want him to. I only ever worried that he might love me too much, that he'd scare himself and not hurt me enough. It had happened a time or two, but he knew better now. I'd tell him to back off if I really needed it. Until then, all I needed was everything. Anything. As long as I could be a slut for it.

Finally he pulled the dress back over my shoulders and the cotton slid down my arms and into a puddle on the floor. Satisfied, he smiled and closed the knife, tossing it onto the chair in the corner before unhooking my bra. I looked in the mirror again, watching his face as he pulled the garment off me, glad that he seemed to appreciate the fact that I'd chosen sheer white lace—

he'd told me once how much he liked the prissy symbolism, how he liked the thrill of feeling like he was making a virgin into a whore.

I didn't dare, or really want, to break my tacit bondage by moving my hands from where he'd stationed them. Suddenly his hand was on my belly, pushing under my panties with a rough twist, two thick fingers forced into me so fast and hard I didn't have time to think. I gasped and spluttered, and he snatched his hand out again, wrenching my panties down my legs as he turned me with the other heavy, hard hand and pushed me toward the bed. I stumbled, tripping on my own underwear, clutching at the curlicues of brass to keep from falling. I steadied myself, and began to stand up again.

"No you don't." I heard the jingle of change in his pockets, the thump of his belt buckle hitting the floor. Out of the corner of my eye, I could see him kick his jeans to the side. "You better hold on with both hands, slut, if you know what's good for you."

He bent down and yanked his belt free of the belt loops, catching my gaze as I tried to see what he was doing. He smiled at me, a wicked leer whose raw, unapologetic possessiveness made my cunt clench. "You know what I want. Spread it, cunt."

I clung to the bedrail as he traced the cleft of my ass, the wide-open space between my legs, with the doubled-over end of the belt. I trembled with lust, aching, muscles in my thighs and calves twitching. I wanted to beg him to fuck me, or hit me, or do something, anything other than tease me with the edge of the leather. It was barely enough to feel, and it frustrated me. I wriggled, trying to provoke him. He didn't react, didn't say a word, just kept stroking the splayed lips of my cunt with the edge of his belt so lightly it was all I could do not to back up against the belt, to try to increase the contact. I whimpered, and still he was impassive. Finally I just stood still, my face flushed, feeling the pulsing of my swollen pussy and trying hard to be good enough, patient enough, that he would proceed.

I did not scream at the first stroke, or the second, or the third that fell across my flesh. I could tell he wanted me to, because he surprised me with it and he hit me hard, no warm-up, no warning. But some willful streak in me reared its head instead. He wouldn't let me react before, and now he was going to have to make me. The belt fell again and again, just at the tops of my thighs, then across the middle of my ass, and I groaned out loud in spite of myself, tears of anguish and need falling heedlessly from my face as I gulped for air.

"What's the matter, Lee? Did that one hurt? Did it make that slutty little cunt of yours get even wetter?" I wouldn't even nod. "Fine," he continued. "Go ahead, try to tough it out, slut. Go right ahead."

As he spoke, his voice teasing and smarmy, he held my ass in both hands. He licked my ass cheek, then rubbed his face across my butt. I winced as his two-day whiskers rubbed the welts but said nothing. Then he growled and I felt his teeth digging into me, crushing, tearing, sinking deep and tight into my battered, stinging ass at the same time that he shoved three fingers deep into my cunt. I yelped, then, bit my lip hard. He kneaded me deep, fingers pushing into me further with an obscenely wet slurp, stirring the depths of my cunt. I moaned as the pain and the deep, primal pleasure swirled together, making me start to feel high. I could still feel his teeth, feel the red flares of pain radiating from where he bit me, but it was indistinguishable from the opaque sheets of pleasure that emanated from where his fingertips massaged me.

Then his jaws clenched harder, vicious, unbearable. I screamed and wrenched away, reflexive, feeling the nasty rip of teeth not quite breaking skin as I bucked away from his mouth. The dark red core of my sex rippled sharp and strong around his fingers just as he yanked them out of me.

"Don't you dare," he snarled, grabbing hold of my hair and pushing me back down as his other hand came down hard on my upturned ass. "I told you to hang on, and you fucking well better do it. Head down, slut. You know you want it."

Yes, I do, I thought as he thrust his cock into me with one long stroke, shoving me forward, pressing my chest against the cold metal. I clung desperately to the bed, grateful for something to hold on to as his cock hammered into me, deep, percussive thrusts that played counterpoint to the buzz of sensation that ebbed from the welts across my ass. He pinched my nipples, twisted them hard until I came, breathless, and as my cunt spasmed around him he reached down to do the same to my clit, working it hard as his hips slapped my lewdly splayed ass. I was his cunt, his slut, his everything, and it all felt so good that all I could do was whimper and come again and again.

Somehow we ended up on the floor, his long body flattening me into the boards. He was trying to hold back, his whole body tense, waiting for something. "Tear me apart," I whispered, wanting to feel him come, my body now hungry for his release. "I'm your slut. I want it. Give it to me." He bit the back of my neck, growling, and slammed the final strokes home, pounding me into the floorboards, bringing tears to my eyes as I burst once more into ecstatic flames. I felt him explode, heard his muffled bellow as he bit between my shoulder blades, and went limp as he did, floating on endorphins and hormones and climax after climax.

Tears drying on my face, sweat cooling on our bodies, I lay beneath him. It felt good to be held down by his tall, strong body, good to be helpless under the voluptuous dead weight of his lassitude. His cock still filled me, not yet soft, reminding me just how much I loved being a slut bottom for him, how glad I was that he understood it, that he reveled in it too.

He gently kissed my ear. "You there?" he whispered, protective and soft.

"Mmmm." I didn't want him to move, not yet. It was too pristine.

"You okay? It wasn't too much?"

"I'm wonderful," I murmured, touched by his sudden, boyish insecurity. "You know I love the way you drive."

Virgin

I don't think you have the slightest clue what you're getting yourself into, boy, with your Michelangelo face and your Stanford Ph.D. and your charming little crooked smile. You've been smiling at me for quite a while now and every time we talk about it, you tell me how you've always felt this submissive urge in you but you've never really had the chance to explore it. So now you've decided you trust me enough, you know me enough, we've dated enough, you're brave enough. I'm gonna be your bad girl, your wrong-side-of-the-tracks, is that it? Dark to your light, ample and round to your wiry and thin, black to your white, the reasonable, nurturing voice of experience to your babe-in-the-woods platitudes about wanting to be pushed, wanting to lose control? I'll be the one who'll show you the ropes, pun intended, and show you all my pretty tricks? Is that how you think it's gonna work?

Think again, my little tourist. You haven't got the first clue about this. This isn't about you anymore, not since you said you wanted to do this, and it sure isn't about whatever the fuck little soft-focus bondage fantasy you have stuck in your head from one too many kitten-with-a-whip porno magazines. I've done this before. A lot. I like it. And I'm good at it. You haven't. And yeah, I know it's scary. It's supposed to be.

But don't back down now. I can see you getting worried. You can see the look in my eye and you know full well that I'm not

165

kidding you when I flash you this hungry, glittering smile. Look me in the eye, I dare you. Come on, look me in the eye. We'll see how brave you are.

Soft, that's what you are. Soft and smooth, sweet and unmarked as a baby's tuchas. Your eyes are a little frightened, a little hopeful. It's clear you have no idea what to make of me, of this side of me you've never seen before, where my eyes narrow like a cat's as I reach out to touch you. I feel my muscles rippling under my skin. I feel like a tiger in the zoo, restlessly pacing out the perimeter of her cage, aching for a chance to use her claws.

You flinch, and I laugh. Soft soft baby, soft sweet thing, little playtoy, little boy, what are you so afraid of? Why do you wince when all I do is reach out to touch your face? Do you really anticipate such cruelty from me? I'm not so bad as all that. I'm worse. I'm a bigger bitch than you've ever dreamed, a crueler top than you can imagine. Not cruel in any mindless crude way, and not because I will make you take it. I know what you don't: You'll take things for me you didn't imagine you would ever take for anyone. It isn't cruel to give you what you want.

The cruelty comes because I'll make you take it, watch you writhing in agonized ecstasy, and keep you there as long as I want. You'll stay there past the point of exhaustion, past the point of your body's ability to respond, long past the point where your cock can rise, past the point where you can even form words to beg me to stop. I'll break you, leave you aching, send your brain to places you never knew existed. I'll make you howl with anger and I'll fill you with the kind of desire you only thought you knew with the other women you've fucked. I can give that to you. And maybe I will. But you've got to ante up. Give me everything you've got and I'll return the favor.

Come here, baby. I pull you close to me, and I slip my arms around your waist. I hold you in the cradle of my arms, rocking you gently with the curve of things, observing the mixed flickers of desire and trepidation in your big blue eyes. I kiss you, thick and growing thicker, as I tug the shirttails from your waistband and slide my hands up your back. You murmur and purr softly, and I bite your lower lip a bit as I let my nails lightly trail back down your torso, pressing hard enough for a shiver, not hard enough for a gasp. Breaking the kiss, I watch you smile, then catch you by the chin, grabbing that achingly boyish grin in my hand and giving it a shake. Don't congratulate yourself so soon, little man. You haven't earned it yet.

I tell you to take off your shirt for me. You do, eager, trying to please, fumbling slightly with the cuffs as I watch. I walk around behind you and I lean you against the wall. Wordlessly, my hand between your shoulder blades pushing you toward the door-frame and wall, I feel you resist even as you give in. I feel your desire to do as I tell you, and your uncertainty at not knowing the etiquette, not quite knowing how. You try to let me pose you. You don't say a thing. Good boy.

I examine your back, running my nails over your skin. You have such pretty skin. Candy-assed rich boys like you always have nice skin. Very pretty, very pale. Your skin will take my marks beautifully one of these days. You've got the type of skin that bears bruises easily, distinctly, and I already know you heal fast. I can see the shadowy outline of a vein below the skin just at the corner of your jaw. I trace it with my eyes when I stroke the side of your throat with my nails.

You wriggle a little. I dig in my nails, sharply. Did I tell you you could do that? I didn't think so. Manners, pet. I lean over you and kiss between your shoulder blades, leaving a lipstick print. Reaching around you, I press my belly into your back and butt, and I feel you reflexively press back, not hard, just looking for reassurance. I chuckle softly, sliding my hands up your belly and over your chest. I trap your nipples between my fingers, gentle pressure enough to make you squirm. My nails dig in like tweezers. You gasp, biting your lip because you know I don't want to hear it. Do I need to tell you? I hope not.

I reach into my skirt pocket for the little yellow rubber cups I hold up to your face. Lick it, I say, bringing one of them to your lips, and you do, but too tentatively, as if you were tasting an unfamiliar candy. You make me laugh. It's not dessert, little boy, you are. I make you lick the rim of the cup again, then I squeeze it and press it to your nipple, releasing it so that it sucks your sweet soft flesh up and into it like a hungry mouth that never lets go. I hold you as you writhe, cooing assurance in your ear, stroking your other, naked nipple while you adjust to the sensation. Does it hurt? A little. Poor baby. It's gonna get a whole lot worse before it gets better.

I have you naked now, suction cups making both your nipples strain, engorged, forced to swell by the vacuum inside. Your cock juts out and up, unforced but swollen nonetheless, darkening, doubtless aching. Hands behind your back, wrists bound securely with broad leather straps, you're trembling. You're weak in the knees. Poor thing. I tease your balls, your thighs, the underside of your cock with the tip of my riding crop, running the smooth leather cracker over your skin. You shiver and your eyelids close, almost overloaded, close to crying. Open your eyes. I didn't give you permission. Don't hesitate. Don't you dare. My crop slices nastily through the air and sharply slaps the wall just to the right of your hip. Now your eyes are wide, your lip quivers. That's better. Pay attention, little boy. Pay attention.

I smile at you and raise the crop, stepping back. Without preamble it twitches below your chin, fast as a cobra strike, and the suction cups are flicked away, one, two. Angry and red, your swollen tits poke out at me. I wonder if I could see them throbbing if I looked more carefully? I gather you up, feeling you quake in my arms as I fold you in, pulling you against me, kissing you hard, harder. You whimper, suck my tongue, let me nip gently along your lip. I capture your lower lip and suck it, edges of my teeth playing with it, deciding what to do with you. Don't fight me. Let me move you. That's a good boy. You'll go where I tell you to go.

You shrink back when I let you go, as if you want to, as if you could, disappear without my touch. What are you when you aren't in my arms? Is there anything left of you? Not right now, no, and you'll do whatever it takes to get back there. I know it better than you do. All you know is that you ache and I can make it better. That's all right. You can do your aching over here, bent over the arm of the couch. I put pillows under your chest, but leave your face exposed. I want to watch you biting your lip and gasping, see you flushed with pleasure and slick with sweat, watch you when you're so far beyond reality that you stare at me, not seeing anything but the force that pushed you into a place you don't recognize and that alone has the power to bring you back to what you know in the mirror. I want to pull the loose threads of you and watch your soul unravel.

Your ass is in the air for me, and a nice ass it is. It will be even nicer once it's been claimed, don't you think? I would blindfold you now, but I want you to see. I show you the flogger, long soft deerskin tails heavy and warm against your skin. It feels reassuring, sensuous, when I trail it down your back, but it's still a scary thing. It is heavy and flows over you like hair. The softness of the black leather makes your butt wiggle when I caress the backs of your thighs and the crack of your ass with it, makes you grind your hard cock into the arm of the couch.

Stop that. You are very uppity, you know. Too goddamned used to having your own way, that's your problem. Don't worry, I won't let you. You don't know shit. You think you know what you want, but I know what you need.

You start screaming when the flogger begins to land lightly on your ass, with only the weight of the leather behind it. I stop instantly. What the fuck do you think you're doing? Stop it right now. You sputter and are silent. Did that hurt you? No, of course it didn't. My hands are on you, my side pressed against you. I reassure you and I scold you for crying wolf. This doesn't even hurt. It doesn't, and you admit it. You're just scared. Don't worry, baby, I whisper gently in your ear. I'll tell you when it's time for you to scream.

I kiss you once, briefly. I touch your hair. Take it for me, then. If it scares you, then take it for me. The flogger lands on your ass again, lightly, long soft leather strands grazing your skin. Slowly we begin to dance, your body, my body, and the flogger making a trio. The sound of leather against skin, the sound of my breath and yours, gentle sighs growing into soft moans flowing from your mouth as the sensation begins to build in your ass, your thighs, your hips. You feel it in your cock now, I know. I imagine the tendrils of my whip reaching through your body to swirl around your cock each time they fall on your ass. I reach through you, through my rhythmic arm, the tips of my leather fingers. You've never felt this before, and I take you slowly outside of yourself with the flesh-and-blood percussion of my will on your body.

You don't resist me, so I push you. Sweat streams down my torso. My shirt sticks to my chest, clings to my breasts, my arm rebels. You are almost screaming again: not pain, not fear, but orgasm. You're so close to coming that your body can't process the sensation as pain, so far from coming because the sensation isn't close enough to your cock. I swing harder, my hunger burning in my throat. The shock of contact makes my arm shake with each stroke.

This has turned into a real flogging. This whip won't cut you, and I am half-blind with wishing it would and with the sweat that runs into my eyes. I want your blood, I want your come, I want your life gushing out for me. This whip won't cut. It isn't supposed to, it's far too soft and really quite gentle, more like a massage, thuddy and deep, than a whipping. The gentleness of my weapons is the only thing that saves me from my lust at times like this. I settle for the dark red of your ass and the desperation with which you moan.

Beg for it, you bastard. Beg me. You want me to let you come. You ask me not to stop, you ask me to fuck you. You beg me to stop, but I don't hear a safeword. You sob. You wail, and I keep going. Unless you say the magic word, this isn't up to you. And then suddenly I let the flogger fall. My hands are on your ass, nails clawing hard over scarlet, and you wail higher, so tender, so sensitive, I can't bear it any longer.

Helpless on the floor, you fall where I push you. Eyes wide and awestruck, you watch but can't speak. I say nothing as I take off the cuffs, roll you onto your back. You're a piece of meat for me now, nothing more. It's precisely what you want to be. I take off my skirt and straddle you, bare ass in your face. Hard, male, wracked with wanting, you growl, impatient, when I roll the condom on. Your ass is hot against the cool hardwood floor, but not as hot as my pussy as I lower it to your mouth. I don't have to tell you what to do. I watch your cock twitch and throb as you lick the length of me, feel you groan into my clit. I'll fuck whatever part of you I want, boy. I tell you so, and tell you again, and you moan your gratitude into me.

When I'm done with your tongue, I turn around for a shimmy down your belly, cunt-wetness painting a stripe. You're still so hard, and I smile. The tip of your sheathed cock nudges between the lips of my cunt. You whimper, bite your lip. You want in. I don't give a fuck what you want. I bite your chin. I kiss your throat. I nip at your chest. I suck your left nipple into my mouth, biting down until you gasp and choke, and then and only then do I begin to sink down, inch by raw-silk inch, onto your cock.

Suddenly you beg without thinking, singing me an obscene litany. You'll give me anything. I'd be more impressed if I didn't already know it. You're desperate. I like it. My fingers rake your shoulders, my teeth gouge your chest, my cunt surrounds you. Biting and clawing, scratching and thrusting, grunting and cursing, I bruise your hips with my need. I don't notice until I begin to descend from orgasm that you are slammed up against me, arched into me with fierce vigor, your ass off the floor holding us both in the air as your cock explodes. I didn't give you permission. But I'll overlook it this time.

You're limp as cafeteria spinach. I stroke you a bit, lightly, amused. I get up and shove my toys into the bag I brought them in. Looking out the window at the narrow street lined with triple-deckers, I put on my skirt, run my fingers through my hair. I feel your eyes on me, but now is not the time for me to return your stare. I'll be ready to go in a moment, just like we talked about. This isn't the time to stay.

Did you say something? Your voice is soft, gentle, but somehow I can tell that you're surer of who you are now than you were when I arrived. You didn't do too badly for a virgin. Perhaps I can make a real bottom of you later, but now I kiss you softly and leave you lying on the floor of your silent living room, alone with the awakened choirs of your own flesh.

Darling Nicky

I was deep in the groove of a road trip, making it up as I went. There was no schedule, no plan, no real destination, just me and a backpack and a road atlas and an increasingly thick stack of truck-stop postcards in the glove compartment. Sam and I had decided to call it quits in March. I moved out in April, and every day that followed was an impatient wait for the end of the school year. That last bell rang, the kids hollered and ran for the door, and two days later I packed my bag, dropped my cat off with a friend, turned in my grades to the principal's office, then headed for the highway, the streets of my arid little town fading behind me like a long sigh.

It had been a long, long time since I'd thought much about sex. I cannot tell a lie: As sweet as he was, Sam never inspired me in bed, and if he was far too nice a guy to pester me about sex if I didn't seem interested, I was far too aware that I'd hurt his feelings if I explained why I wasn't. The urge flickered for a while, but time went by, turning us into something much closer to siblings than lovers, and eventually it just went away. It's like fasting: After a few days you don't get hungry anymore.

And then came that clear afternoon when I found myself up in some Colorado hills or other, daydreaming of sex as I let the wheel slip between my fingers. In my two-lane pipe dream I would swear I could feel stubble brushing the inside of my thigh, hot breath against my skin. My hips pressed toward the steering wheel before I realized what I was doing, and I nearly closed my eyes for a moment to savor the tautening sensation before I remembered I was driving. The images and sensations—half-remembered, half-imagined—turned from a trickle to a torrent, until finally I pulled off onto some old logging road and sat on a tree stump, one hand down my pants, savoring the air and the sun on my face, warm as imagined flesh. Soon my phantom lover had come and gone and so had I, peeling down the highway, heading for the nearest flyspeck on my road map. Something had to give.

That night, in a tidy logging town, I flirted with men who smile a little rather than laugh a lot, men who still say "ma'am." At the border of the parking lot an insolent neon finger fuck-youed Drinks Dancing at the high, impassive sky. Inside, I sat behind a watery Bud, cruising the boys at the bar.

Some were ugly or drunk or boring, too old, too young, too weather-beaten or rough. I was the only woman in the bar beside the barmaid. She was the only one who didn't stare at me. Some of the men blushed when I stared back. I sipped my beer, simmering with exhilarating indecision. I could take whichever one I wanted, or none of them at all. I disqualified the one who approached me first. This was my show. Watching them drink and talk, I disqualified some more—too shy, too lewd, and the inevitable one who would never shut up. One or two seemed too married for what I had in mind, too much prey to their own conscience to look me in the eye when looked their way and smiled.

The one I picked came in later than most. I chose him for his broad, long-fingered hands and the way his jeans faded along his lean thighs, and because he smiled as if he understood exactly what I was looking for. The wind was almost cold when I took him out to the parking lot, but he kissed like a champ, movie-worthy nipple-stiffening mouthfuls of cream and muscle, leaning me up against the side of his pickup. I nodded and wrapped my arms around his neck when he tugged my shirt from my waistband, shivered and clutched his shoulders, sighing, when he unbuttoned my jeans and slid a hand inside. When I bucked hard and spasmed against his thick fingers, grinding violently against the callused hand in my panties, his eyes opened wide as pies and he kissed me even harder than before.

My breathing slowed, a long-awaited calm seeping into my marrow as he stood with his thigh against mine, glancing watchfully, even protectively over his shoulder when a few men left the bar and went to their trucks. I took his wrist and pulled his hand from my clothes, zipping up my fly, not tucking in my shirt.

"Thanks, handsome," I said. My smile was serene as I stood on tiptoe to kiss him. I tasted his jaw line, and the roughness of stubble on my tongue almost made me ask him to follow me back out onto the main drag down toward the highway. There are always motels right off the interstate, places where they only charge you thirty bucks or so a night, the kinds of places you don't dare stay when you're in a city. Out on the road, though, they're definitely affordable and generally safe, and if you don't mind the noises of truckers and crew foremen grunting countless blue-collar generations into the talented mouths of bleached-blond working girls in the rooms on either side, tucking yourself in between those frequently bleached sheets is a comfort.

I had stayed in quite a few of them on the road, had grown to enjoy hearing strangers fucking through the walls, sloppy and anonymous, their noises gradually rousing my cunt from her slumber. Now all I could think about was being a part of it, slick with the funk of the drive-through fuck, high on the freedom of knowing you'll be gone in the morning.

The schoolteacher in me wasn't bold enough yet. "You sure you don't wanna?" trailed behind me as I began to walk away, moving out from between him and the truck to rejoin the slipstream, car keys in my hand.

"Already did," I shrugged, flashing him a smile as I opened the car door.

The next night, in another town, I told my inner schoolmarm to get stuffed, and promptly did what I hadn't had the guts to do the night before. I did it shamelessly, and then I did it again. I had one opening night after another, each in a different town.

Eleven first kisses, eleven eager mouths, twenty-two roving hands, ten excitable, headstrong cocks. It was startlingly easy. Without half-trying, I picked out eleven men who thanked me again and again, their eyes shining with gratitude when I was finished, when I graciously kicked them out of the motel rooms they'd paid for. I'm no supermodel, but still it seemed that they could hardly believe their good fortune.

I'd pick them out of the lineup at some bar or other, drag them back to some nameless motel room, exhaust them doing all the things they'd never thought existed outside the pages of porno magazines, things I hadn't done since well before Sam came into the picture, some things I'd never done before at all. Their condom-sheathed pricks muscled into my asshole, fucked between my baby-oiled breasts, rubbed against my clit until I succumbed to feverish thrashing and begged them to shove it in. Two years of complete celibacy disappeared like smoke. It was just like riding a bicycle.

I chose them, I told them what I wanted, I put them through their paces. Heat rippled from my skin as they kissed me sloppily, hungrily, as they kneaded my tits hard and rammed into me with single-minded cocks. They were rough and unsophisticated and their selfishness pleased me because it matched my own. I knew how to make them blind with lust. They knew all the ways to overwhelm me, to batter me with the force of their desire and leave me glad and exhausted and covered with sweat.

Nothing they asked of me frightened me, nothing they wanted worried me. I handed out dreams like Halloween treats, high on their wonder and awe as the men helped themselves to my cunt, my tits, my willingness. Blushing as red as the cheap velour bedspread in the motel room we shared on the seventh night, one asked to spank me. I looked between my legs as I knelt on all fours, legs spread, feeling my cunt get hotter and wetter, my clit grow harder and more insistent, as he paddled my butt with the flat of his hand. He talked about how pink my ass was getting, how red, his voice never more than a reverent whisper. Meditative and steady, he hit me again and again and I stroked my clit until I came, thrashing as he hit me harder still. He didn't ask permission to fuck me from behind then, snarling like a dog as he sped toward his own climax, or to blister my ass with the hairbrush he grabbed off the bedside table while he did, but he didn't really need to: I never stopped coming.

On another night, in a city on the far edge of the mountains, there was a man about my age with a playful green-eyed wink and a glorious voice of chocolate and smoke. Number nine. He knew how to kiss me, how to work me into an aroused daze with his lips and his tongue, his teasing bites on the side of my neck. I wanted to fuck him then and there, in the alley, in the backseat of his car. He insisted we go to the grocery store, and then to a motel.

I waited in my car, parked next to his in the grocery-store parking lot, two ships moored together on a blacktop sea. He brought two bags to the motel room. He said he didn't want to fuck me with his cock, that he couldn't anyway, he hadn't gotten it up in years. I shrugged and told him whatever, that it was okay with me. He tucked grapes, cool and green, into the red folds of my pussy, then ate them out one by one. An unripe, unpeeled banana was brought to bear on my G-spot until I gushed a puddle on the polyester bedspread, then he plunged into me with hard, smooth cucumbers, one in each hand, until I did it again. He put me on my hands and knees and decorated my ass with whipped cream from a spray can, licking it clean and making me squirm while he pumped my pussy full of an icy juice bar, raspberry trickling down my thighs and making a massacre of the sheets. Gleeful, he slurped my fruit-flavored pussy until I trembled, my cunt feeling so open and empty that I snarled at him to fill me up again, snarling again when he started to thank me. I think he never thought anyone would let him do what he did to me that night. I just wanted to get fucked. I spread my legs wider and let him concentrate on slowly stretching my cunt with a fat, heavy zucchini. It took time and lube, and no small amount of frustrated wriggling on my part, but finally he got the thick green thing into me and fucked me hard, licking my clit until I screamed.

Driving along during the afternoons, I wondered when I

would start to feel used, defiled, hollow as a cheap chocolate Easter egg. I had felt that way sometimes when I was young, when I thought vaulting out of the vapidness of atomic-age subdivisions meant letting intellectual upperclassmen get me drunk and take me to strange beds at other people's parties for an inept obligatory screw. But I didn't feel that way now. I felt shiny, as if I glittered in the sun, tinkling with the sharpness of climax after climax. It had been years since I had felt the slightest temptation to just wallow in my own animal possibility, but now every man I chose, every cock that pierced me, every solitary night's sleep amid sheets that smelled like sweat and aftershave made me feel as triumphant as winning a fight.

And so I made my way from Cowdrey to Sandpoint to Tesuque, leaving a trail of used condoms, exhausted cocks, and braggin' rights behind me. I was proud of the fact that my asshole was still sore from the night before as I sped down the road, every bump and pothole reminding me of number eleven's relentless abandon, his thickness pounding into my ass as my fingers ground my clit. And I was proud of them, every man I chose, every smear of testosterone sweat that slicked my skin, proud that I'd given the finger to my good-girl training and several years of being the stereotypical sexless schoolmarm. I was tickled to death to think of myself as a slut, as a predator, as a gift or a vision, an unanticipated carnal miracle that a handful of men would remember for the rest of their lives.

The desert unfurled dry as suede as I crossed another mesa, and as the sun dipped toward the distant sea, I licked my lips. I had broken up with Sam months ago, but to really leave him, it seemed, took another man, and another, and another, each fresh cock an antidote to the slow poisons of a long-dead marriage. Soon it would be nighttime again, another night to fill with the smell of fresh sweat, an unopened twelve-pack of condoms and a new bottle of lube in my backpack promising the rhythmic smack and slurp of rut. I wanted a hard, sharp fuck. We'd share a raw hour or two of battle, man versus woman, and then we'd both be gone. I'd pick a good one tonight, I told myself, one with a fat cock, a tireless tongue, and strong thighs.

Number twelve had all those things, as it happened, but that wasn't what attracted me at first. I was drawn to his tattoos, vivid, sharp, and artistic, covering his arms from his wrists on up to where the sleeves of his T-shirt cut them off. His hair was short and lay in orderly waves, his beard trimmed close, redder than his hair, and his fine young body was compact, limbs sleek and smoothly muscled, hinting at power and stamina. Around his left arm a leisurely dragon wound upward among rocks and water, his right bore stylized black, tribal arcs and blades. I smiled at him and gave him the eye. He bought me a drink. His name was Nick, and after we chatted a bit, I told him I wanted to see the rest of his tattoos. He took the hint, smiling and show-ing white, even teeth, and asked me if I wanted to go for a walk.

It wasn't far from the bar to a moon-silvered vacant lot where a van was parked, an awning raised above its wide side door and extending toward a ring of rocks and ashes where a fire had been laid. Nick was traveling, too, it turned out, resting up for a few days while his mail caught up to him, grabbing a little work in the meantime. He'd been in town a few days, and there was a foam sleeping pad that he'd rolled out on the ground, topped with a bedroll that smelled of smoke and maleness and earth.

I sat down with him, but I felt a bit confused. He hadn't tried to kiss me yet. It wasn't supposed to work that way. I'd become used to a certain trajectory in these things, a logical arch that began the first instant I smiled encouragement. There would be the hand on my arm, the kiss, the press of abdomen against hip, and then it would just get quicker and harder, fiercer, pushing toward its logical limits. Instead, Nick and I sat and talked, words hovering in the air, occasionally hearing cars or distant televisions on the slight breeze. After a while he took off his shirt to show me his tattoos, turning his back so that I could see bet-ter how the dragon on his arm chased another that flowed over his shoulder and down his spine, then turning so that I could see the designs that continued across his chest.

Impatient, I caught his shoulders and kissed him, hoping to catch him in my willingness. His mouth opened to mine, but slowly, his tongue almost thoughtful as it spiraled against my own. "I see," he said when I broke the kiss, and smiled at me. Soon enough he'd unbuttoned my shirt, his lips and tongue caressing the curves of bared breasts as he pushed down the cups of my bra. He bit my nipple until I sighed, rolling it lightly along the edges of those even, meticulous teeth, and his fingers found the buttons of my jeans, enacting the beginnings of the ritual with slow, deliberate precision. I shivered with enjoyment and relief, back on familiar ground.

Nick bit my lower lip as he cupped my bare breasts, buffed my nipples with the palms of his warm, sturdy hands. He kissed me firm and warm and wet and kept on kissing me as he stroked my chest, my sides, my belly, bringing me into my skin so that every caress made me feel a sharp twinge somewhere deep inside. Our tongues traded secrets as we sank down on the bedroll, Nick's thigh between mine at first, then his hands on my hips, pulling me over and on top of him.

He was huge and hard beneath his button fly, thick enough to make my pussy clench at the mere thought of how his cock would feel inside me. I rocked against him, feeling his rigidity through the crotch of my jeans, and though he smiled and bit his lip with pleasure, he seemed to be in no hurry. He didn't grind his hips up into me, didn't make a show of moaning encouragement when I ground myself against his cock. It seemed somehow perverse for him to be so hard, and so huge, and not seem to be in a rush to do anything about it, but his hands were too busy for me to care for long. He pulled me down to kiss me, rolling me over as his tongue teased my earlobe, my neck, and his hand peeled down my jeans and panties, leaving me naked to the night.

Strong fingers found their way between my slippery folds, first two, then three, his thumb on my clit as he kissed and bit his way across my chest and belly. My womb turned to lava as he fluttered his fingers fast and firm in my depths. He knew what he was doing. He liked what he was doing, too, and it showed, his beard rubbing over my nipples, his teeth scraping along my hipbone, fingerfucking me into repeated oblivion, purring his delight at my pleasure. The more those knowing, indulgent hands touched me, the more that wicked, skillful mouth teased me, the more expansive my appetites became. I shuddered luxuriously when he suckled the fat, puffy lips of my cunt, chewing them just slightly before latching on to my clit. I wallowed in it, in the intensity, the purity of my tattooed stranger's mouth and fingers, my whole body vibrating with bliss.

"What about you?" I finally asked as I lay panting, his fingers still inside me, his face nestled in the valley between my breasts as he nuzzled their inner curves. I reached for his cock and stroked it through his jeans, impressed. Nick gasped and bit his lip, his eyes closing for a moment as the sensation thrilled through him. How ironic, I thought, that the only man I'd ever encountered with a truly blue-ribbon schlong seemed almost reticent about getting it serviced. It only made me want it more. He knelt between my thighs, casting a long heavy shadow across me. I couldn't really see his face, but I could hear the warm, virile pleasure in his voice.

"How bad do you want it?" he teased, fondling himself as he looked down at me, backlit by the distant moon. I begged, instant and unabashed, the ache in my cunt so deep and so thick I was sure that if he withheld it for another instant I would almost certainly die.

Nick didn't bother to take his jeans off, just unbuttoned his fly, took aim, and hit bottom in a single easy push. Impaled and breathless, I watched his face above mine as he began to thrust into me, now harder, now faster as he ascertained just how hard and how deep I could take it. His eyes were on mine, his mouth widening into a wolfish grin as he realized I'd gladly accept whatever he had to give. The lust I felt was deeper than the simple urge to be filled, something else altogether than the customary fast frenzy of mutual need to come. Something simmered within me as the tattooed man's cock thrust down into my hungry cunt, as his dark pupils focused on mine. I wanted *him* inside me, not just his cock.

I reached up, grabbed his shoulders, pulled him down to me as I lifted my legs, opening to him as wide and deep as I could. As we kissed, I rode the intense pleasure of his thrusts against my cervix, rhythmic and firm, and my orgasm swelled and burst into laughter that flooded his mouth, giggling and cackling. It was simple, it was delirious, delightful, hysterical. Together we rocked, slamming our hips together, moaning and gasping, laughing our asses off under the endless spangled canopy of the night.

I came and came until I could hardly tell whether I'd just come or was just about to come again. Nick came too, shuddering and pushing himself in me so deep it hurt, but that incredible cock of his stayed hard. He pinched my clit as he recovered and I giggled into his mouth as we kissed, wallowing in the giddy joy of it as his sweat dripped onto my body and he fucked me with punishing thoroughness, a last gritty tango toward paradise.

Afterward, we lay on the bedroll, spooned together beneath the blankets, midnight desert air cool against our faces. Curled against my bare ass, I could still feel Nick's bulge under his jeans.

"You're still hard?" I was amazed.

"Takes a while for it to go down sometimes," he said. "You know how it is."

It was new to me, but I supposed everyone was different. We drowsed a bit, then, when Nick got up to go behind the van and take a leak, I offered to leave and let him get some sleep.

"Don't be silly," he said, returning to the bedroll after a few minutes and lying down alongside me again. He wrapped an arm around my middle and a leg around my hip, sweet and snuggly. I wriggled and purred at the warmth of him radiating into my bare skin, enjoying the reassuring weight of his dragon-embroidered arm around my waist and his blue-jeaned thigh on top of mine.

Time passed, and I dozed a bit in Nick's embrace. And then I noticed that his cock was gone. It was an accident—I honestly hadn't suspected anything until I sleepily adjusted my arm for comfort and my hand brushed against a crotch that was flat where it shouldn't have been. Suddenly I wasn't sleepy. I gently felt the front of his jeans, not firmly enough to wake him. There was nothing there to feel, not even the jiggly softness of a tired scrotum, and certainly not the monster with which he'd so delectably ravished me. Inspecting his chest as closely as I dared in the moonlight, I saw a trace of a long scar, carefully worked into part of a tattoo. And it all made sense. Of course.

I felt stupid for not having noticed earlier. It bothered me that I hadn't figured it out. Shouldn't I have been able to tell the difference between a real dick and a fake one when I had it inside me? I guessed circumstances had proven that the answer was no. Besides, I'd wanted to have him inside me bad enough that I hadn't even paused to ask him to put on a condom. I'd been far enough out of my head with lust that I hadn't apparently cared what was going into my pussy, only that it did so as soon as possible. Perhaps it was for the best that Nick's cock wasn't capable of spreading seed or anything else. I was suddenly, strangely thankful for Nick's ersatz cock, wherever he'd stashed it for the night.

Only it hadn't been fake. It didn't feel fake. Nick hadn't acted like it was fake. He came with it inside me. I felt him come. And it felt amazing. His cock might not have been permanently attached, but it had certainly been real. I craned my head to look at Nick, sleeping soft with his cheek against my shoulder, his breath even and slow. His beard trapped the dark of the night against his skin, and his arm encircled me with a simple, faithful, tender affection. It was hard to imagine him as a woman, as a girl. I wondered what he'd looked like when he wasn't a boy, whether the lines of his face had gotten sharper or whether he'd always had those high cheekbones, that defiant jaw. I wondered why he hadn't told me. He shifted slightly, and the smell of him drifted to my nose, warm and deliciously masculine in a way that instantly reminded me of how his fingers felt inside me. Then I realized I was musing about what he had aside from a great big cock and whether he ever let anyone touch it, whatever it was. No, he didn't have a flesh-and-blood cock. But it didn't matter. I closed my eyes and snuggled against him for the night.

The next day dawned cool and clear as glass. Nick was up when I opened my eyes, shirt on, his mouth toothpaste-fresh. I struggled back into my clothes and combed my hair, aching in unfamiliar places.

I yawned as I walked over to where Nick stood by the van. He grinned and encircled my waist with one arm as I kissed him on the cheek, then softly on the lips. Holding his gaze, I reached down and gently I put my hand on his crotch, confirming what I'd suspected. His cock was back, huge and hard behind his button fly. He flinched and grimaced, his ears turning bright red. I gave his cock a firm squeeze, laying the fingers of my other hand gently across his agitated frown, shushing him before he could say anything.

"You don't have to say it. You weren't born a boy," I said, affectionately patting the enormous cock through the denim. "And I don't care."

He started to stammer. I kissed him hard.

"Never apologize, Nicky. You're a hot fuck. And you're one hell of a man."

He looked at me to see if I meant it. I did, and he beamed.

A short while later we laughed and joked our way across the vacant lot, down the deserted early-morning street to my car. I gave him my address and my phone number scrawled on the back of a postcard, and he promised he'd look me up if he could.

I was done with the nameless men and towns and bars, I realized as I backed out of my parking space. I'd had enough of frantic solitary climaxes in the company of strangers. I was sore and chafed, hungry as hell, and in desperate need of a shower. But I was satisfied. Nick had given me something I needed, and it seemed that perhaps I had returned the favor. Perhaps I'd get to again. In the meantime there was a road ahead of me, and that was good enough.

Different with Your Kind

It's so different with your kind. The ecstatic gulps you take with hands and eyes, lips and fingers brushing my curves, my belly, the swell at the bottom of my rib cage, gliding over my breasts are so different from the fond but passing touches of a man who doesn't seem to find the same wonder in what he touches. I become so greedy with the ones who, like you, want me enough that you're willing just to wallow in what caresses I do permit.

I'm greedy because I can't imagine wanting it to end, all the stroke-and-pet, knead-and-tease, the murmurs of "oh how sexy" and "you're so beautiful" and all the other words that you never hear enough when you grow up believing that you'll never hear them at all. I want to take this further, to go from teasing to earthy smacking gusts of wrenching, torrential satisfaction; I want to fuck you, yes, and I can and do imagine it. But I do not . . . not at the expense of getting to the other side of this exquisite bridge too soon, this arching span of wanting and newness and almost-disbelief that hangs between us, the cables of lust shivering with tension where they pierce the foggy fact that we barely know one another. I'm not ready for this part to end. Not yet.

It is that, almost more than the practical concerns—how I lead my life, the husband to whom I have pledged my first allegiance—that makes me pause with you, that makes me draw the line, thus far, and no further. Almost. But only almost, and the feeling of your hands on my hips when you pull me to you, so enthusiastic, so unapologetic, makes me shiver in spite of myself. It makes me wonder what it would have been like if it had always been like this, if I had learned earlier to be made love to instead of being the one to reach out and bestow pleasure first, if I had known that there were those who would gladly pay this homage. If the first man I had loved had been like you, perhaps I would not have come so often to see sex only as a hopeful transaction in which I would give and give, and hope I'd get what I wanted in return, as if handing over coins stamped with the wishful words "In Reciprocity We Trust." There have been so many times that lovers desired me with their minds, their ears, their hearts, then later, only when love taught them how, learned that they might love me with their hands, their eyes, their lips, their cocks. There have been so few times, by comparison, that the vision, the lust, the avarice have come first. I know I'm not supposed to want to be objectified. But there is a pleasure there, a cleanness, a purity of intent, an appreciation of the simple animal facts of things that cannot be denied, and perhaps it tastes all the sweeter to me because I found it so late.

Fine, you called me, sultry, *thick,* and it went straight to my clit just like the half-whispered "I can't bear it when you smolder like that" I heard once from another man's mouth in another city where the hours pass as slowly as old men read the evening paper. You and he, and some few others, all quite different, some browner or pinker, some more or less married, some grayer than others, yet all so happy to get your hands on me, your mouths on me, all of a kind. What would it be like now if the one I married were like you, if his eyes and hands and lips transformed his endless delight at my Palouse-hillside hips into yielding sliding bliss? Would I still understand how crucial lust is, how you wither without it? Or would I just be jaded, spoiled like fruit left to rot, juices oozing stickily in the sun?

But this is no time to think too far, not with the strange new warm winds of you surrounding my roundness, caressing, taking so much joy in what I sometimes think of as an embarrassment of riches. Your delight unmoors me, and with that rude freedom

I can't help what rises from my throat when your fingers pluck my nipples like grapes. Can you touch my belly? You want to know, and the answer is noyes, or is it yesno, and damn it anyway, you know you're making me melt. Still, there's that belly again. And you? You want to touch it, to see and stroke it, your eyes shining and pupils wide with desire (it softens you, makes you tender in a way I was not sure you could appear). But you're too new for me to bear the sight of it, that part of my own body I can only sometimes bear to contain. I can't look at it now, not next to your brand-new face, your mad-monkish fervor, the oiled-teak gleam of your shaven-smooth skull.

So I flip my skirt down and you push it up again over garters and stockings, purple velvet thong panties that cover (cover?) almost nothing, just a girly gesture stretched against the amplitude of belly, mons, and juicy fat lips. Or perhaps that's the point, that no matter how thin, fabric does mean something. Dress to impress, but remember: Leave a watchman at the gates.

You nuzzle the velvet, it catches on abrasive pips of stubble but slides smooth against your moustache. Do I want you to push it aside, to sneak your fingers into me in a way that puts meaning back into the word "snatch," to feel the incontrovertible evidence of what your touches, of what your words and the faintest edge of your teeth, of what your tongue and lips have done to me?

Of course I do, but to say it would be too much. In so many words it would cross the bridge, and I would lose the crazy vertigo of being here with you, lose the dangerous knowledge that there's just as far to fall up as there is to fall down. I'm no longer sure if there's much difference. So we shift to the couch and I arch back against you, perched on the edge, sitting between your knees. Your wide hands roam up under my sweater, and mean it, fingers deftly tormenting my nipples, composing symphonies with my groans and cries, making me twist and strain until I can only give in and I come for you, and a moment later it's just the first time of many.

Champagne glasses shatter, flashbulbs pop, sequins slither, throwing cascades of stars against the wall, white like the moon's bones. Sparklers on the Fourth of July and a hail of ripe cherries, a night of Northern Lights reflecting off the snow. These gasps you draw from me remind me of so many things, of other times when it has been like this, other ones of your tribe. Like it was with the knowing, corduroyed professor who waited until the end of the semester before he made me breathless in his living room while his skinny wife made canapés in the kitchen. Like it was with the shy, bearded Texan whose tenor sounded so sweet in my ear and whose arms held my hips as if he cradled the sun.

And just like with the others I eventually let you touch my cunt, at the moment when I can't bear not to. As if I can hear the liquid simmer of stockings rustling over the blood in my veins, I spread my thighs and listen, tongue twined with yours, catching your breath in my teeth. Your reach is fast, poised to rush in each time my slow greed unfolds to let you find the next cache of treasure. You split the seam of me and I gush forth heavy with juice, and I want to howl the delectable backseat don't-tell-mama of it, the sacred scrape of your fingerprint over the seal-slick chubby tip of my clit. Nostalgia cradles me in fragrant fog, like the smell of opening my Nana's bureau, a pedal point to the driven rhythm of you pushing me louder and closer, and I hear the rasp of your voice and I feel you sag as you come just from the tension and the joy of touching me, of knowing I'm so close, of feeling your fingers surrounded by my delight.

Afterward, I will think about these things, and wonder whether I dare take another chance with you. Some nights I will imagine you over me, becoming my dark storm sky as you thrust hard between my cunt lips and I melt helplessly at each piston-statement of the desire in your thighs. Some mornings, still swaddled in dreams and the warm familiar scent of sleeping husband under the comforter, I will feel your lips again, and your fingers so alive inside me and the yielding of your skin beneath my teeth and through it all, the impossible-to-refute need of it all, I will hear your voice, and all the words I drank in so eagerly. I will hear them not in my ears but in my bones, and I will recall the instants in which I was so beautiful and I will remember: It is so different with your kind.

About the Author

Raised in Cleveland, Ohio, and trained as a classical musician and cultural historian, Hanne Blank is a writer, editor, public speaker, activist, and educator whose books include *Best Transgender Erotica* (with Raven Kalder, Circlet Press), *Zaftig: Well Rounded Erotica* (Cleis Press), and the groundbreaking *Big Big Love: A Sourcebook on Sex for People of Size and Those Who Love Them* (Greenery Press). Her socially progressive, intellectually- and emotionally-engaged approach to sexuality has been characterized as "sophisticated . . . does for for sex what feminism does for women: it gives us context." Proud proprietrix of one hell of a variegated resume, hanne is co-editor (with Heather Corinna) of literary erotica standard bearer *Scarlet Letters* (scarletletters.com), the former associate editor of the feminist newsmonthly *Sojourner: The Women's Forum*, and has been an educator at institutions including Whitworth College, Tufts University and Brandeis University. Her fiction, essays, reviews, and other writings are published in a wide range of venues, ranging from erotica anthologies, travel magazines, indie newspapers, zines, feminist and Jewish journals, books on music and culture, and beyond. Hanne and her work have been featured on radio and television in the United States, Canada, and the United Kingdom, and she is a frequent public speaker and workshop leader on topics literary, sexual, and otherwise.

Hanne Blank lives near Baltimore, Maryland. She also maintains an outpost at www.hanne.net where you may, if you wish, find out more.

SELECTED TITLES FROM SEAL PRESS

For more than thirty years, Seal Press has published groundbreaking books. By women. For women. Visit our website at www.sealpress.com.

INDECENT: HOW I MAKE IT AND FAKE IT AS A GIRL FOR HIRE by Sarah Katherine Lewis. $14.95, 1-58005-169-3. An insider reveals the gritty reality behind the alluring facade of the sex industry.

SINGLE STATE OF THE UNION: SINGLE WOMEN SPEAK OUT ON LIFE, LOVE, AND THE PURSUIT OF HAPPINESS edited by Diane Mapes. $14.95, 1-58005-202-9. Written by an impressive roster of single (and some formerly single) women, this collection portrays single women as individuals whose lives extend well beyond Match.com and Manolo Blahniks.

CONFESSIONS OF A NAUGHTY MOMMY: HOW I FOUND MY LOST LIBIDO by Heidi Raykeil. $14.95, 1-58005-157-X. The Naughty Mommy shares her bedroom woes and woo-hoos with other mamas who are rediscovering their sex lives after baby and are ready to think about it, talk about it, and DO it.

INAPPROPRIATE RANDOM: STORIES ON SEX AND LOVE edited by Amy Prior. $13.95, 1-58005-099-9. This collection of short fiction by women writers takes a hard look at love today—exposing its flaws with unflinching, often hilarious, candor.

DIRTY GIRLS: EROTICA FOR WOMEN edited by Rachel Kramer Bussel. $15.95, 1-58005-251-1. A collection of tantalizing and steamy stories compiled by prolific erotica writer Rachel Kramer Bussel.

SHAMELESS: WOMEN'S INTIMATE EROTICA edited by Hanne Blank. $14.95, 1-58005-060-3. Diverse and delicious memoir-style erotica by today's hottest fiction writers.

CPSIA information can be obtained
at www.ICGtesting.com
Printed in the USA
LVHW041943090622
720811LV00004B/461

9 781580 050814